AFTER DARKNESS FELL

AFTER DARKNESS, LIGHT

David Berardelli

AFTER DARKNESS FELL

GRAVESTONE PRESS

ISBN: 978 1 78695 715 3

Gravestone Press
is an imprint of
Fiction4All
www.fiction4all.com

This Edition
Published 2021

PROLOGUE

Nearly three months have passed since the plague of death had wiped out most of the world's population. The exact numbers, of course, could not be calculated, since there was no one left to work the computers or maintain the databanks. Even so, most computers were rendered inoperable due to mass power failures, and those still capable of using their mental facilities realized long ago that such responsibilities no longer mattered in the great scheme of things. Survival had taken precedence, and the phrase "survival of the fittest," trampled years ago and left in the cloud of indifference generated by the mass chaos of modern technology and sophisticated living, had returned triumphantly, bringing with it a primordial behavior that had long been hidden for decades.

PART ONE: DARKNESS

CHAPTER ONE

I felt rather than heard someone wandering around outside.

Under normal conditions, such a sensation didn't warrant immediate attention. However, since conditions hadn't been normal for some time, I knew I had to investigate.

The early hour of the day most likely contributed to the red flag that went off in my head. The clock on the kitchen wall said 8:42. I hadn't been sleeping soundly the last couple of months; knowing I had to be on my guard twenty-four hours a day made the natural process of sleeping a thing of the past. By the time I'd gotten up, showered and dressed, I was fully alert.

As I stood in front of the gas stove, the eggs simmering quietly in the skillet, the familiar tingling in the back of my head jolted me, and I abruptly put down the spatula, turned off the burner and placed a cover on the skillet.

I'd learned twenty years earlier to listen to my senses; they'd served me well during my three-year stint in the Army. They'd also served me well during my trip from Orlando three very long, arduous months ago. Using my instincts—and also aided by Reed McCallum and Brooke Fields, my two best friends—I managed to escape the underground Government facility run by a handful of psychos intent on creating a superior civilization by killing off most of the population.

The last three months had been unbearably grim. Living quietly with your partner in normal conditions can be a wonderful thing, but in a world where everyone is dead or dying, life becomes a nightmare. You're on constant alert, and fully aware that every move you make could be your last. When you stumble upon someone who doesn't appear to be doped, your defenses immediately go up. If this person seems okay and is armed for his own protection, he can accidentally kill you if he panics, or is unfamiliar with his weapon. If he is acting sick or doped, he can have an accomplice hiding close by, ready to kill you.

In the last three months, Fields and I had killed six people—four men and two women. The men ambushed us when Fields and I were at an abandoned filling station in Bakerstown, pushing containers of gas onto the bed of Uncle Joe's Silverado. Luckily, we managed to kill all four without blowing up the truck or the station.

The women we encountered had faked a breakdown on the Bakerstown-Culmerville Road, as we were coming home from the first of our two monthly shopping excursions. The older of the two distracted us by asking directions while her sister rushed at Fields with a machete when our backs were turned.

Surviving a holocaust is horrible. Its effects are so far-reaching, the survivor spends much of his time angry with himself for surviving and longing for a peaceful death. But the will to survive takes precedence, and feelings of guilt and self-pity quickly return to the back of the mind.

The will to survive manifests itself in many forms, often becoming paranoia in times of extreme stress. I kept loaded guns in each and every room in the house. I'd nailed certain windows and doors shut, locked others and rigged simple booby traps inside the front and back doors that would cause a string of empty tin cans to come crashing down onto the linoleum.

Although Fields was still sleeping when I'd slipped out of the bed, I heard the shower going only minutes after I'd gone downstairs to fix breakfast. It was still going, and I saw no reason to disturb her. I wasn't a hundred percent sure there was anything to worry about. For all I knew, a stray dog or coyote could be roaming the property, sniffing for food. Besides, I didn't want to waste time running up the stairs and telling her my intentions. She'd argue with me and tell me to wait until she put on some clothes so she could investigate with me. It would take too long. If someone *was* prowling around, I needed to find out as quickly as possible. And since I was over forty, the extra scrambling would tire me unnecessarily, giving a would-be trespasser a deadly edge.

I told myself that even if I was imagining things, it still wouldn't hurt to check the property. It would only take a minute, and I'd come right back and finish making breakfast. Anyway, I knew I couldn't concentrate on anything else until I'd gone outside and found out if my instincts were right.

Before leaving the house, I picked up the compact .380 Beretta Cheetah lying beneath the towel on the kitchen counter less than a foot from the rear door. It was small enough to keep hidden in my hand but quite capable of knocking someone down at forty or fifty yards. I'd used it before and was willing to use it again if the occasion arose.

I sincerely hoped my instincts were wrong. If they were right, and someone was indeed outside, Fields would never forgive me. But I knew that if the latter rang true, time was of the essence, and I had to find out as quickly as possible.

I pushed open the screen door an inch at a time and slipped outside, into the back yard, moving quietly up the walk leading to the stone steps that extended to the long, winding gravel drive. I stopped about ten feet from the door and stood there, listening. I heard a few birds singing from the trees and a distant barking dog.

So far, so good. I resumed my trip to the end of the walk.

As soon as I cleared the corner of the house, I saw a lone slender figure wandering up the drive.

It was Reed McCallum.

***

My heart stopped. I could only stand there numbly and watch as the apparition drew nearer. *Was* it Reed? No. It simply couldn't be.

Fields and I had buried Reed in the shade of the buckeye tree my mother had climbed as a child, up the hill at the end of the drive. Mom's body rested there as well, right beside Uncle Joe, whom Fields, Reed, and I had buried earlier. Shortly after Uncle Joe had died, one of my mother's Quarter Horse mares accidentally killed Reed when something spooked her in her stall, slamming Reed into the wall. Reed died shortly after, filling our dark, frightening world with an overwhelming sadness I'd never experienced before. I thought of him every day since, feeling his presence at odd moments and reminding myself that even though he'd gone, his spirit would remain with us.

Perhaps this was why I thought the stranger walking up our drive was Reed. The image of his slenderness, his unkempt reddish-brown hair, would forever remain fixed in my consciousness. The sight alarmed me, and it was then that I suddenly remembered the gun in my hand. When reality intervened, I knew I should pull myself together. The man coming up the drive was trespassing, and I needed to take full control of the situation immediately.

Once the morning sunlight poking between the trees that lined the driveway had settled on the stranger's features, I knew right then that this wasn't Reed at all, just someone resembling him.

I faced him at an angle, with my right side turned toward the right, my right arm hidden from his view. The .380 rested snugly in my hand, pressing comfortably against my thigh. As a precaution, I carefully pulled back the hammer while keeping my gaze steady on the stranger. I sincerely hoped this would turn out innocently. I hadn't yet been forced to kill anyone on my own property and hoped the trend would continue.

"Nice morning," he said, coming up the drive.

I nodded. As he drew nearer, his resemblance to Reed diminished totally, and I knew then that the only thing they had in common was their hair and slenderness. He wore a white tee shirt beneath a light-blue windbreaker, jeans a little large around the waist, and black tennis shoes.

I knew full well that I could be facing a psychopath. He moved normally, which told me he was obviously not doped. This, of course, made him even more dangerous. I stopped thinking of Reed altogether and concentrated on the here and now.

When he was about twenty feet away, I motioned for him to stop.

He took two more steps—which I didn't like. It was most likely a control thing, suggesting that he was playing a head game with me. He was trespassing and I wasn't in the mood for games.

"Where are you coming from and why are you here?" I asked.

"Don't get tense. I'm not here to cause any trouble."

"Then answer my question."

"I'm just down the road." He jabbed a thumb to his left, toward the intersection at the top of the hill. "I had a breakdown and was wonderin' if you could give me a jump."

This didn't feel right. Our house sat nearly a hundred yards off the road, hidden by pines and buckeyes. The pasture was just as secluded, the line of pines spanning the perimeter providing the farm with heavy camouflage. This stranger had either been watching the property with binoculars or had followed us from our shopping excursion last week.

Either way, this was not good. The idea of someone watching us intensified the tingling in my neck. The trees keeping the front yard of the house hidden from view could easily conceal others this man may have brought with him. For all I knew, there could be half a dozen others hiding in the woods, waiting for his signal. I didn't dare take my eyes off him.

I realized I could be dead very shortly. If I managed to survive, Fields was going to kill me. At the very least, I'd never hear the end of it. But her safety was my big concern. Hopefully she'd stay in the house and would be close enough to a gun when she heard gunshots. If there were only a couple of trespassers, I had no doubt she'd be able to get them all. I didn't want to consider the possibility that there could be a dozen or more.

I took a deep breath and forced myself not to show fear. I knew all about fear and how to handle it. In the military, we all learned that you ignored it and worked through it. You grabbed it and shoved it out of the way as quickly as possible. It was necessary. Once the enemy saw it, you were dead.

"How'd you know anyone lives here?"

He grinned. "Just took a wild guess. Car's just a quarter-mile up the road, near the intersection. That gas station didn't look occupied. Neither did the tire place across the road. Nothing in either place. Guess they've both been picked clean."

There were more than a dozen houses at the top of that hill. It didn't make sense for him to walk all the way back here when he could have just gone a little farther up the hill and checked any of the dwellings there.

"Sorry," I said. "I can't help you."

"You don't have something to jump me with?"

"Nope."

"You've got a barn."

"That doesn't mean anything."

"How 'bout that garage up that hill behind you?" He pointed.

I could tell he wanted me to turn around, but I didn't have to; I knew where it was. "What about it?"

"No battery charger? Cables?"

"I'm not exactly a car guy."

He laughed. "Nowadays? Everyone's gotta know a little about everything, fella."

I didn't reply. I'd managed to sneak a peek at the pine grove in front of the house. I didn't see anything move, didn't see glints of anything. But that didn't mean much. The growth ran pretty wild and thick in spots.

"Maybe you could give me directions."

He was obviously stalling, possibly making sure someone was getting into position for a clear shot. I relaxed the tension in my knees and gripped the .380 more tightly. I was now ready to move quickly. If I didn't get hit by someone in the grove, he'd get my first shot. "Where to?"

"I'm just headin' through, but I don't know where Route 8 is from here. I've got a friend—well; I used to have a buddy up near Butler, but who knows anymore? Anyway, I'm tryin' to look him up so maybe we can…"

"West of here, two miles." I used my left hand to point to my right.

"West?" Without taking his eyes off me, he turned to his left. "And you say it's that way?" He extended his right arm across his chest. I couldn't see his left.

Then I saw the tip of his left elbow rising behind his back. This told me he was doing basically the same thing I was. The issue of his baggy jeans came into the equation. Baggy jeans meant more room to conceal a small firearm as well as more ease in getting it out in a hurry.

In that same instant, I heard the crunch of dead leaves about twenty feet to my left, near the hedges at the corner of the house in the front yard. Two loud, familiar clicks snapped in my ears—one from the hedges, another from the upstairs bedroom window. I knew instantly that they were the sounds of gun hammers being cocked.

The harsh bark of Fields' voice, about twenty feet above my head and forty feet to my left, chilled the marrow in my bones: "*Duck*!"

I put a .380 hollow-oint slug neatly into the center of the stranger's forehead and fell face-first to the hard gravel. Two loud shots exploded almost simultaneously. The first buzzed inches above my head. The second echoed down the drive, to the wall of the barn, coming back up again and reverberating. I heard a loud gasp, and something slammed into the hedges near the house.

***

I lay motionless on the gravel, but all I could hear was my heart hammering deafeningly in my chest. I didn't want to get up and show myself; these two might have brought along someone else. But once my heart finally settled down and I still heard nothing, I decided I might be in the clear. Besides, Fields was probably still watching.

I crawled over to the dead man. A quick search revealed that he was heavily armed. In addition to the compact .22 revolver he'd tried taking from his left side pocket, I found a tiny long-barreled .25 derringer in his right, a .45 snub-nosed automatic in a pancake holster in the small of his back, beneath his windbreaker, and a 9 millimeter automatic in an ankle holster. When I found the courage to look at his face, I realized that despite the hair color and build, he didn't remotely resemble Reed. He was much younger, probably no more than thirty, and I saw nothing warm or inviting in the gaping chestnut eyes.

I took the 9 millimeter and checked the mag for ammo. One was missing from the mag; one remained in the pipe. Ready to go, obviously, and a quick sniff of the barrel told me it had recently been fired. I tossed the others into the hedges near the stone walk.

Still wary, I crawled over to the long row of bushes lining the drive. I hoped Fields would stay in the house so I could concentrate on the yard. If someone tried sneaking in through the front or back, she'd nail them.

I moved over to the bushes. Pushing a jagged clump aside, I peered through the small opening and scanned the front yard.

No movement. No glints from glasses, binoculars, plastic or gunmetal. No rustling sounds from the bushes or the pine grove.

I crawled along the hedge line, toward the barn, and stopped at the break in the hedges leading to the sidewalk extending to the front of the house. I continued listening but heard nothing louder than the heavy beating of my own heart.

As far as I could tell, there were only two of them. But I knew better than leave anything to chance. I decided to continue to crawl to the end of the hedge line, where it stopped at the corner of the barn. I could then slip through the gap and, using the wild underbrush as cover, veer toward the pines.

I began crawling.

"There were only two of them."

The sound of her voice startled me. I pushed myself up and carefully snuck a peek over the top of the hedges. Fields stood on the front porch, a hunting rifle cradled in her arms. She wore a pink tank top and faded jeans. Her hair was loose and wet from her shower, and glistened in the morning sun. Less than ten feet from her, the body of the second intruder lay face-down in the bush. Fields didn't seem to care about him; she was much too busy glaring at me. I'd seen that expression before; each time I saw it, I felt my testicles quiver and knew I was in serious trouble.

I approached the house. Fields remained stock-still; her glare did not soften. Even though I was nearly a hundred feet from her, I could feel the dark vibes coming from her. For a moment I feared she might even raise the rifle and shoot me. But she merely watched me as I drew closer.

I knew that my most sensible option was to walk up the steps and apologize. If I was lucky, the matter would be closed and eventually forgotten. I'd been married before and had learned that an apology went a long way in a relationship. Hopefully, an apology would be all Fields wanted.

Still, I realized how stupid I'd been about handling this, and that a mere apology might not be enough. I'd done something we'd promised one another we'd never do: I'd taken an unnecessary, dangerous risk. And no matter how I explained my reasoning, I knew it wouldn't suffice. I'd crossed the line and had to face the consequences.

I reached the top step and stopped about five feet from her. Her glare still hadn't softened, and I knew right then just how upset she actually was. This worried me much more than someone hiding in the grove behind me. "You sure no one else is..."

She nodded.

"I guess you would have seen someone if..."

Another nod.

"Listen, Fields. I know what I did was..."

"Why'd you do it?"

I shrugged. "I didn't want to disturb you. You were taking your shower, and I wasn't really sure anything was wrong."

"You came real close to never disturbing me again."

"I know, and I'm really..."

"The eggs are probably burnt."

"Probably."

"So is the coffee."

"I'll make fresh..."

"You owe me breakfast."

"I owe you much more than that."

She turned toward the front door. "Right now I'll settle for breakfast." She opened the door and turned back around. For long moments she stared at me, that same coldness penetrating my flesh. Her anger seemed to resonate the same way it had in Breezewood, when she'd aimed a giant revolver at my face. But this was different. Her cold green eyes were moist. I almost expected her to start crying. Fields didn't cry much, but it sure looked like she was about to do something along those lines.

She glared at me a little while longer. Then, without warning, her right hand came up and swatted me.

A knot of fire exploded in my jaw. My eyes snapped shut; when they opened, they were wet, and I noticed my vision had gone double. I closed them again and waited for the pain to subside. It took its time, and I finally opened my eyes. She was still standing there. The glare remained, and her eyes were still wet.

"Understand now?" she asked, her sandy brows rising.

"Sure do." I knew better than say or do anything to heat her up again.

"You're sure?"

"I think one of those is plenty, thanks."

"You needed it."

"I know."

"If it'll keep you from doing it again, it was worth it, don't you think?"

"Definitely."

She moved closer and planted a warm kiss on my lips. "You can be a bastard, you know."

"I know."

"Let's have breakfast. Then we have some unpleasant work to do."

CHAPTER TWO

Fields was right; we had to get rid of the two bodies, for obvious reasons. We also had to find out where they'd come from. If a vehicle was sitting off the road nearby, we had to find it. Two of them had snuck onto the property to do us harm; there could be others. If they were members of a wandering gang, it wouldn't be long before the others found out about us.

After Fields and I finished with the breakfast dishes, we set out to do what was necessary. I brought along my .357 Smith & Wesson revolver, as well as the tiny .22 Beretta Bobcat automatic, which fit snugly in my side pocket. I also brought along a Mossberg 12-gauge single barrel shotgun, which held six -00- buckshot cartridges and one up the pipe. Fields brought along her .38 Ladysmith hammerless revolver, which she carried in a pancake holster hidden in the small of her back, and the 1911 model Colt .45 automatic in a black Uncle Mike's holster strapped to her belt above her right hip. The .45 was heavy, bulky, and packed terrific stopping power. Over the last few months, she'd learned to handle the weapon quite well by taking it into the woods behind the garage and spending half a dozen afternoons splintering a square sheet of plywood I'd nailed to the stump of a dead tree.

Before leaving the house, we made sure all the windows were nailed shut. I turned off the generator and unplugged the appliances before double-locking the doors. Then we went up the hill, where the four-car block garage sat at the end of the drive. Uncle Joe's three-quarter-ton Silverado rested in its stall beside the van I'd stolen in St. Cloud to use for my trip up here. The pickup was sturdy, strong, and dependable. Uncle Joe had kept it in excellent condition, and it had never failed us. Aside from keeping a close eye on the fluids and making sure it had gas, oil and antifreeze, maintaining it was no problem.

I'd installed a gun carrier beneath the dash, fashioning it from a piece of plywood about a foot square, connecting it to the dash with spring hinges and fitted with clamps to hold two loaded .9 millimeter automatics. A simple button rigged to a short metal rod beneath the console released a clip, dropping the carrier and making the guns instantly accessible.

Fields and I had also sewn holsters beneath the front seats, fitting each with a .38 Smith & Wesson revolver loaded with full metal jacket bullets.

A short double-barrel coach-style shotgun lay on the floor beneath the driver's seat, its handle sawed off just behind the pistol grip, its barrel sawed off to a length of twelve inches. If more than one or two people approached the truck, the scatter would cause considerable damage.

For food, we stocked the console with cans of tuna and chicken, as well as bottled water and a small bottle of Kentucky bourbon. We also placed a small first-aid kit in the glove box and other essentials, such as penlights, flashlights and security lights, in the bags behind the seats and the slide-out compartments beneath the back seats.

In Uncle Joe's galvanized metal toolbox, which stretched across the width of the bed, I'd placed a two-gallon container of gas, two empty containers, four pints of high-grade engine oil, windshield washer fluid, a small toolbox, jumper cables and a tire patch kit.

Before climbing in, I lowered the tailgate. Our plan was to pick up the two bodies on the way down the drive and put them in the bed. Then we could find their ride and work from there.

As I got in, I noticed the dark expression on Fields' face. She was still obviously upset about the morning's fiasco. She'd been quiet at breakfast, barely touching her eggs and toast. Despite my crude attempts at conversation, she'd limited her responses and remained distracted.

A more perceptive guy would have chosen to let her anger run its natural course. I, on the other hand, didn't like the silence—or the tension between us—and decided to bring the issue to the surface as soon as we climbed in the truck.

"Still upset?"

She sat back in her seat. "What do you think?"

"I think you're still upset."

"If you already know, why ask?"

"I want you to start talking to me again."

She didn't reply.

I didn't press the issue as I fired up the ignition. I knew she'd snap out of it when the time was right.

Fields had a temper, but her storms never lasted long.

After backing out of the garage, getting back out and closing and padlocking the garage door, I got back in the truck, put it in reverse and backed it down the long, thirty-degree drive. When we were just a few feet from the first body, I put it in park and climbed down. I heard the other door click open behind me.

"You can't blame me, can you?" Fields stood behind the bed, watching me. Her anger had softened a little; her expression now looked more like sadness. Although her slap had given me a strong dose of reality, her expression right now told me even more. My actions had not only been reckless and foolish, but also deadly. Because of my decision to sneak out of the house alone, we were almost killed.

The horror of the situation swept through me. One simple decision had nearly resulted in our deaths. At the time, I thought I was acting sensibly. My paranoia had apparently reared its ugly head. It had been doing that a lot lately, but that didn't mean it was always right. Sometimes there *was* no threat. Sure, life had gone down the tubes, but that didn't mean death awaited me each time I left the house. There weren't many people walking around anymore. That fact alone should tell me something.

But not in this case. My instincts weren't wrong at all. Maybe there weren't many people walking around anymore, but that didn't mean there were fewer dangers. Powerful monsters had been set loose on society, killing an enormous amount of the population. Fields and I had somehow survived. It was up to both of us to take care of one another and treat each moment as if it could be our last. This meant I could not be reckless or take anything for granted.

In the old days, being reckless meant getting drunk, being pulled over on the way home and facing jail, a ticket and a fine. Or falling off a ladder and being taken to the Emergency Room. Or picking up a strange woman at a bar and taking her home.

Being reckless in this new world had become something totally different. There were no cops to pull you over. No Emergency Rooms to take you in. No one to stitch you up if you fell, or examine you if you felt something was wrong. And picking up a strange woman now meant finding yourself in the company of someone who carried around an arsenal and a container of severed penises behind her back seat.

I went over to her and put my hands on her shoulders. "I can't blame you at all. That was stupid of me. I thought I was being considerate. But things are different now, and every once in a while, the optimist in me seems to forget that, and for a moment I think things haven't changed at all. But they *have* changed, and now I know that what I did was probably one of the stupidest things I've ever done in my life."

She shook her head. "No. It *was* the stupidest thing you ever did. If I hadn't gotten to the bedroom window when I had, that moron in the bushes would have killed you."

"How'd you know anything was going on?"

"I came out of the bathroom and went downstairs, and when I smelled the eggs and the coffee and didn't see you, I went into the living room and checked the window. Then I ran back upstairs, got one of the rifles, and had a peek out the spare room window. I saw that other guy crawling in the grass, toward the house."

"How'd you get the screen open? I thought I nailed it shut."

"I didn't. I shot right through it. That was okay, wasn't it? I didn't have enough time to look for a knife..."

I hugged her. I was pleased that she hugged me back.

After kissing her, I turned, picked up the first body and slid him into the bed of the truck. Luckily, he only weighed around one-fifty, so handling him wasn't that difficult. I got back in the truck, backed it down to the front walk, grabbed the other body by the ankles and dragged him out of the bushes. He was slightly smaller than his partner; I had no problem dragging him across the lawn. When we reached the concrete stoop, I pulled him into a sitting position. I noticed then that Fields had got him directly in the center of the back. The exit wound was somewhere between his groin and left hip. She must have gotten him right in the heart.

I also noticed that he looked no more than twenty.

"Kind of young," I said.

"He was old enough to shoot a gun," Fields said softly.

I squatted, lifted him and carried him over my right shoulder to the truck. I set him down on the tailgate and let him fall backward, his head thumping the bed. I slid him the rest of the way beside his dead partner. When his tennis shoes cleared the bed, I slammed the tailgate shut.

***

I made a right onto the main road and we went west, up the mile-long hill that brought us to the intersection of Bakerstown-Culmerville Road and Deer Creek Road. As I'd suspected, there were no vehicles in sight, and aside from the junk cars and pickups languishing in the abandoned front yards up the hill, we saw nothing. The two men who'd wandered onto our property and tried to kill us had obviously come from a different direction.

I pulled into the deteriorating lot of the old abandoned garage, turned around and sat there a few moments, thinking. Those two had obviously come from somewhere. Had they driven here? Or walked? If they'd driven, they could have come from anywhere. If they'd walked, that meant they'd lived close by.

Two psychos living so close frightened me. I knew it was possible, I just didn't like it. It meant there could be others. It also meant that what happened this morning could happen again.

For obvious reasons, I didn't want to tell Fields my fears.

"Where exactly did he say he broke down?" she asked.

"From what he told me, we should have passed their ride on our way up this hill. He said he checked both garages, saw they were abandoned, and walked back down the hill."

"I think he lied to you."

"Looks that way, doesn't it?"

"If it were me, I would've checked those houses up the hill. They all look empty, but you never know. Someone could still be moving around in one of them."

"We both know what they were after."

"He and his friend obviously followed us from Bakerstown the other day."

That made me feel much better than the possibility of a gang of psychos living close. "And they've been biding their time, waiting for the right moment."

"So where do you think they came from?"

I eased back out onto the road and we went back down the hill, past the farm. At the horseshoe curve rounding the barn and front pasture, the road went down a fairly steep decline for about a mile before bottoming out and starting another gradual ascent up the next hill. At the bottom, about sixty feet from the road and in the middle of a narrow dirt road, a battered station wagon sat hidden behind wild brush, its body riddled with dents, scrapes and holes, its windows covered with dust and dirt.

I pulled onto the dirt road and brought the truck to a stop about twenty feet from the front of the vehicle. We sat in tense silence for several minutes, staring at it. I expected dark shapes to suddenly kick open the doors and leap from the cab, guns blazing.

There was no movement and no sign of life, but I knew better than lower my guard. I grabbed the .357 from the console. "I'm gonna check it out."

"Not alone, you won't." She snatched the .45 out of her Uncle Mike's and cocked the hammer. She meant business. I felt sorry for anyone naive enough to give her trouble.

"Okay. But we do this my way, all right?"

"Unless you plan to do something stupid again."

I sighed. She wasn't going to let me live that down. "Let's get this right, then. We'll get out the same time and leave both doors open."

"Why?"

"If someone jumps out of the car or the woods and starts shooting, we can get behind the doors. They're not bullet-proof, but they'll provide some protection."

"All right."

"We'll approach the wagon at the same time— me on this side, you on your side. Keep your gun pointed at the wagon. Keep as close to the door as you can while I check out the passenger's side. If it's clear, I'll signal and you can join me. Okay?"

"Yes."

"Now ... before we move, any other questions?"

"Just one. What's the procedure if we hear another vehicle coming this way?"

29

I didn't want to think about that, but I was glad she'd asked. "Get behind the truck, hit the dirt, and be ready to open up if the vehicle slows down."

"Where will you be?"

"Right beside you."

"Sounds like a plan."

"Any questions about what we do if someone's hiding in this wagon?"

She shrugged. "I was just gonna blow them away—unless you don't want me to."

"Just make sure I'm not in the line of fire when you do."

"Then make sure you're out of the way before I start shooting."

I wanted to smile. "I'll try to remember that, thanks."

***

Together, we crept alongside the truck, one cautious step at a time, our gaze fixed on the dirt-smeared windshield. My heart did a drum roll. Twenty years had gone by since my old Army days, when I handled riot control in Little Odessa, hunted down terrorist cells in Pakistani Brighton, and watched for illegals behind a barricade of sand bags near the Arizona Border.

Back then, I'd killed terrorists, suicide bombers, snipers, illegals working for the drug cartels, and innocents caught in the line of fire. I hadn't thought much about it at the time, attributing my actions to duty, love of country and the rationalization that if I didn't kill the enemy, the enemy would kill me. Even so, the act of killing had darkened my spirit, and I promised myself that once I was discharged, I would never kill anyone again.

In spite of my promise, I'd killed more than a dozen people in the last few months. Each killing had been necessary for my survival, as well as the survival of Reed and Fields. But even though these killings were completely justified, my spirit continued to darken just as it had twenty years earlier.

Fields kept the .45 trained on the windshield of the station wagon as I crept closer. Due to the dirt and dust covering a good portion of the glass, it was impossible to see inside. This made me wonder if the two had purposely darkened the windows. This could mean they'd been doing some nasty things.

The .357 was a heavy, cumbersome revolver, and often required both hands even for a large man. It delivered a substantial kick, and unless the cylinder was loaded with .38 bullets, the best way of maintaining control was to support the wrist of your firing hand with the palm of your non-firing hand.

Since I had to pull open the passenger door, I didn't have the luxury of keeping both hands on the gun. As a precaution, I mashed my upper arm tightly against my side for more stability. Taking a deep breath, I reached out, grasped the door handle and yanked it open.

The stench of marijuana, cigarette smoke and stale beer assaulted my nostrils.

The empty interior sneered at me.

The automatic held straight out, Fields moved closer. She pulled open the driver's door as I stuck my head inside and had a quick look at the interior. Food and candy wrappers, as well as empty beer cans, covered the floor. The dash ashtray overflowed with butts. Plastic bags of what looked like marijuana sat in a heap on the console. The back seat was covered with bundles of clothing. Canned goods and boxes of cereal and other foodstuffs lay in a pile behind the back seat.

I went around to the back of the wagon and lowered the tailgate. Three Styrofoam coolers sat behind the seat. A large open cardboard box sat by itself, toward the tailgate. Curious, I moved closer for a better look.

The box was crammed with hair—and strips of bloody flesh.

Scalps?

I thought of Carla and her collection of severed penises. This discovery made the hair stand up on the back of my neck.

Fields came around. "What's wrong?"

I just shook my head.

She moved closer; her eyes grew. "*My God*!" She pulled back and turned away. "Those two actually *were* psychos."

"Looks like it."

"Well, at least there were only two of them."

I didn't want to voice my opinion that there might have been more, or that others could have gone looking for more victims. Judging by the cramped quarters in the wagon, I strongly believed there were only two of them.

"I guess we just pile them in back and leave them here," she said.

"I have to see what's in those coolers."

"Are you sure about that?"

"No ..."

"Why do it, then?"

She was right. There could be something even worse than scalps floating around in them.

"You're right. We don't need to know."

Fifteen minutes later, after I'd pulled the two out of the truck, dragged them back to their ride and stuffed them in back, I closed the tailgate and we went back to the open doors see what else we could find. While Fields checked beneath the driver's seat, I opened the glove box. It was crammed with wallets. I counted seventeen. They must have taken them from their victims.

"Nothing here but a crack pipe and six or seven bottles of drugs," she said.

"What sort of drugs?"

She read the labels. "All sorts of meds."

"Same person?"

"Different people. Uppers. Downers. Tranquillizers. There are even some poppers here."

I opened two wallets. The second one caught my attention. The driver's license photo was of the man I'd shot. His name was Willis K. Simpson, he was 29, and lived in Saxonburg. I pulled out his registration, insurance card, and a few other cards. Suddenly things seemed much worse.

"What is it?" Fields asked.

"The man I shot. His name was Willis K. Simpson, and he was a doctor. He's got a card here from Saxonburg Regional Medical Clinic."

Fields just shrugged.

"You don't seem surprised."

"Nowadays I'm not surprised about anything."

I didn't know why this bothered me so much. Maybe it was because I didn't want to think a doctor capable of doing such horrible things. Or maybe I just didn't want to admit that I'd shot a doctor in the head. But I had to face facts. He might have been a doctor once, but he'd spent his last days breaking into people's homes, robbing them, killing them, and taking their scalps as grisly souvenirs.

"It really puts a new light on things." Fields laughed a humorless laugh. "A doctor robbing, killing, and scalping people. This plague sure has brought out the worst in everyone."

"This keeps getting more and more difficult." I didn't want to know about the other guy; the fact that he was a kid was too much to handle as it was. I dropped the wallets on the seat and slammed the door shut. I wanted to get away from here, drive back to the farm and have a big glass of bourbon.

"Personally, I think..." Fields suddenly stopped.

I froze. We both heard it.

The distant sound of a moving vehicle was coming from the east, down the long hill.

If my guess was right, it would be passing us in less than a minute.

CHAPTER THREE

"Get the truck doors closed! *Now!*"

While Fields ran for the truck, I closed the doors of the station wagon and ran up to her just as she pushed the driver's door shut. Grabbing her by the arm, I pulled her across the dirt road and through the bushes, to the six-foot ditch on the other side that ran parallel to the main road. We slid down the weed-choked slope, landing on the muddy bank just above the creek running through the culvert. The ground was damp and cold. Fields disappeared in the wild growth of the grassy slope and lay on her stomach. I stayed close to her, on my left side, my right hand tightly gripping the .357, which was aimed at the road less than ten feet away.

The sound of the approaching vehicle grew louder.

"What's the plan?" she whispered. Although most of her was hidden in the tall grass, I could see her eyes, which had grown quite large. She was frightened, as was I.

"If the vehicle stops and someone gets out and comes over to the truck, we drop them, no questions asked."

"Gotcha."

Luckily, the high weeds hid us from view, but by pushing some of the heavy growth aside we could see the road surface.

The hum of the vehicle grew louder. As it came down the hill, it began slowing down. I placed the barrel of the .357 on my forearm, which lay on the ground about six inches in front of my face. Then I cocked the hammer.

The vehicle, a light-blue compact, came into view. Judging by its soft, steady whine, it was some sort of hybrid. Its darkly-tinted windows hid the driver from view. It slowed as it drew closer, easing to a crawl as it neared the turnoff, where the truck sat off the main road. When it was about thirty feet away, it stopped.

For long, agonizing minutes, it sat totally still, its engine only slightly louder than the silence. It was a two-door—one of those models manufactured years ago for optimal fuel efficiency, when America began breaking off its ties with OPEC. The back seat was tiny, used mainly to house its many batteries, the trunk much too small to accommodate anything larger than a suitcase, or a bag of groceries. However, that was not the issue. The driver could be armed. And if someone was sitting beside him, he, too, could be armed.

After what seemed an eternity, the driver's window eased down a couple of inches.

I tensed up, just as I'd done in the Arizona desert twenty years ago, as a sniper for Border Patrol. Back then, when I spotted a shadow moving around in my infrared scope, I did not move or even breathe until I'd squeezed the trigger.

Right now I chose not to fire the gun. I didn't want to kill anyone unless it was absolutely necessary. The driver could be an old woman, for all I knew. Or even a kid. To survive nowadays, I had to assume everyone was a potentially dangerous threat, but that didn't mean I should become a homicidal maniac.

So I waited, just lying there, not moving, barely breathing, the .357 aimed at the driver's window. I caught a glint of something and decided it was most likely sunglasses. Even if I was correct in that assumption, I didn't know if a man or woman sat behind the wheel or if he or she was armed. I knew only that I should wait.

About five long, tense minutes later, the window eased down another inch.

My heart skipped a beat. I realized only then that I'd been sweating. The ground was cold, yet my limbs were hot, my face and arm covered in sweat. Cold beads drifted down my forehead, gathering in my eyes. I forced them shut. In spite of the panic building up within me, I didn't dare move. I guessed Fields was sweating as well, but I knew better than turn my head and risk betraying my position. I knew not to worry; Fields had good nerves.

I blinked a few times, squeezing away the sweat in my eyes. My vision finally cleared just as the car window eased back up. Moments later, the clicking of gears issued sharply from the vehicle. It eased away, abruptly increasing its pace as it ascended the hill.

The silence returned, heavy and inviting.

Fields turned to face me. "That was close."

"Too close." Something about that made no sense.

"What's wrong?"

"If you'd been in that car, would you have stopped?"

"No."

"Me neither."

"But at least no one got out. That was good, wasn't it? We didn't have to kill anyone else this morning."

"They probably didn't get out because they might have thought it could be an ambush."

"I'm just glad they left. I really don't care about their motives."

"I do."

"Does it matter?"

I couldn't believe she'd asked me that. "The three of us passed dozens of abandoned vehicles sitting along the roads on our way here. We didn't stop."

"We had other things on our minds. If you recall, we were trying to get away."

"I remember."

"Then what's bothering you?"

"There's only one reason for stopping nowadays."

"But they didn't get out, did they?"

"That's what I can't figure."

"You think they wanted to get out but didn't because they were afraid to?"

"Yes."

"Well, they're gone, and I don't hear anyone."

"That doesn't mean they're gone."

"I think you're being paranoid."

"Being paranoid doesn't mean someone isn't after you."

Fields didn't say anything for a little while. She seemed to be listening. "I still don't hear anyone."

"They could have gone up to the top of the hill, rounded the bend, and pulled over."

"What would they be doing?"

"Waiting."

"For what?"

"I don't know. I think we need to stay here."

"How long?"

"Twenty minutes. I think they'll come back, and twenty minutes seems a good length of time to test them. If they did stop somewhere up there, they'll probably wait five or ten minutes before circling back."

"If they do come back, we're gonna have to kill them, aren't we?"

"Only if they stop, get out and walk over to the truck."

"What if they don't come back at all?"

"Then everything will be all right. If nothing happens in twenty minutes, we'll get back in the truck, but I think we should head east and take another way back."

"Why?"

"If they're somewhere up that hill, watching, I don't want them seeing us pulling into the drive. They'll know where we live. We really don't want that."

**

We waited in the ditch, listening to the birds fussing in the trees, an occasional afternoon breeze drifting by, and the intermittent silence.

No sign of the compact. The road remained deserted.

Still, I couldn't lower my guard. Something just wasn't right, and no matter how hard I tried, I couldn't believe the danger had passed. Even though Fields' comment about my paranoia had me wondering, my gut continued telling me something was amiss.

"It's twenty minutes." Fields had pushed aside a clump of weeds to peek at her wrist watch. "Can we please get back in the truck?"

"I suppose." I sat up and, turning, gave the road a long, cautious scan. I saw nothing, heard nothing. As far as I could tell, Fields and I were the only two people in the area.

Fields straightened and brushed herself off. Still holding the .45 at her side, she climbed the steep grade and went back to the truck.

I followed, glancing in both directions as I approached the driver's side. Fields had already climbed in and was eyeing the hill as she buckled her seat belt. The .45 rested in her lap.

I got behind the wheel, laid the .357 on the console and buckled up. I made one last scan of the hill before firing up the ignition. Then I pulled out onto the road, pointed the truck east and climbed the hill that would take us to Saxonburg Boulevard.

I tried convincing myself that this was indeed paranoia rearing its ugly head, and that we were wasting precious gas for nothing. If I was sensible, I'd pull into the first drive we came to, turn around and head back west. We could get back to the farm and I could have my bourbon and forget about this ugly mess.

We didn't even reach the top of the hill before I noticed the light-blue speck in my rearview, about a mile behind us.

***

Fields glanced at her side mirror. "Why can't you be wrong once in a while?"

"How can you say something like that? Look what happened this morning."

Winding and treacherous in spots, Bakerstown-Culmerville Road snaked through the Pennsylvania hills for five or six miles before Saxonburg Boulevard cut through it, where a country store and filling station sat for as long as I could remember. Fields and I had gone there just a few weeks ago, looking for gas. The pumps still worked and the store still carried some supplies that hadn't yet been taken by the few survivors in the area.

The two-lane country road was lined with trees and heavy brush. Most of the houses sat far off from the road, with only portions of rooftops visible from the highway. Grass and weeds had grown wild during the last few months, hiding much of the land and properties from view. If I could gain a little distance, I could pull into a drive and use the cover of the overgrown brush to hide, then wait until I was sure we were no longer being followed.

Once again I wondered what this was all about. I sincerely hoped I could put this down as an innocent action. For all I knew, the driver might have gone up the hill and driven another five or ten minutes before remembering that he might have forgotten something. A map, perhaps, or bottle of water. Or maybe he hadn't brought along enough cigarettes for his trip.

Or maybe he was driving simply to keep his vehicle in working condition. Nowadays, this sort of thing made perfect sense. There were no more jobs, no more services. The only reasons to leave the house were for food and supplies. For that, you needed reliable wheels. Abandoned vehicles sat everywhere nowadays, but you couldn't be sure if they would start. And you ran the risk of being hunted down if you ventured out of the house on foot.

Although not exactly the perfect vehicle for heavy shopping, the compact could be used for other purposes. It was economical and thus perfect for looking for supplies or abandoned houses to ransack. Once the driver found something interesting, he could return home, switch to the truck or van, drive back to the target site and load up.

I wanted to believe that the driver of the compact was not a killer, but I just couldn't toss the possibility aside. Each time I considered the errand theory, I had to dismiss it. It didn't make sense that someone looking for food or other supplies would stop on the road and stare at a parked truck for five minutes, drive away and turn back around twenty minutes later. It made more sense that the driver had wanted to investigate, but didn't like the odds. Something about the setup had caused him to drive away. It felt like a possible ambush. Someone could be hiding in the truck, the station wagon, or even in the trees or ditch. Too much of a risk. Best leave and wait for a few minutes, come back and see if the truck was still there.

Then what? Follow the truck? Find out where it's going, drive on by, sneak back a little later and try to steal it? Or hide in the bushes and shoot the driver when he returned, then rob the body and take the truck?

As I drove, I kept glancing in my rearview, trying very hard to pull vibes from the tiny light-blue object nearly a mile behind us. I had gut instinct and a sixth sense, but as hard as I struggled, I just couldn't pull other people's thoughts or intentions out of the air.

"He doesn't seem to be in a hurry." Her long brown hair flying next to the open window, Fields kept a watchful eye on her side mirror.

"We're the only other vehicle on this road. He'd have to be a moron to lose sight of us."

Fields sat back in her seat and pushed hair out of her face. "He could be just an innocent guy driving around, for all we know."

"We can't assume anyone's innocent anymore. Now that we know they're coming up the driveway, we have to suspect everyone we see."

Fields didn't reply. I could tell she didn't like what I just said. I couldn't blame her; I hadn't liked it, either.

"If all he wants is to rob people, why didn't he stop and check out the station wagon?" she asked.

"It looked ratty."

"So? You can pile a bunch of things in that wagon."

"I think he's more interested in the truck."

"Why? Because it's in good condition, has balls and can carry a ton of stuff?"

"Maybe."

"Too bad we don't have Reed with us anymore. His friend could..."

"I know." I was thinking the same thing. Reed's invisible friend could have told us what was going on in the compact. But I didn't want to think of Reed right now. I missed him and wished he was here, but he was dead and Fields and I were still alive, and we had to do what we could to stay that way.

"I miss him, too." Fields touched my arm.

I considered our options. We had to lose the compact. If its driver didn't have any murderous intentions, he would have just driven on by. But he'd turned around and was now following us. Because of this, I no longer felt the need to rationalize this any further.

"Got anything in mind?"

"I'm gonna speed up around the next bend and look for a place to turn off. There's enough foliage around here to conceal us. If I can pull off quickly enough, I might be able to find enough trees to hide the truck from the road. Then we can wait until he drives on by."

"And if he pulls the same thing he did before?"

She was right. We couldn't spend the morning dodging some anonymous driver with unknown motives. The time would come when I'd had enough and decided to call his bluff. I didn't want to kill anyone else today, but if he forced my hand, I'd have to deal with it.

"We'll see what happens. If we spot him again, we'll just pull over and find out what he wants."

Fields said nothing. I knew what she was thinking. I was probably thinking along the same lines. Even though there weren't many people left in the world, monsters still existed. I found the concept aggravating as well as frightening.

I eased my foot off the gas as we rounded the bend and immediately pressed down on the pedal, upping our speed from 45 to 50 then 55. I punched it to 60, keeping it there for about half a mile, until we approached another bend. Just before we reached it, I pulled my foot off the gas and snuck a quick glance in the mirror. There was no sign of the compact. They probably hadn't yet reached the last bend.

As soon as we hit the next curve, I slammed down my foot again and got the truck back up to 55. A turnoff on the right, about a quarter of a mile straight ahead, beckoned to us. It sat directly behind a grove of pines. Beyond it and perpendicular to the main road, a small two-and-a-half-story brick house

45

with a steep shingle roof sat at the foot of a winding drive behind another grove of pines, about a hundred yards from the road. Large bushes concealed most of the house. The bushes and lawn hadn't been tended to in a great while—a clear sign that the place was abandoned. A narrow gravel drive veered around the corner of the house, to the back. It looked like the perfect place to hide.

When we were less than a hundred yards from the turnoff, I pulled my foot off the gas and applied it to the brake. Just as we inched past the dented white mailbox, I jerked the wheel, jerking the truck sharply around the bend while taking my foot off the brake. I hit the gas again, and we rushed down the winding drive, past the tall weeds of the unkempt lawn. We rushed down to the grove of pines, veered around the corner of the house, and came to an abrupt stop a few feet from the two-door garage.

"Stay here." I slammed it in park and rested only a moment to let my nerves settle down. I had to check the road. Snatching the .357, I pushed open the door, climbed down and snuck over to the side of the house just as the light-blue compact came into view on the main road, whining past the long line of pines at a clip of around fifty miles an hour.

I sighed in relief but knew it wasn't over just yet. We had to stay here for a little while and make sure the compact didn't show again. Then we could head back to the farm.

But first, I needed to assess our present situation. There were no other vehicles in the drive.

If a car or truck was parked in the garage, it might indicate that someone was inside the house. This person could be alive or dead. We wouldn't know for sure unless we investigated. I didn't want to go inside, but I had to find out what was going on. I didn't want to spend time sitting in the drive of someone's house if there was someone inside, aiming a gun at us.

I crept over the garage door. It was painted white, but the paint had faded long ago, and had peeled all over. I was just about to peer inside the dirt-smudged window when Fields said, "Moss, I think you'd better turn around."

The tone in her voice cut through me. I did as she said.

A small, slender old man around seventy years old sat at a battered wooden picnic table in the patio at the top of the stone steps leading to the French doors of the house. He wore a plaid shirt, suspenders and baggy pants. However, his mode of dress wasn't what alarmed me. Inches from his gnarled hands, which gripped a stained white coffee mug, a double barrel shotgun lay on the bench in front of him.

The barrels were pointed in our direction.

CHAPTER FOUR

I knew better than make any sudden movements. I still gripped the .357, but didn't want to shoot the old man. This was his house, and we were trespassing. Over the last year, life had reached its ultimate extreme, but that didn't mean I could kill an old man having a cup of coffee in his own back yard.

The shotgun looked like a twelve-gauge: a caliber I truly respected, since I'd seen the damage it could do. I didn't want to do or say anything that would cause the old man to pull the trigger. I had no desire to test his reflexes or his mood. The odds were in his favor. He didn't even have to pick it up; all he had to do was move his hand a few inches away from the coffee mug and squeeze the trigger. The gun was already pointed toward us—more toward Fields than me—and its scatter pattern would surely get her. This was much like our dilemma on the road just a few months earlier, when we'd encountered a unit of TABs armed with shotguns.

In this case, we faced an old man, not a superhuman TAB. He was out in his patio, enjoying his morning with a cup of coffee. He'd brought the shotgun along because he obviously knew what Fields and I had learned earlier this morning: you weren't safe in your own back yard.

He wasn't smiling, nor was he frowning. He just sat there, watching us curiously. He could be wondering if he should shoot us. We were trespassing, and I was holding a gun. We'd obviously come to rob and kill him, and I'd already walked over to open the garage door so we could enter and pick the place clean. He'd be well within his rights to shoot us. Just an hour or so earlier, Fields and I had defended ourselves when two men had wandered onto our place.

What was the difference?

The difference was that Fields and I were not psychos and hadn't come here to rob this old man. We didn't want to be followed and didn't want to kill whoever was following us. We'd come here strictly to avoid a confrontation.

Unfortunately, the old man didn't know any of this.

I had to somehow convince him that we meant him no harm. If he was a decent man, we might not have anything to worry about. If he realized that we'd come here just to hide out for a few minutes, he might even let us go.

"Hello." I smiled and tried to look pleasant.

No response. The old man didn't move. Neither did Fields. She was gawking at me, possibly for reassurance—or maybe because she didn't want to be looking directly at the gun if the old man decided to reach for it.

"We didn't come here to hurt anyone."

Still no response.

The old man was watching Fields. This made no sense. I was the greater threat. I was armed, and standing close enough to the truck to jump behind it for cover ... yet his gaze remained on Fields. I didn't know what was on his mind, if there was something about her that interested him—other than the obvious, of course. Fields was extremely easy on the eyes. But in a situation like this, anyone with combat training or experience would automatically concentrate on the immediate threat, and would fight to keep distraction out of the picture. This told me the old man had no military training. I didn't know if that gave us the advantage or posed another threat.

But that didn't matter right now. I had to shift his attention from Fields—to get him to look at me. This way, if things turned horrible, Fields would have time to duck and let the door absorb most of the buckshot.

I decided to keep talking and try to get him focused on me.

"We only came here to..."

"Hi," he said finally, and sat up on the bench seat. About ten seconds later, he grinned. It happened slowly, as if each muscle had to be activated individually. When the grin reached its level of intensity, I saw that he had no teeth.

The realization hit Fields and me at the same time.

The old man was doped.

***

"Why're you kids ... here?" he asked.

"We're hiding." I didn't want to lie to the old guy. "Someone's been following us."

50

He nodded several times, thinking it over. I wondered how far gone his brain was. "Where ya comin' from?"

"Just down the road." I used my left hand to point. As I pointed, I tilted my body to hide my right side from view, as I'd done with Willis K. Simpson. In this case, I wanted to appear less threatening. The old man was doped, but many of his faculties obviously still remained. He'd dressed himself, made a cup of coffee, and brought the shotgun outside with him. His reflexes were slow, but he had the presence of mind to ask why we'd come here.

"That's a big one." He pointed to the .357.

"I have it for protection."

He nodded again. "Someone followin' ya?"

"I don't like killing people, but sometimes they don't give you much of a choice."

The old man cackled laughter. "You can say *that* again." He abruptly stopped laughing. "My kid ... he's got a big one, too. Know Don?"

"I don't think so. Is he here?"

"Naw ... Don ... he ain't out here ..." The old man began grinning at Fields. "You the missus?"

Fields nodded.

"You're pretty, got nice hair ..."

"Thank you."

"Peggy had nice hair, bless her heart." He lowered his head. I felt sorry for the guy. Fields turned to me and shook her head. I was about to ask him about her when he looked up a moment later and raised his bushy gray brows. "Want some coffee?"

"No, thanks. We've got to..."

"Don't get much company now ... Don ... he makes good coffee ..."

"Do you have any made?" Fields asked.

He nodded. "Don ... he makes ... yeah, there's some left ... in the pot. In there." He pointed toward the French doors. "Made some last..." He scratched the back of his neck, trying to remember. "Wasn't too long ago."

"That would be very nice." Fields turned to me. She obviously felt badly for the poor guy, too. Before she opened her door, she tilted toward her left, to slide the .45 out of sight beneath the seat. I went over and slid the .357 beneath the driver's seat.

The old man grunted into a standing position. He was short, about five-four, and probably weighed in at one-thirty after a heavy meal. But he still appeared fairly alert, even though he was doped. After he'd picked up his mug, he grabbed the weapon and held it loosely at his side, barrels pointing toward the ground. "Bring it out with me all a time." He shook his head. "Never know now, folks runnin' around, crazier than shithouse rats." He held up the shotgun. "Don ... he found it for me."

"I'm glad you didn't shoot us," I said.

He grinned. "A fella can tell. Even when he's old and losin' his nut, he can still figure things out once in a while." He shuffled across the large, jagged stones of the patio floor, to the French doors.

As I followed Fields, I felt a heavy wave of cold darkness pulling us inside.

* * *

A heavy mix of stale cigarette smoke, burnt coffee, urine and something faintly rancid made my eyes water as soon as we'd gone inside. As Fields and I followed the old man through the piles of clutter and boxes stacked six feet high, the darkness surrounding me grew.

Stepping over empty beer cans and a couple of golf clubs, we went through the small dining room. At least I thought it was the dining room, judging by the French doors and what appeared to be an oval table and four chairs in the center of the area. However, the junk piled on the table and chairs and the boxes scattered everywhere made me disoriented. The floor was covered with strewn newspapers, magazines, laundry, beer cans, old toys, and cat litter. Two small kittens scurried across the floor as we went inside. A full-grown cat darted down the hall.

The dark, messy kitchen smelled strongly of urine and rotting food. The linoleum floor was covered with stains. The only light source came in through the window above the sink. Dirty dishes and pots and pans stacked two feet high filled the sink. A dish smeared with remnants of food sat on the counter. A calico cat crouched over it, licking its contents. A percolator bubbled quietly on the counter, its contents black and burnt.

53

The old man laid the shotgun on the island counter. He found two cups in the dish drainer, placed them on the counter and poured some steaming battery acid into them, as well as his own cup. "Sugar? Cream?"

A small milk carton sat on the counter. A sour smell emanated strongly from it. It had undoubtedly expired long ago.

"Sugar's fine, thanks." Fields glanced at me.

The old man placed both cups on the island counter, spilling some as he slid them over. The coffee was rank, but we nonetheless accepted his kind offer graciously. I was pleased that he'd decided we weren't a threat, and welcomed this kindness, hoping it might lead to a casual friendship, and that it could be an omen of a future that might not be as bleak as we'd all originally feared. After this morning's nightmare, Fields and I needed some sign, however small, that the human race hadn't gone entirely belly-up. I hoped this turn of events would be such a sign.

I didn't know if Fields felt the same, but I was curious about Don. If he was as cordial as his father, there could be a possible friendship in the making there as well. I wondered if he lived here as well. We couldn't tell by the cluttered interior of the house. Boxes, dirty laundry, canned goods, toys and beer cans filled every inch of available space. Judging by the sheer volume of board games, model airplane kits, unopened packages of shirts, underwear and dog-eared paperbacks tossed everywhere, the old man had been accumulating this stuff long before the plague had come about. But it didn't tell me if anyone else lived here. From what I'd learned about hoarders, this mess could easily belong to one person.

The old man gestured for us to drink the coffee.

Fields and I both watched him as we raised our cups. We brought the cup to within two inches of our lips, but no closer. The stench of the brew was horrible. I held my breath and I could tell Fields had done the same thing. We both lowered our cups as he sipped from his own. The cat had finished cleaning the food from the plate and tiptoed across the sink, to the carton of milk, where a few drops had splattered the counter in front of it. The cat lapped it up, jumped down to the floor and ran out of the room.

"Scruffy." The old man grinned. "Came here one day, lookin' for vittles."

"Are all the cats yours?" Fields asked.

"Don ... he brought one home the other day." He scratched his jaw. "Naw. Last week, mebbe?" He grinned. "Two weeks. Yep, two weeks ago, I think ..."

"Does Don live here with you?" I asked.

He laughed. "Don? Naw, got his own place three roads down. Betsy didn't like it, him movin' out, but what the hell? Kids, right?" He shrugged. "It's okay, he comes here once in a while, brings me ciggies and beer. Smoke?" He pulled a crumpled pack of Pall Malls out of his plaid shirt pocket. Fields and I shook our heads. He pulled a crooked smoke from the pack and dropped it on the counter.

He picked it up and dropped it again. I picked it up for him. He took it, put it in his mouth and struggled with a match. I took the book from him and lit it. He nodded his thanks, pulled in a thick lungful and hacked away. Gray smoke danced around him. He stopped coughing and had another quick puff.

"Where ya from?" he asked again, coughing again.

"Down the road a few miles," I said.

He nodded. "Used to ... I worked on cars ... before this ... before everyone started ... dyin' off ..."

"Did Don work with you?" I asked.

He grinned. "Yeah, Don's a big, strappin' boy, always around when ol' Dad was workin' on a car, learnin' all kinds of stuff so he could be like his daddy ..." The old man shook his head at some memory and sighed. "Now?" He shrugged. "He goes out now, once in a while, lookin' for folks. Don's always liked people, especially the ladies ..."

"Then Don lives here with you." Apparently Fields was just as confused as I was.

A nod. "My boy ... he goes out for beer and ciggies, but sometimes he'll find someone along the way, bring 'em back, and we'll have a nice little get-together, like in the day ..." He winked at Fields. "He'd like you. You're pretty. My Betsy was pretty ... I've got a picture of 'er ... somewhere ..."

The darkness around me grew heavier. At that point I decided that we should be leaving. "It's been nice, but I think we need to be getting back to..."

"Don's here, ain't he?" He was staring at me as if I knew the answer.

"I don't know. You just told us..."

"That's right." He nodded, remembering. "He came over the other night, said he was all done in, wanted me to meet a lady, only he forgot to bring 'er ..."

I turned to Fields. She was eyeing the back door.

"The other night ..." The old man scratched the back of his neck. "Naw, it was last week ... or mebbe two weeks—wanna meet Don?"

Fields and I gawked at one another. I didn't like where this was going.

"Came back the other night, said he was tired, real tired." A chuckle. "Done tuckered out, all that drivin' and all, lookin' for beer and ciggies for the old man."

"That's all right," I said. "Like I said, we've got to be..."

"Only take a sec. Don's here somewhere." He put down his coffee cup and went through the doorway. "Don?" He turned, gesturing. "C'mon, you'll like 'im, he's always been a good kid. Don?" He shuffled down the hall. More cats emerged from doorways, scattering. I counted at least eight of them.

"Should we follow him?" Fields whispered.

"I think we should leave. I don't think he'll even miss us..."

"*There* he is! Just *knew* ya hadn't left yet. Hey Don, we got company!" The old man reappeared in the hall. He was gesturing again. "Don's in his room, restin'. C'mon, now. He's tired, but wants to meet ya."

Fields shrugged. "We don't want to be a bother..."

"No bother. C'mon." The old man disappeared into the room at the end of the hall.

Fields and I went cautiously down the hall, stepping over scattered underwear, newspapers, and beer cans. More cats darted out of doorways.

We reached the doorway at the end of the hall.

The room was even more cluttered and foul than the rest of the house. The stench coming from it overwhelmed both of us. Fields covered her mouth and turned away.

"Don? We got company. A lady, and she's real pretty!" The old man stood over a bed covered with clothes, coats, and blankets. A man about my own age lay in the bed, not moving. His colorless face was covered with maggots. A dead cat, also covered with maggots, lay beside the body. The dead man's arm was curled around its matted corpse.

Gasping, Fields rushed past me.

As I followed her, I heard the old man talking to Don, telling him to get out of the bed to greet their guests.

***

Fields and I sat in stunned silence as I got back onto the main road. No words could justify—or lessen—the image of the old man's son lying dead in the bed. The bone-white face. The dull eyes, frozen in death, staring at the ceiling. The maggots feasting on the man's cold, bloated flesh. The dead cat lying next to the corpse's arm.

I imagined that the old man was still trying to coax his son out of the bed. Then, after several horrifying moments, the dark cloud in the old man's muddled head would clear and he'd realize the boy was dead. Remnants of memory would flicker among the darkness. The images would stay there just within his grasp, if only temporarily. The darkness would then dissipate, revealing glittering shards of reality.

He'd sit on the edge of the bed, holding the boy's cold, lifeless hand and sobbing quietly. Fond memories would seep out of the fog, and confusion would thunder through him. The clouds would come back, smothering the memories, and he'd realize that his son needed his rest. He'd get up quietly and tiptoe from the room. He might want to talk to his dead wife Betsy, perhaps to clear up a few things. But he'd gradually remember that the house was empty, and then he'd have to take a few moments to recall where she was the last time he saw her.

She could be lying in their bed, taking a nap ... or sprawled in a chair in a spare room ... She might even be out in the garden, tending to her flowers.

As he went through the house, trying not to panic, a photo would catch his eye. He'd pick it up and stare at it for a few minutes, tears gathering in his eyes moments before his mind betrayed him again by clouding up. He'd put down the photo and stand there, wondering what he was trying to remember. As he did so, a cat would rush by, and his thoughts would clear. Yes. The cats needed to be fed. And he'd be off to the kitchen.

Fields sat forward in her seat, her face buried in her hands. She hadn't said a word. As I pulled onto the main road and headed east, she remained bent forward. I didn't know if she was trying to hide from what she'd just seen, from reality itself, or from me. It was the first time I'd seen her break down like that. Fields was strong and generally unshakable by nature. She'd survived an assault by three roving TABs when I first met her in Breezewood. She not only got away from them, she'd also found a place of refuge and a gun, and was able to gain the advantage when I stumbled into the gas station office and posed a viable threat.

This last event had been too horrible for either of us to easily dismiss. Although I'd seen death in many different forms, I fully expected nightmares from this, possibly for years to come. There was no reason why Fields, a former RN who'd no doubt seen just as much death as I had, should feel any differently.

I left her be, partly because I understood and also because I needed to tend to my own quiet reflection. This plague had reared its ugly head once again, revealing yet another page in its lengthy tome of unspeakable horrors. It had been months since Reed, Fields and I had escaped the underground government facility. We'd deleted their programs, which, as a result, destroyed their last-ditch attempt at mass genocide, but the results of their corrupt legacy lived on. I sincerely hoped the time would come when we could safely say we'd seen the last of it.

"That poor man." Fields lowered her hands. "I know how cruel this sounds, but I honestly hope he doesn't last much longer."

"If the cigarettes don't get him, the rotten food will. I'm surprised the stench of the cat urine hasn't already damaged his lungs."

"I counted eight cats. From what I've learned in the health profession, the more severe cases—those causing lung and respiratory disease and failure—usually result from constant exposure to a substantially higher number. I didn't see mouse or rat droppings anywhere, so at least he's safe in that area. But even so, daily exposure to cat feces is deadly."

"There are probably more than eight. Cats breed a lot. I saw two kittens, so there might be a lot more hiding. There could also be a few dead ones lying around. Don't forget the one on the bed with Don."

Fields shivered. "That's something I could have lived without."

"Actually, I think the old man's mind is already pretty well gone. He was really distracted—especially when he tried remembering things. I'll give him another couple of weeks before he stops using the toilet and forgets to eat, or feed the cats. Then he'll probably curl up in the bed with his son and stay there."

As I drove, I kept my eye out for the light-blue compact, but there was no sign of anyone else on the road or in any of the yards. We passed a few dead bodies and the carcasses of three dogs lying in the high grass near the road, but no one else still moving. But I continued to be cautious, and decided to stick with my plan of driving to Saxonburg, taking the loop around, and coming back on Deer Creek Road.

"I'd like to stop at the store at the Saxonburg crossroads," I said. "Since they had propane the last time we checked, I think we should take anything that's left. This way, we'll have enough to last us through the winter."

"How's the fuel tank for the truck? You haven't filled up in a while."

It read slightly below three-quarters, which was more than enough. We had twenty gallons stored in the garage, so we weren't hurting. But it made sense to build up the stockpile. We had no idea what awaited us. The power grid servicing the County continued to produce intermittent trickles, but it wouldn't last much longer. Once the station went dark, the pumps would no longer work, and the only gas left in the tanks would go bad and turn useless in just a few weeks.

It took us about ten minutes to reach the crossroads. I pulled off the main road, where the side entrance led to the rear lot, which held about two dozen vehicles. Abandoned trucks, cars, ATVs and SUVs sat along the curb and in the gravel lot behind the store. I eased past a dirt-covered van sitting off the curb, the driver slumped over the wheel. Two more bodies lay on the ground across the street, in the front yard of a small one-story brick house with its windows broken out. Weeds had taken over. A rusty push mower stood just a few feet from one of the bodies.

I eased into the rear lot of the store and parked a fair distance from the block building, between an old Ford pickup and a rusty El Camino. I parked there in case we had to hide out. I'd learned long ago about anonymity, and always thought of ways of keeping hidden, or at least inconspicuous. The best place I knew of to hide a truck was to park it amongst other trucks.

We got out and went up the gravel lot to the back of the store. The cool breeze drifted across the road, bringing with it some sourness. It wasn't very strong, so I assumed the bodies hadn't been dead very long. I carried my .357, Fields her .45. The propane tanks sat on a concrete slab on the far side of the building, inside a small chain-link pen that had been forced open some time ago.

"Do you want to check the tanks first?" Fields asked.

"Whatever we do, we need to do it quickly."

"I don't see anyone."

"I'm still a little uneasy since this morning. Besides, I expect that damned light-blue compact to pop up again."

"So I guess we'll check the tanks."

"If they're full, I'll find a cart or dolly, wheel out the tanks and set them out here. I'll go back for the truck, bring it over, and we can load them onto the bed."

"What do you want me to do while you're checking for propane?"

"You can go around the front to see if the pumps are working."

"Sounds like a plan. What's the strategy if we spot that compact again?"

"We can hide out in the store. If someone pulls in and starts looking around, that's when we'll have to..."

I stopped talking when I heard the harsh sound. Fields spun on her heel in its direction.

Motorcycles. Several of them. Their roar grew louder by the second.

CHAPTER FIVE

A display of lawn mowers and farming implements covered a concrete slab across the aisle from the propane tanks. Beyond it, the loading dock doorway opened into a large area around two thousand square feet. Ten feet from the doorway, 55-gallon metal barrels sat upright in four rows of twelve, covering the wall on the right. A few from the front row had been knocked over, and lay in the aisle amongst strewn candy and food wrappers, broken palettes, forty-pound sacks of concrete and a carton of rat poison that had been broken open, its tiny blue pellets scattered all over the floor.

The angry roar of the motorcycles increased as the riders drew closer.

"The barrels." I pointed behind Fields. "We can hide behind them."

We ran for the loading dock, jumping over rolls of fencing and dodging a manure spreader. I led the way, with Fields close behind me. We reached the barrels just as the first chopper pulled off the main road and coasted down the gravel slope, to the rear lot. The last row of barrels sat close to the wall, but we were able to squeeze behind two at the far end. We ducked down, lowering our butts to the concrete floor and wedging ourselves into the triangular spaces between them.

By this time, two more choppers had entered the rear lot, their rough, loud engines making the walls of the loading dock vibrate. From our cramped quarters, we couldn't see anything but horse feed and dog food sitting on palettes piled ten feet high, against the back wall.

I carefully adjusted my position, until I was sitting with my knees against my chest, my right side mashed against the wall, my left shoulder pressing the barrel. I kept the .357 pressed tightly against my chest, its barrel pointing at the ceiling. Fields sat in a similar hunched-over position, her back just inches from my knees. I couldn't see how she held the .45 but was confident she could get it blasting away immediately.

The deafening idling of the choppers prevented us from communicating with one another. I didn't want to shout at her and risk being heard if the machines were suddenly switched off. To reassure her, I gently squeezed her shoulder. Although she was warm and trembled a little, she nodded slightly, reassuring me that she was okay. I honestly felt we would survive this, provided no one came in to search the barrels.

But we had no idea what these people would do, how many there were, what they wanted, or if they were armed. All we did know was that if they were able to operate their choppers, they weren't doped. Hopefully they'd come here strictly for supplies. Or gas. They might not even be interested in hurting anyone, for that matter.

I knew right off that my reasoning was seriously flawed. For some stupid, inexplicable reason, I was still holding fast to the idea that not everyone left was a potential killer. What was wrong with me? After what had happened in Orlando, St. Cloud, and on the trip up here, I still found myself struggling to remain optimistic. And after escaping the underground government facility, I still held out hope for the survival of the human race.

Even after this morning's events, I still felt this way. I knew I shouldn't, but I did. And though Fields and I were hiding from a gang of bikers, I struggled to convince myself that it might be possible to walk out there and talk to them.

I quickly dismissed that notion, knowing full well that it would be certain suicide to show ourselves. Nothing and no one was safe anymore. No matter how anything looked or felt or seemed, we had to assume the worst. These were bikers, and everyone knew what they were like. In this new age of death and destruction, we faced roving gangs doing whatever they wanted. I could only assume this group was heavily armed, and would not hesitate to kill us.

Except something told me they might not want to kill Fields.

Not right off, anyway.

The choppers stopped idling. In moments, a heavy, eerie silence dropped over us like a smothering blanket.

My nerves twitched as Fields and I heard heavy footsteps.

***

"Hey! Anyone hangin' around?"

67

The footfalls sounded like heavy boots. The sounds grew louder and stopped abruptly near the loading dock doorway. I heard what sounded like glass being broken farther down, in the back lot. Someone chuckled. Someone else coughed wetly and spat. The heavy footfalls resumed, growing louder before stopping again. "Anyone here?"

More glass shattering. It sounded like someone was smashing bottles onto the concrete. Another cough; someone hawked loudly. The clicking of a gun hammer issued near the doorway, making us both shudder, and we heard another cough.

The heavy footfalls resumed, moving toward us. Several steps later they stopped, around twenty feet away. A hissing sound, followed by a loud, barking cough resonated so loudly that it hurt my ears. A loud hawking sound preceded a *splat*! onto the concrete floor in front of the barrels. Another cough, then the clearing of someone's voice.

"Hey, Trapper! Where the fuck didja find this shit? Jammed up a dead dog's ass?"

"You're smokin' it, ain'tcha?" came the distant reply.

"Only 'cause we can't find nothin' better!"

A heavy whiff of marijuana smoke drifted our way as it crawled over the barrels. I lowered my head so I wouldn't sneeze. Fields lowered her head as well.

"Ya don't like it?" The distant voice grew louder as the second biker approached the dock. "Take a dump and snort it instead."

"Funny, asshole. Real funny."

A different voice out back said, "Anything in there worth takin'?"

The footfalls started up again. It sounded like whoever was in the room with us was looking around. A loud bang resonated, and something slammed into the barrels. Fields stiffened. The biker had probably kicked one of the barrels lying on its side. "Just horse feed, dog food, straw—nothin' but farm shit."

More footfalls. A second biker climbed the slab leading into the dock. Fields pressed her right side against the wall.

"There's gotta be a chick around here somewhere. I'm so fuckin' horny, my balls are gettin' all swollen and fucked up, rubbin' against my knees."

"Use your fuckin' hand, ya wuss."

"Tired of that shit."

"Get used to it, dude. Ain't no fuckin' chicks around here. We been lookin' for two days."

"*Got* to be..." More footfalls.

Fields tensed up, pressing harder against the wall. I felt badly that I couldn't reassure her. I didn't want to jump up and start blasting away. I had no idea how many bikers were out there or where they were, and didn't want to start up a firefight. The .357 carried six; Fields' .45 held eight. The Beretta in my pocket also had eight, but was useless for anything beyond ten or twelve feet, and would probably take most of the mag to stop one big biker wearing heavy leather.

69

The footfalls stopped. Someone was sniffing. "I can always tell when there's pussy around ..."

"You're full of shit."

"What the fuck's *that* have to do with anything?"

"You're losin' it, dude. Suck it up."

"That last bitch wasn't worth the trouble, couldn't even remember she even had a pussy."

A chuckle. "She just needed reminded. Didn't take much."

"Ain't no fun doin' a chick when she don't even know what's happenin'."

"The way it is, dude. Gotta nail what we find while it's fresh. Wait too long and they get so fuckin' stupid, they ain't even worth the time."

"Ain't nothin' fresh no more, goddammit."

More coughing and hacking somewhere out in the back lot.

"That fucker Morgan's gettin' it bad."

"Leave 'im alone. He don't have long."

"I say cap 'im now, before we head for Pittsburgh. Excess baggage."

"Then they'll only be four of us."

"So? He ain't no good no more, and he's gettin' worse. Pissed his pants last night, didn't even know it. I had to tell 'im, smelled so bad."

"So? It happens."

"Ain't happenin' to *this* boy." A snort.

"Wanna bet?"

"Hey, I piss my pants? That's when I eat a bullet."

"Lemme know when you're ready for chow, dude. *I'll* serve it up for ya."

"You're all fart, Trapper."

More coughing and hawking out back.

"Fucker's gross. Real gross, coughin' up his insides so much."

"C'mon, we gotta check the store. Then we'll get some gas and head on back to camp."

"What about Morgan?"

"What about 'im? He's a brother, dude."

"He craps his pants, *you're* the one beddin' down with 'im."

"Go fuck yourself." The footfalls resumed.

"Gonna have to. No fuckin' chicks around no more."

"Stop your whinin'. They'll be chicks in Pittsburgh."

"Ya sure?"

"Course I'm not fuckin' sure, dude. Who the fuck ya think I am? One of those fuckin' mental dudes they used to show on the TV?"

The footfalls grew fainter.

***

About a minute after the two left the dock, someone came back and tossed something at the palettes of horse feed. I couldn't make out what it was but decided it was something large and fairly heavy, like a strip of rebar, or a piece of fencing. Then silence. We waited tensely, but no one else came back.

Outside, the bikers yelled to one another near the gas pumps.

"Hey, Trapper ... What the fuck's *this*?"

"No tellin', dude. If ya can't eat it or smoke it, leave it be."

"Looks like a strip of beef jerky some dickhead tossed in the dirt."

"Eat it, then."

"Kinda funky ..."

"Then *don't* eat it."

"Where ya goin' Morgan? Get back here."

A loud, wet cough. "Wanna check out those trucks in the back!"

Fields and I tensed up.

"Forget it, dude. We gotta get back to camp."

"Pops, you gotta quit tellin' me what to do. I don't wanna go to school no more!"

"I ain't your old man, Morgan. How many times I gotta tell ya?"

"Shit, he's losin' it again, dammit. *Told* ya he's a fuckin' fruitcake."

"Billy ain't eatin' his peas, Moms. Can I have 'em?"

"Get your fuckin' ass on that hog right now!"

"Comin', Pops ..."

A chopper exploded into rough idle. A few seconds after that, another chopper fired up, followed by a third.

A gunshot rang out, slamming through the area and causing the walls and floor to vibrate.

Fields and I both cringed.

More shouting, but the idling of the choppers drowned it all out. It sounded like a heated argument but didn't last very long.

72

Then, one by one, the shifting of gears lowered the volume of chaos. The cycles eased back out onto the main road, quickly opening up as they roared south on Saxonburg Boulevard.

After about a minute, the wonderful silence returned, sweetening the air while lifting our spirits. Fields eased out of her crouched position and let her head fall back, causing her hair to slide down my thighs. I left my gun in my lap and rubbed her shoulders. She was warm and damp with sweat, and still trembled.

"Think they're really gone?" she whispered.

"I think so." I was hesitant about saying anything else. We'd been through a lot in just a few hours.

"They left ... someone behind, didn't they?"

"Yeah."

She was silent for a few moments. "I wonder where they ... left him."

I didn't want her to see another corpse so soon after the incident with Don, but I couldn't very well protect her from the horrors of daily reality.

"I'm sure we'll find out when we get ready to drive out of here."

"They might have ... he could be lying there ... in the middle of..."

"We can't sit here and worry about this. We've got things to do."

We both got up. For me, it was slow-going and painful. We'd both been wedged in a tightly cramped position for close to an hour and I'd lost the circulation in my legs. I used the edge of the barrel for leverage to push myself up. Then I shoved the .357 under my belt in the small of my back and leaned against the wall for support while waiting for the feeling to return in my limbs.

Fields got right up and shoved the .45 in the Uncle Mike's holster above her hip. She vigorously rubbed feeling into her thighs and alternately raised her feet and shook them. Then she began moving around again and waiting for me. She was, after all, several years younger than me, and in better shape.

Once the tingling in my legs and feet had subsided, I took a few tentative steps and stretched. Soon I began feeling more like myself.

We went over to the open doorway and scanned the lot. Other than the shattered shards of glass made from the bottles the bikers had tossed, the place looked no different. Most important, the truck remained where we'd left it.

Without warning, Fields wrapped her arms around my neck and clung tightly to me. She was shivering. I put my arms around her waist and hugged her back. I could tell she was coming to grips with our close call. Needless to say, the sudden contact made me feel much better.

"Thank you," she whispered, her hot breath in my ear.

Despite my own ebbing tension, I couldn't help becoming aroused. But this wasn't exactly the right time or place for romance.

"For what?" I asked.

"For being there ... with me."

"I just happened to be in the neighborhood, so ..."

She rested her head on my shoulder. "You were right there, beside me. You didn't come apart. You ... well, you're always strong. You're always thinking. You never panic or let things overwhelm you. It helps."

"Everything's gonna be okay." The military had taught me that keeping a clear head can mean the difference between life and death. In this new world, there could be no room for panic. Daily horrors and tragedies had become commonplace. Zoning out, along with instant denial, meant death.

Fields sighed. "Are we still doing the propane?"

"Since we're here, we might as well."

"Still want me to check the pumps?"

I could tell that she didn't want to go around the building. The dead biker probably lay in plain sight.

"No need. The bikers used them, so they're probably still working. Stay right here and keep watch while I hunt for a dolly. If you see or hear anything, let me know right away. Then get out of sight. Unless something else happens, I'll let you know when I need you to help me load up."

"No. I can't see anything from here, and by the time I hear something, it'll be too late. I've got to be out front, near the road..."

"You don't have to."

"Yes I do. I really do."

"Fields, there's no need..."

"I'm a big girl. I've already seen three bodies today. I even made one of them, remember?"

Despite my fears, I couldn't tell her not to do this. We all had to fight our own demons in our own way. "Just don't spend too much time looking at the body. His problems are over. Concentrate on keeping an eye on the road."

She kissed me lightly on the cheek and mussed my hair. Without another word she went down the steps and crossed the lot, keeping away from the broken glass and other things scattered on the ground. While she went up toward the gate, I went over to where the tanks sat in their fenced-in pen on the slab.

"*Moss!*" Her terror-filled voice stabbed me sharply between the shoulder blades.

I spun around and pulled the .357 out from under my belt. My nerves jumped wildly as I raced across the lot. When I peered around the corner of the building, I stopped cold.

A biker sprawled on the ground, bleeding from a bullet wound in his gut. His hands and forearms were covered in blood as he gripped a sawed-off shotgun. Its blood-smeared barrels were aimed at Fields.

CHAPTER SIX

My thoughts raced as I clumsily jammed the .357 behind my back, underneath my belt. I couldn't risk the man seeing it. He'd panic and shoot Fields. Or both of us.

"I'm right here," I said as I stepped around the corner of the building, my hands up.

"N-No, Moss..." Her voice sounded choked.

"It'll be okay," I said softly, hoping my voice would reassure her.

As soon as the wounded man saw me, he jerked the shotgun sharply to his left, away from Fields. He did it clumsily, nearly losing his balance. The process took him considerable effort, and he squealed loudly. His entire torso was soaked, making any sudden movement extremely painful. I couldn't see the bullet wound but could judge by the blood pattern that he'd been hit dead-center—somewhere below his ribcage and above the groin area. Since Fields and I hadn't seen what happened, we didn't know what gun or caliber had been used. The blast sounded like a .44 mag, perhaps, or .357. The damage was massive and fatal, involving the intestines and other vital organs. He wouldn't last long.

But that didn't mean Fields and I had nothing to worry about.

I was standing at least thirty feet away and had to keep him focused on me. The shotgun barrels were no more than a foot in length; the spray pattern would be wide enough for me to survive. However, Fields was standing less than ten feet from the weapon and wouldn't be so lucky.

Somehow, in spite of the fear growing rapidly inside me, I found my voice. "Are you Morgan?"

He cringed; the shotgun lowered an inch. He squinted through the tears and the sweat pouring down his face and his broad, dirt-smeared forehead. Thick strands of long, greasy black hair had fallen over his face, mingling with his beard. "W-Who the fuck ... are you?"

"Trapper sent me." I hoped that confusing him would give us time. Maybe all we'd need was a few minutes before he start slipping away.

He squinted. "*Huh*?"

"He told me he didn't mean for you to be shot."

Morgan coughed but kept the shotgun aimed in my direction. "Fucker ... he *let* that dickhead Aaron shoot me, you dumb shit ..."

"Trapper said Aaron shouldn't have done it. He said your dad wouldn't have let that happen."

"Pops?" The man's voice changed, grew softer, higher-pitched. "I hurt ... I really *hurt*!"

"Anything I can get you, son?"

"Pops?" He sniffed; the shotgun lowered another couple of inches. He shook his head to get his hair away from his eyes. "Moms around? I don't ... want her to ... she don't like me ... gettin' into..."

"I'll talk to her." I wanted Fields to move to her left, but I couldn't give her a signal. The man would certainly lose what little sense he had left and shoot one of us.

Morgan coughed wetly. "Promise?"

"I sure do." I hoped I could get to the .357 quickly enough. Fields wore her .45 in her hip; she kept her hands held high and wouldn't be able to get to her piece before Morgan could shoot her. I had to somehow keep this guy talking and coax Fields out of the way. I couldn't risk waiting any longer. This man could last ten minutes or more. "Everything'll be all right, son."

"N-No ..." Morgan shook his head, his hair skipping across the shoulders of his leather jacket. More blood trickled onto his left hand. "Fuck. Fuck!"

"What's wrong, son?"

He groaned. "Just shit my fuckin' *pants*!"

A heavy fecal odor drifted in our direction.

Fields slowly turned to look at me. Her face was white, her eyes filling the sockets. She didn't move. Her eyes screamed at me. I forced myself to put as much reassurance into my expression as I possibly could. Fields was strong, but even a blind man could tell she was hovering dangerously close to the panic mode.

I took a deep breath. "It's ... okay. You've just been shot..."

"It *ain't* fuckin' okay, Jack!" The barrels jerked back up. He glared at me. "It *ain't* fuckin' okay. It really sucks!" Then he abruptly shifted his eyes back to Fields and raised the shotgun again. It took him considerable effort, and he groaned weakly.

"It's *her* fault, dammit! Moms, it's *your* fault! *Your* fuckin' fault! *You* did this! Damn you, *you* did this to me!"

"It's *not* her fault." I struggled to keep the panic out of my voice. "She doesn't have anything to do with this. This is my fault. And if you want to do something about it, you have to deal with me."

He turned awkwardly in my direction. His eyes closed and his head bobbed as he struggled to stay awake. As he fought to keep from collapsing, I brought my right hand down and behind my back. Despite my growing fear, my experience took over, steadying my hand and closing it tightly around the comforting grips of the .357.

Fields instinctively leaped to her left.

Morgan's eyes shot open; he jerked his head in her direction.

I pulled out the .357 and shot him in the head. The force of the powerful caliber slammed his right side into the pavement. The shotgun clattered to the cracked concrete three feet from him, just beyond the blood and brain splatter.

Fields pushed herself up and studied the scene on her hands and knees. She looked at me, turned back to the dead biker, groaned, bent over and threw up.

***

While I waited for Fields to recover, I struggled to keep myself in control. The woman I loved was almost killed with a shotgun, and this would have happened just ten feet away from where I was standing. In spite of my military training and

80

everything I'd faced in the last six months, the fear swept violently through me, and I felt the blood turn to ice in my veins. I had to fight it. *Take down the enemy*, my inner voice kept telling me, over and over. *Forget the fear, the urge to run away, and take him down.*

That was what I just did, and now that it was all over, I had to listen to the inner voice once again. This time it said, *Do it and forget about it. Put it behind you and move on.*

Move on. Somehow, that important tidbit just wasn't working right now. Not with what I was looking at.

Her head down, Fields knelt on the ground, her arms crossed as she hugged herself. She sobbed quietly and made no effort to look up and see where I was, or if I was still there. I recognized shock when I saw it, and knew that people dealt with it in many different ways. Fields was fighting it in her own way. She was surrendering, holding everything in while coming to grips with what she'd just been through.

Although she needed time, we couldn't stay here. The bikers could be coming back, for all we knew. Or that damned compact. Whatever the case, we had to get back on the road.

I knew something about interrupting people in their grief or shock. I also realized how dangerous it was. But I had no choice. I approached her quietly. If I could get her back to the truck, we could get out of here. She could continue crying in the safety of the truck, and I'd let her have her privacy. It would take at least twenty minutes to get back to the farm. Once there, she could lie down and rest.

"Brooke? It's me. I think we'd better leave."

No response.

"Brooke? Please ..."

Still no response.

Taking a deep breath, I reached down and gently touched her right shoulder.

She pulled back sharply, as if bitten by a poisonous snake. She spun around to face me and through the long tangles of her hair covering parts of her face I could see the terror blazing from her large glossy eyes. Drool beaded from her lower lip and had gathered on her chin. She looked like someone who had just been given a frightening glimpse of Hell.

I'd seen this same expression many times before, years ago. I'd seen it on vest killers just before they activated the bomb. I'd seen it on gang members when a police assault weapon turned their way. I'd also seen it on children packed tightly into vans for export in the slave and prostitution trade, as the rear doors opened and sunlight shined on their faces for the first time since their confinement. This expression had haunted me for many years, and I didn't care to see it ever again.

I surely hadn't wanted to see it on Fields.

I didn't move. I continued to watch her, hoping that the horror that had taken over her spirit would eventually fade, and that my image would come back and remove some of the fear and terror she'd just experienced. I'd already returned the .357 to its place beneath my belt behind my back. When the darkness enveloping her ebbed and my image appeared to her again, she wouldn't see the gun, and thus remember the horror.

She remained frozen, her gaze never leaving me. Then, finally, she blinked several times, as if awakening from a dream, and began breathing normally. She shivered. The dead biker lay about ten feet directly to her left. She continued to stare at the pavement directly in front of her. She grew still and didn't move. Then, just as I began wondering if she would ever move again, she slowly raised her head. Her hair had fallen over her face. She slowly brought up her hands and pushed it away, letting it fall down her back.

When I saw her face again, I sighed in relief. The terror had left her eyes. She sighed, and as she looked at me, I could have sworn I saw a smile struggling to soften her features.

I knelt beside her. "Brooke?"

She tilted her head. "You ... never call me that ..."

"You scared me."

"It ... sounded nice."

Her closeness began making me lose focus, but at least I found my self-confidence returning. Still, I knew we had to get out of here. "C'mon." I took her arm. "We have to go."

She let me help her up and guide her back down the slope, where the truck awaited us in the parking lot. She moved stiffly at first and then relaxed, keeping close to me, her side pressed against mine as I led her back to the truck. She even let me hold her around the waist while I pulled open her door. I helped her up the step and made sure she was settled in comfortably as I strapped her in. Her head fell back onto the neck rest. Her eyes were closed while I circled the front of the truck and climbed in beside her.

I saw no reason to continue with our propane run. It was much more important to leave this place. I fired up the ignition, backed out and eased down the gravel aisle, where the opened gate led back up the sloped hill, to the main road.

The dead figure sprawled in the middle of the pavement, less than twenty yards ahead. I'd have to veer the truck to the left, brushing the bushes in front of the property fence. The truck's tires would straddle the shotgun, which lay a few feet from the corpse. It wouldn't take long to pass the grisly scene, especially if I hurried through. But I didn't want her to watch.

I stopped the truck.

Fields sat up. "What's...?

"Close your eyes."

"What's going...?

"Just do it. Please?"

She stared at me in silence. She'd become quite skilled at reading me during the last three months; it didn't take her a moment in this case. She closed her eyes and let her head fall back onto the neck rest.

I brought the truck up the hill, moved over to the bushes and slipped past the dead biker. Once we'd cleared the gory scene, I eased up to the curb and immediately pulled out onto the main road.

Fields' eyes remained shut.

It only took me a few moments to realize she'd fallen asleep.

***

After just a few minutes, Fields began to stir. About a minute later she sat forward and brought her hands up to her face.

Keeping my attention on the winding road ahead, I gently grasped her forearm. She pulled back; her eyes grew. When she realized it was me she relaxed and pushed some hair away from her face. "How long have I ... I must have dozed off ..."

"You're gonna be okay. We'll be home in about fifteen minutes, and..."

"And then what?" The spark in her eyes told me I'd just triggered something.

"Then we can relax, have a drink."

"Moss, we were almost *killed* back there!"

"I know."

"Doesn't that mean anything to you?"

"It means a lot."

"Really?" She sounded skeptical.

"Yes. It does."

"I know you, Moss. I know how you look at things, how you think. This didn't bother you at all, did it?"

I didn't want to tell her how much it bothered me. How much I'd wanted to crawl inside my own skin and stay there. I knew I had to be the strong one in this case, even if it meant taking the brunt of

85

her wrath. "Of course it bothered me. Why would you even think...?

"You're acting just like you always act."

"I don't think I understand."

"That's the problem."

"What?"

"Look how you handled that back there."

"I thought I handled it pretty well."

"As always, you handled it perfectly." Her voice trailed off; she turned away and stared at her window. "Nothing is ever a big deal for you. You rushed right over as soon as you heard me. Then you waited for the right moment to kill that man. You even talked to him as though he was a *friend*."

I was surprised and hurt by her tone. It sounded almost as if she thought I'd *caused* what happened back there. "I talked to him so he'd..."

"I know. You got him to aim the gun at you. I know you. It's how you work."

I couldn't believe she was acting like this. "How I *work*? I didn't *cause* this, you know."

"I know."

"I just did the best I could."

"You always do. It's why we're still alive after all we've been through."

"Then why does it sound like...?

"I don't know."

I knew better than argue about this with her. She was still fighting with herself about what happened, trying to make sense of it. But she needed to be reminded that she wasn't the victim, and hadn't been helpless. She needed to know that I couldn't have done this without her help. "I can't take *all* the credit here, you know. You were the one who distracted him, got him to move his gun."

"I was about to faint, Moss. I felt woozy and light-headed."

I didn't want to tell her how close I'd come to fainting as well. "Well, you certainly moved out of the way at the perfect..."

"I didn't plan it that way—it just happened. I knew you'd kill him, so I wasn't too concerned about being shot by that time. All you needed was a second to get at your gun. Once you grabbed the gun, he was as good as dead."

"However it happened, the main thing was that we survived."

"Yes. You killed the bad guy. And everything was fine and dandy again, so you came right over and tried to snap me out of it. The danger was over, and it was time to leave."

"It *was* over."

"For you, maybe."

For you, maybe? I'd been right; she was struggling with the panic.

"It was a much bigger deal for me, Moss. It would have been a much bigger deal for mostly everyone else, too."

I kept silent.

"You helped me back to the truck. You were sweet and kind, a true gentleman. You held the door open for me, helped me up. You even told me how everything would be just fine." Her eyes turned cold. "I hate to bring this up, Moss, but everything is *not* fine! Everything is just about as *un*-fine as it can possibly get! The world is gone, society is gone, all the good people we ever knew are gone ... and the people still alive, the ones we still have to deal with, are cold-blooded savages!"

The encounter with the biker had made the nightmare too real, reminding her how death would continue stalking us. Harsh reality had let her have it right in the face, harder than ever, and for the first time, she fully understood what it all meant.

This brought back the conversation I'd had with Reed on the way up here, after I'd killed three young thugs in Cocoa. At that time, Reed couldn't understand how easily killing had been for me. Reed was a school teacher—a quiet, unassuming man with a wife and kids. For him, death and murder had been something he'd seen only on the news or read about in the papers. By the time we'd hooked up, his wife and kids were dead, and he'd been mugged and nearly run over by a gang of punks. Just hours later, after we'd driven to Cocoa, he found himself standing in someone's living room, his arm covered in blood and brain matter from one of the thugs I'd killed. He was looking at me as if I was some monster that had crawled out of a nightmare.

I'd tried to tell him that my military training had come into play, that survival was second nature to me. Reed said he understood, but I could tell he didn't. Only those who had been through something similar could grasp the cold reality of killing someone in self-defense.

In the few short months since Reed's death, things had gotten much worse. Survival had turned into constant terror—a chilling, merciless horror that followed us everywhere we went. And despite Fields' contention that it didn't bother me, I couldn't shake the nagging fear that we couldn't go on like this. There were only two of us now, and since Reed was gone, the strange voice he'd often heard, that same voice that had saved our lives more than once, was gone as well. And although my instincts remained basically sharp, there was no way I could make any of this more tolerable—no matter how much I wanted to.

"I can't help what's happened," I told her. "I can only try as hard as I can to make things a little ... well, not as bad."

"I appreciate it, I really do."

"I'm sorry if I seem, well, optimistic. It's just that I'm trying to make you feel..."

"It won't work, Moss. Can't you see that? It's too late for anything to be fine or okay. This is something that will never ever happen again."

"You know that already. You've known it for some time. You knew it when we were trying to get out of that the underground facility."

"Of course I knew it. My head wasn't in a fog. They even had me assisting in their horrid experiments. I'd have to be comatose to not realize what's going on, what we've been through."

"Then what's different now? You and I are a team. Together, we can survive this. We proved it this morning, didn't we?"

"Yes. This morning, we both killed someone. I stepped out of my shower, toweled myself dry, looked out the front window and saw someone with a gun sneaking around in the front yard. I grabbed a rifle and shot him. Then we had breakfast. Two normal, healthy people sitting at the kitchen table with our eggs and bacon and toast and coffee, while the two bodies lay dead outside."

"We had no choice."

"No. We didn't."

"Then what's all this *really* about?"

"I used to be a nurse, Moss. I used to *help* people; I assisted daily in *saving* their lives. I wish I could tell you the number of times I saved the lives of patients when their doctors couldn't be right there when they were needed. Now? I'm *killing* people, for God's sake. *Killing* them!"

"I know you're killing them. Believe me, I know. Look at me. I used to be a soldier. It happened twenty years ago. I was just a kid then. Twenty years old and full of myself. In my three-year stint, I killed people, lots of them, but it did something to me, and I promised myself that once I got out, I'd never have to kill anyone again. Now here I am, twenty years later, killing again. But that's what life has become, and we've got to accept it."

"I know that."

"We've been living like this for several months now. What's changed?"

"Nothing."

"I know it's bad."

"It's worse than bad."

"I know it is. But we've been surviving very well under the circumstances. We've got a roof over our heads, food..."

"I understand that. I appreciate it, too."

"Then what's the problem?"

"It's getting to me. It really is."

"It was the biker, wasn't it?"

"Among other things, yes. It was the biker. It was also Don, lying dead in his father's house with a dead cat in his arms. But mostly it was the biker. He had both barrels aimed at my face, Moss. My *face*. And he really wanted to shoot me. I saw the blind rage in his eyes, and if it hadn't been for the severity of his wound, he would've shot me. Right before you came around the corner, he was aiming, ready to shoot ... and then he coughed. If he hadn't coughed..."

"But he did."

"It was too close. *Way* too close." She rubbed her eyes. "It's getting to me, Moss, and I'm not sure I can handle it anymore."

"We *have* to handle it. We've got no choice."

She buried her face in her hands and began sobbing quietly again.

I stayed silent for the rest of the ride, struggling with myself to figure out something I could say that would help her.

But what could be said about any of this that would make it more tolerable? How could I possibly make her feel better when we both knew that what had already happened on this miserable day would most likely happen again tomorrow?

CHAPTER SEVEN

It was 4:30 when we reached Bakerstown-Culmerville Road. Before driving down the hill that led to the farm, I pulled into the abandoned garage at the top of the hill and sat in the truck with my window lowered, listening. Fields sat staring at the abandoned two-story house on the side of the hill directly across the road. I forced myself to stop worrying about her, at least for now, and focused on the present issue. I still wondered about that light-blue compact. Although I didn't see it anywhere, my gut told me it wasn't too far away.

I spent the next fifteen minutes listening and watching. When I was certain we hadn't been followed and that there wasn't anyone else close by, I put the truck back in gear and went down the road, to the bottom of the hill. Before turning off, I stopped again and listened another minute or so. Then, confident everything was as it should be, I took the truck up the long, winding drive.

Fields still stared straight ahead. Her eyes were wet, her face flushed. Her hair was dirty and matted. Thick strands dangled in front of her face. She made no move to push it back or even nudge it away. In fact, as I opened my door and glanced at her, I faced the cold realization that the woman sitting beside me was no longer aware of anything but what was going on in her troubled mind.

This disturbed me, but I fully understood. Fields had been through hell and was seriously wounded. Judging by her glazed eyes and empty look, I could tell she'd ventured much too close to the brink of her own sanity. I'd seen it too many times before. Some never come back. Others do, leaving vital parts of themselves behind. Still others bring much of their trauma back with them and let it dominate them for the rest of their lives.

Fields was a strong person; I was confident she'd survive this and bounce right back. We'd endured other horrors before and would be forced to struggle through many more. If she wanted to handle this by herself, I'd step back and let her. If not, I wouldn't hesitate to help her.

I climbed down, approached the garage door and got out my keys. Behind me, the passenger door slammed shut. I turned. Fields had already climbed down and was shuffling down the drive. As she neared the stoop that led to the concrete walk, she stopped abruptly and stood quite still, her head lowered. It took me a few moments to realize she was gazing at blood and brain matter from this morning's battle. After just a few seconds, she straightened and veered left, toward the stoop. She then climbed the step and went down the concrete path leading to the kitchen door.

I climbed back in the truck, pulled into the garage and killed the engine. Grabbing the .357, I climbed back out, then closed and locked the garage door.

Fields was standing a few feet from the kitchen door when I got back to the house. She stood with her back to me, facing the pine trees on the other side of the property.

I opened the screen and unlocked the back door. I waited for her to turn around and join me, but she didn't move. I went inside and put the .357 on the table. I crossed the kitchen and picked up a flashlight on my way downstairs to the cellar, where the generator was hooked up. I turned it on, went back upstairs and opened the door to the chest cooler, where we kept our ice and cold stuff. I got out two beers and set them on the table. When the power returned, I'd ask if she wanted me to fix dinner. She was probably not hungry, but I thought I'd give her the option anyway. An attempt to return to normalcy seemed a good way of helping her through this.

I was just about to approach the screen door when she came in and stopped in the doorway. I didn't like the cold expression on her face; she was looking at me as if she was about to break up with me. But I told myself to put my feelings aside. She was going through some heavy stuff; the last thing she needed was for me to make things worse.

"I'm going for a walk."

"Aren't you thirsty? We could both use a drink."

"I need to be alone for a little while."

I didn't like any of this but knew better than argue. But I couldn't forget this morning's fiasco, when I decided to take a look outside. I'd earned a harsh slap for that decision but knew that wouldn't work at all in this case.

"We never go anywhere alone," I reminded her.

"I know."

"You just said..."

"I'll be all right." She removed the Uncle Mike's holster and set it and the .45 on the kitchen table beside the .357.

Alarm shot through me. I didn't like that at all. "You'll need a..."

"I've got this." She reached behind her and patted the .38 Ladysmith in the pancake holster in the small of her back.

This wasn't like her. After what happened this morning, I hadn't expected her to act like this. She'd apparently built up some sort of wall on the way home and had locked me out. Part of me felt that way, while another part told me otherwise. She was going through hell and needed some time to sort things out. If I didn't stand in her way, she'd have an easier time of it. As a result, her wall might come down easier and much sooner. But if I made things difficult, both of us would suffer.

If all she needed was a little time, the least I could do was let her do what she wanted, even if it meant standing helplessly by and watching her walk away.

A sense of dread hovered around me like a heavy cloak. It was past dinnertime and would be dark in an hour or so. I knew I didn't want her walking around out there in the dark all alone. "Are you sure you don't want me to..."

"I'm sure, Moss."

"Then you'd better take a flashlight."

96

"I won't be that long."

That made me feel a *little* better. "I could make some sandwiches for later. You'll probably be hungry by the time you..."

"I really need to be alone." She turned and went back outside.

My heart raced as I hurried over to the kitchen window. I pushed aside the sheer curtains and watched as she passed, climbed the stoop and went up the drive that led to the woods.

I went back to the table and stared at her .45 sitting in its Uncle Mike's right beside my .357. The significance of what Fields had just done registered strongly, and I quickly found that I couldn't look at her gun without my stomach turning into knots. I turned away and eyed the clock on the wall. 4:55. I'd give her half an hour. That would give her plenty of time. When she came back, we could talk this out over a drink or two before dinner.

I had no idea what I could do to help her process what happened, or what I could say that would help her rid herself of her demons. I didn't know what I'd done to cause all this. I'd reacted to the crisis in my usual way, handling the situation the best way I knew. I may have done everything right, but it still couldn't help Fields.

She was breaking down. According to my own personal observation, several things had contributed to this. What happened outside this morning undoubtedly headed the list. The shotgun aimed at her face had certainly been a major factor. The biker's gut wound had helped things along as well.

97

Our nightmare in the loading dock, as we hid behind the barrels, had also contributed in giving her own personal horror a slight nudge.

It might have been all of that ... or none of it. Her nerves might have started tearing down even before we drove to the store. This could very well have happened in the bedroom of the house we'd visited earlier, when we saw someone named Don lying dead in his bed, cradling a dead cat, while his father bent over him, urging him to wake up.

In this new world of every unimaginable horror, I couldn't expect someone like Fields, who'd spent her life caring for people, to adjust very well. I'd always been afraid that it would only be a matter of time before a spirit like her would rebel, before logic and reasoning would cause her to break down.

But I couldn't just stand by and watch it happen. I had to somehow bring her back. We were a team; we'd been handling things ever since we first met. Together, we could handle anything.

At 5:30, I got up, grabbed the .380 Cheetah and a flashlight, and went outside. It was already cooler than it was when we'd come back. It would be dark in less than an hour. I stuck the .380 in my pocket, got out my keys, and locked and bolted the back door. Then I ran down the walk and hurried up the hill.

I expected to see her as soon as I reached the clearing, but there was no sign of her. A sudden inner coldness made me shiver, but I forced myself to ignore it, and kept walking. A hundred yards later, just as I'd entered the woods encompassing of the heart of the property, I began calling for her.

"Fields!"

I stopped walking and waited.

Silence.

I told myself it was much too soon to panic, so I kept on. I had a ways to go before I'd reached the rear of the woods, which turned into lush pastureland my grandparents used many years ago to graze their cattle. This was the same path Uncle Joe and I used during our talks those few weeks we'd spent together before the doping finally took his life. Those afternoon walks held fond memories for me. I hoped nothing happening tonight would change them for me.

Still no sign of her.

The sun began setting, and my scalp buzzed. *No. I won't panic. Fields is out here. She's working out her problems and has lost all track of time.*

I called for her again, this time louder. *"Fields!"*

No answer.

The buzzing in my scalp grew. I moved more quickly, the flashlight beam darting everywhere as I covered the narrow sloped trail that cut through the pines. I was careful to lift my feet to avoid deadfalls, tangled weeds and fallen limbs. Now was not a good time to twist an ankle.

The sudden possibility made me wonder. What if Fields had suffered a mishap? She might have twisted an ankle, or tripped on a fallen branch. If so, she would have answered my calls, right?

Unless, of course, she'd hit her head.

I struggled to dismiss that possibility. This was woods and pastureland; if she fell, she'd land on weeds, or soft grass.

Deadfalls were lying everywhere. She could have twisted her ankle, fell, and hit her head.

No. She *didn't* fall and hit her head. Fields was careful. She took care of herself. She was a *nurse*, for God's sake. She was coordinated. And graceful. She wasn't lying unconscious on the ground out here; she was walking around, trying to sort things out. And she wouldn't run off, wouldn't desert me. She was upset and scared and confused. She needed time to think, to rationalize. She needed time to be by herself.

But she'd *never* leave me.

It suddenly occurred to me that Fields might have already gone back to the house. It was possible, wasn't it? She could have circled around on the other side of the trees and gone back that way. I might have reached the woods at the same time, and missed her completely. For all I knew, she could have already unlocked the door and gone inside.

She was probably wondering where I was. Hopefully, she wouldn't come back out and look for me. She'd realize that I'd gone out looking for her and would return soon.

I glanced at my watch. It was now 6:15—forty-five minutes since I'd left the house. If I didn't soon get back, Fields would definitely think something happened to me and would come back out and start looking for me. I needed to turn around and hurry back...

My thoughts stopped abruptly when the toe of my tennis shoe connected with something that made me lose my balance. I fell flat on my face in the thick underbrush.

Luckily, I'd fallen onto soft earth and hadn't hurt myself. I hadn't even dropped the flashlight. I sat up and crawled back to search for the object that had caused my mishap. The ground was much too dark. I switched on the flashlight and slowly moved the heavy white beam around in a wide arc. As soon as I saw the dead limb protruding from the grass, pointing to the dead tree stump directly to my right, my head grew hot, and I told myself that what I was seeing wasn't actually what was really there. My fear had obviously decided to take over. It had switched on my imagination, making me see something that actually wasn't there.

My nerves quivered as I forced myself to crawl closer. I kept the beam trained on the object sitting on top of the stump, ordering it to change, to turn into something else.

But it didn't change. It remained there, defying me.

When I forced myself to admit what I was looking at, my blood turned cold and my heart thundered.

Fields'.38 Ladysmith sat in its pancake holster on the tree stump.

CHAPTER EIGHT

I stared in total disbelief, my mind refusing to accept the horrible sight. I couldn't touch it, couldn't pull the flashlight beam away. All I could do was stare helplessly and force myself to accept the fact that Fields' .38 was indeed lying on a stump five feet in front of me.

My first thought was that it had fallen out of her holster during her walk.

No. That wouldn't wash. The holster clipped onto her belt and snapped into place. If the gun wasn't fastened properly, a fall or sudden stumble might cause it to wrench loose, but the holster would stay hooked to her belt.

If the gun had accidentally fallen out of its holster, Fields would surely have noticed. She would have picked it up, shoved it back in place and snapped it shut.

The .38 was a light-weight, compact pistol. The only one way it could have been placed on the stump was if Fields had taken it off and left it there.

I couldn't accept that possibility. Fields would never have removed her gun and holster. If someone had snuck up on her, she would have grabbed the gun, whipped it out and used it.

But what if she hadn't had enough time?

What if it had happened too quickly for her to react?

I didn't want that image floating around in my head. This would mean there were others wandering around like the two we'd killed this morning.

But even if there were others out there, I still couldn't accept such a scenario. Fields was upset and depressed, but that didn't mean she wasn't alert. She had great eyes, superb hearing, and terrific instincts. If someone had snuck up on her, they would have had to be close. Perhaps they were hiding in the brush. Even so, they would have had to be moving fast, and would need a Taser...

Stop it. You're being paranoid. You need to think this thing out rationally. Just because Fields' pistol is lying here doesn't necessarily mean there's a band of psychos roaming around in these woods.

First of all, I had to determine what happened. If someone had snuck up on her, he would've taken her gun. But it was right there, and since it hadn't been fired...

Had it been fired? I hadn't heard anything while she was gone. The sound a gun made could be heard at a considerable distance. Even if Fields had fired it while I was in the house, I would have probably heard it.

In any event, I had to pick it up and study it. I couldn't tell if it had been fired just by looking at it.

My left hand shook horribly as I reached out for it. Just before my index finger connected with its cold, smooth surface, I froze. Something inside me told me I couldn't do it, that I really didn't want to, while another voice told me it didn't matter what I wanted, or that I couldn't do it. I *had* to do it.

I finally forced myself to grab it, cringing at first, as if I'd just been scalded, then groaning as my fingers closed painfully around it. I held my breath, fighting to maintain my grip, to resist the urge to open my hand and let it drop silently to the soft grass.

You can't let it go. It belongs to Fields. If you let it go, you let her go, because right now, it's your only link to her ...

The insane reasoning worked, and I tried picking it up. It was much heavier than it should have been, and actually fought to keep me from pulling it. I realized right then that a corner of the holster had caught on vines growing next to the stump. I pulled it free, and before I knew it, I had the cursed weapon in my left hand.

Then I closed my eyes and forced myself to sniff the barrel. It took me two seconds to conclude that the gun hadn't been fired.

Fields had apparently heard something, unsnapped the holster, and placed it on the stump.

But why? What had she seen? Had she heard something? If she'd seen or heard a threat, why hadn't she used the gun?

I had to figure this out, to consider all possibilities.

The first one, of course, was the one I really wanted to believe—that she might have actually gone back to the house. But that made no sense because she wouldn't have left her gun.

She might have heard something in the bushes, grabbed the gun, heard another sound and grew frightened. In her panic, she could have dropped the gun and forgotten it entirely while racing back to the house. She'd been in a troubled state most of the morning and afternoon; the sound of a rabbit or squirrel scampering about in the brush could have sent her over the edge.

That wouldn't wash, either. The gun hadn't been dropped, but carefully unclipped from her belt and placed in the center of a tree stump not far from a deadfall blocking a path we'd used several times before.

It was getting darker. In another twenty minutes, I wouldn't be able to see ten feet in front of me.

Keeping the flashlight beam ahead of me, I moved quickly through the thick brush, back to the house. Fields was there—I could feel it in my bones. If I was lucky, I'd find her sitting at the kitchen table, sipping beer or Jim Beam. There would be sandwiches made, and the smell of coffee would be strong. When I walked in, she'd give me her usual coy smile and say, "And where have *you* been?" I'd laugh, hold up her pistol, and ask if she forgot something. She'd redden and laugh in embarrassment. I'd sit down beside her and pour myself a drink. Then I'd ask her about her walk, and everything would be okay again.

I reached the clearing about ten minutes later. I couldn't see any lights coming from the house, but that didn't tell me anything. We'd been careful about that since we'd moved here. Using lights at night could be seen for miles and would attract roaming predators. If Fields was in the bathroom, she could have taken a small kerosene lamp with her and placed it on the sink. The blinds and heavy drapes in the window would hide the light. From the outside, you couldn't see anything.

I hurried down the hill and ran across the concrete stoop, stopping abruptly when I caught sight of the padlock securing the back door. Heavy chills overtook me, and I nearly dropped her gun as well as the flashlight.

Fields hadn't come back to the house.

She was still out there somewhere, unarmed and helpless.

***

My thoughts raced as I struggled to keep my wits about me. I knew I'd be of no use to Fields or myself if I just gave up. I forced myself to ignore the cold wave of panic threatening to wash over me.

I had to find her and bring her back.

First off, I had to unlock the door and go inside. There were things I needed to take with me when I looked for Fields. These things were inside the house.

I shoved my left hand inside the pocket of my jeans. No keys. The other pocket, perhaps? This would require me to use my other hand, which held Fields' .38.

Clear your head and switch the gun. It couldn't be simpler.

After a few awkward moments of blackness, I let my head clear. I placed the pistol in my left hand and used my right to search the other pocket. I began staring at the .38 and suddenly lost track of what I was doing.

Idiot. Focus. Get the damned keys, unlock the door and get your ass inside.

Then what? What was I supposed to do when I went inside?

Grab whatever you'll need to take with you to go find Fields, dammit!

After taking another deep breath, I was finally able to focus long enough to pull the keys out of my pocket and open the door.

The kitchen, of course, was empty, the soft, steady hum from the fridge reminding me that the home generator was up and running. The room was dark except for the three small nightlights I kept plugged in, which cast hazy yellow halos on the floor near the hall and dining room doorways.

I stood glaring at the darkness, longing to hear her voice or smell the perfume of her hair. It hadn't been that long since Fields had stood right here just moments before she'd left the house to go on her walk.

The hum of the fridge intensified the silence, making me feel even more alone. For a moment I thought that if I flicked on the flashlight, her image would materialize on the other side of the table.

I tried, but of course it didn't work. The dark emptiness continued mocking me.

I wanted to scramble down the hall, into the living room, and collapse on the sofa. I wanted to lie there on my side in fetal position, safe and warm and at a safe distance from the nightmares. I wanted to close my eyes and dream about Fields and me doing all the things we'd done since we'd arrived at the farm an eternity ago, when Reed and Uncle Joe were still in our lives. In my dream, Fields and I would be together again, and our fears would never...

Moss, stop all this crap and start looking!

I stiffened. Was that her voice I'd just heard? Or was it my own?

Or was it my conscience telling me to stop the self-pity and start acting like myself again?

This wasn't me at all. If Fields came through that door right now, she wouldn't believe what she saw. If I saw my own reflection, I wouldn't believe it either. I didn't feel anything like the man who twenty years earlier hunted down suicide bombers, slave traders and Mexican drug runners. I'd been stabbed and shot, and had stared down the barrel of a gun more times than I cared to remember.

Right now I didn't think I could cope with much of anything.

I felt useless and invisible, like a stick of old furniture no one wanted anymore.

I'd come a long way in the last couple of hours.

Fields told me I handled things too easily. Reed had said the same thing just a few months before that. Emergency situations were second nature for me. When a crisis arose, I reacted with the speed and efficiency of a highly-tuned machine. I reacted coldly and economically, my gun out and ready. In an instant, someone was dead, the emergency successfully abated.

If only Fields or Reed could see me standing in the kitchen doorway, gawking stupidly at the darkness, teetering on the brink of hysterics ...

Moss, stop this!

Was it her voice again?

It didn't matter whose voice it was. I had to somehow regain my composure, pull myself together and focus. I had to do what I was trained to do, what I'd done in the military and what I'd been doing the last six months.

Surviving. Picking up the pieces. Shrugging off my wounds and tending to business.

I had to become a soldier again. That same cold-blooded killer I'd been when I was a foolish kid who took dangerous chances because I'd thought I was invincible, and would live forever.

But now I was no longer a kid, had seen death in all its forms, and knew I wouldn't live forever. The love of my life had just vanished, and my gut told me it wasn't her idea.

Fields had been taken. Kidnapped. On our own property ...

Someone had snuck up to her, overpowered her and taken her away.

Fired up and shaking with rage, I felt my former self coming back quickly. I knew right then that I'd been a dickhead for showing weakness. Fields depended on me and I wouldn't let her down. We were a team, and when one of the team was attacked, the other burst into action.

I slammed the kitchen door behind me. With the aid of the flashlight, I immediately set about gathering a few things. I had no idea how long my search would take or how long I'd be gone, but I was reasonably sure I'd be hunting for Fields through the night. But how long would it take before I'd covered the entire 88 acres? How long would it be before I picked up her trail?

I knew right then that it didn't matter.

I was going to find her and didn't care how long it took.

I picked up two cans of tuna, some beef jerky and three small bottles of water. I found a metal flask and got a pint of bourbon from the cupboard. I filled the flask and grabbed a hunting knife from the top of the dresser. From the medicine cabinet in the bathroom across the hall from the kitchen, I grabbed a small first-aid kit. From my grandmother's sewing stuff in a kitchen drawer I picked up a small emergency kit containing needles and thread. I put everything on the kitchen table and went upstairs to look for the small black backpack I'd found a few weeks ago in an abandoned store in Bakerstown.

Satisfied I'd found everything I needed, I loaded the backpack.

Since I didn't know what I faced, I decided that the best ammo would be the standard .22. It was small and light, and also good for long range shooting. For closer, more effective work, I'd need a lighter weapon with a larger caliber. For extremely close work, I decided on a gun small enough to fit in my pants pocket.

I grabbed Fields' .38 Ladysmith and clipped it and its pancake holster onto my belt in the small of my back. I also selected the tiny .22 Beretta Bobcat, and the .22 Ruger Mark II target pistol with a 6-inch slab barrel and shoulder holster. I shrugged into the holster, adjusting the strap until I barely felt it over my sweatshirt. I found two extra mags for the Beretta, two for the Ruger, four speed loaders for the .38, and loaded them into the backpack. Then I picked up a box containing a thousand rounds of .22 long rifle ammo and packed that as well.

I slipped on an ammo belt I'd picked up at a local sporting goods store. The belt contained pouches for four mags, two pouches for knives and a larger one for loose ammo. I filled the pouches with two speed loaders and two penknives and dumped about forty rounds of .22 mini mag ammo into the pouch.

This done, I went down to the cellar to turn off the generator, came back upstairs and put on my lightweight jacket. I found three penlights, put two in my breast pocket, one in the backpack, and zipped everything shut. I shrugged into the backpack and adjusted the straps, positioning it high on my back so it didn't interfere with the Ruger under my jacket.

Less than half an hour after I'd entered the house, I went back outside, locked the door and rushed over to the small rock garden that sat at the foot of the hill, about fifty feet from the kitchen door. Several weeks ago, I'd placed a small plastic Tupperware container beneath one of the rocks. The container held a set of spare keys to the house, garage and vehicles, as well as a small .38 snub nosed revolver loaded with six hollowpoint rounds. Using light from a pocket flashlight, I put the keys in the container, snapped the lid shut and dropped it in its shallow dirt bed. After covering it with dirt, I rolled the rock back over it.

Straightening, I flicked off the flashlight and hung it from a ring fixed to my ammo belt. I grabbed a penlight from the pocket of my jacket and used it to guide my way down the concrete walk. When I reached the driveway, I faced the top of the hill and took a deep breath.

Before setting out, I said in a soft voice, "Fields, I don't know what happened tonight or where you are, but I'll find you. I'll find you if it's the last thing I ever do, and I promise that if anyone hurt you in any way, they'll pay dearly."

My anger surged within me, but I fought it down, knowing this wasn't the right time to let it out.

I had more important things on my agenda.

***

My eyes quickly adjusted to the darkness. Flicking off the penlight, I climbed the hill that went past the garage, and in just a few minutes reached the clearing leading to the woods that made up a third of my grandparents' 88-acre farm. The huge black fortress of pines and buckeyes looming a hundred yards straight ahead resembled a shapeless demon waiting to devour me. I hesitated, nearly stumbling, but kept my focus on the narrow winding trail cutting through its center.

112

I kept the long-barreled Ruger in my right hand as I crept silently over the tall brush, my ears pricked for the slightest disturbance in the eerie silence of the night. The whispering of the wind through the trees and the distant hooting of an owl barely penetrated the cool stillness.

As I approached the harsh underbrush leading into the woods, I slowed my pace and kept the beam of the penlight directly in front of me. Before venturing on, I studied the solid black mass of the trees towering above me and let my eyes acclimate. Alert for sudden glints, as well as rustling sounds, I resumed walking. The Ruger was perfect for this type of work. It was light yet sturdy; its long slab barrel could be used as a club if I was unable to shoot in time.

Soon I was among the trees. The clearness of the night turned black and cold, and my visibility diminished drastically. I slowed my pace, scanning all around me and turning around frequently to make sure no one was sneaking up to me. I wanted to call out for Fields but knew that would be dangerous. I wanted to believe she wasn't far, but had to consider the facts. If she'd fallen and twisted an ankle, I would have already found her. This alone told me she might have become victim of foul play. She could have been knocked unconscious and carried or dragged away. At this moment, while I searched for her, she could be imprisoned in some psycho's basement a mere mile away ... and who knew what could be happening...

Stop this ... It will only frustrate you and take your attention away from your mission.

I stopped moving and spent the next couple of minutes taking deep breaths to calm myself. I was going to find her. No matter what happened, I was going to find Fields, and she was going to be okay.

Feeling more confident, I began moving again.

About twenty minutes later, just as I was about to reach the general area near where I'd found her Ladysmith, the toe of my tennis shoe bumped something protruding from the weeds. I fell forward and landed on my right side. In an instant I rolled onto my back, the Ruger up and ready as I feverishly scanned my surroundings.

I remained on my back, the Ruger in my right hand, the penlight in my left, sliding the slender white beam carefully over both sides of the trail as I listened for movement. I heard nothing. I stayed there, alert for rustling, soft footsteps—anything that would warn me someone was coming.

The silence continued.

I sat up and stuck the penlight between my teeth. Then I grabbed the pocket flashlight from my ammo belt and began exploring the area more thoroughly.

I quickly discovered that I'd tripped on an exposed root.

I remained on the cold ground for a few moments, exploring my surroundings. Satisfied I was still safe and alone, I replaced the flashlight and switched off the penlight. Then I glanced up at the sky and noticed a star northeast of my position twinkling brightly. This struck me as odd. Stars filled the sky, yet only one of them sparkled, appearing significantly brighter than the rest. Judging by its position, it wasn't the North Star, nor was it part of any of the few constellations I was familiar with. Its position seemed to be northeast of where I was...

Why was this suddenly familiar to me?

It continued twinkling. It was almost as if...

No. It couldn't be ...

I remembered something Fields had told me not long after we'd buried Reed. Her parents had died in a car accident when she was a little girl, and when she was told about it, she went through a period of deep depression. She was convinced her parents were coming back for her, and she wanted to be awake when they did. After several sleepless nights, her uncle and aunt, who'd become her legal guardians, grew frantic to find some way of calming her.

Her uncle told her that when someone died, their spirit went up into the sky and latched onto a star, and you could see them at night if you looked up at the stars. Fields asked how she'd know which stars were which. He'd said you could tell because it would be the brightest, and would twinkle when you looked at it.

Fields believed it at the time, but as she grew older, realized how silly it was. I hadn't thought it was silly. At the time, I'd been looking for something to believe in, to help me process all the death, the destruction. I'd lost my mother, my uncle,

115

and Reed, all in a very short period of time. Fields' bedtime story did much to soften the blow.

But now the story seemed to be doing something else, and as I gazed up into the eternal darkness, I could only wonder about that one star glittering so brightly amongst the millions of others surrounding it.

"Reed?" My heart raced. "Is that you? Or is it you, Uncle Joe? Or Mom? Are you guys trying to tell me something?"

Was it really their spirits trying to communicate with me? Or was my imagination doing strange things to my troubled state of mind?

The star continued twinkling. Others flickered while others dimmed, but the one in question continued twinkling brightly.

Coincidence? Probably. Silly? Most definitely. Childish? Yes.

So why was I entertaining the notion?

Is it because Fields is out there somewhere, and you need all the help you can get? Is it because once you reach the end of your grandparents' property, you'll have no idea where to go from there?

Or is it because deep down inside you, you honestly don't think the notion is silly or childish at all, because ever since your mother, Uncle Joe and Reed died, you truly feel that they really haven't gone away at all?

It was because of all of this. But most of all, it was because I honestly believed Fields would want me to do this.

My gut—as well as my heart—quickly made the decision for me.

I got up from the ground and veered off the main path.

***

I reached the barbed wire fence that formed the boundary of my grandparents' property just a hundred feet or so from Deer Creek Road.

A large two-story brick house sat directly across the road, its dark windows gazing unseeingly at a front yard overrun with weeds and trash. A child's wagon sat on its side in front of the living room window. A basketball pole leaned against the side of the two-car garage, its rim bent at an extreme angle. Dark, eerie shapes sat among the weeds and bushes, as well as near the front door. They appeared to be garbage bags, but I couldn't tell for sure.

Mindful of my backpack and ammo belt, I slipped carefully through the loose strands of rusty barbed wire and crossed the deserted two-lane road. Fields and I had been on this road just a couple of hours ago. Now it seemed like it had happened an eternity ago.

I didn't know if I should cut across the overgrown yard and continue my hunt through the woods behind the house, or stay on the road. The woods ran north for more than a mile and extended to the east, reaching the main road on the other side of the bend about a mile or so farther down. If Fields had been taken to the rear of the property and forced to slip through the fence, I suspected she

117

hadn't been very far from where I was standing right now.

But where had they taken her?

Judging by my twinkling star, I should keep heading northeast. But how? The road? Or the woods? Had Fields been shoved into a car or van? Was it parked here, waiting? I flicked on my penlight. I didn't see fresh tracks or tire marks on the grass, but that didn't mean anything. Since traffic was no longer an issue, anyone could park wherever they wished. Whoever had kidnapped Fields could have left their ride right here in the middle of the road.

This frightening fact sent a sharp blade of icy terror slicing through me. If they'd taken her away in a car or van, I didn't have a prayer. They'd be miles away by now.

I couldn't let that defeat me. I had to stay focused.

Fields had been gone nearly an hour before I left the house and went looking for her. Then I went back to the house and spent another half-hour filling up my backpack. That added up to a grand total of nearly ninety minutes in which I was in the house, and unable to hear an engine on this side of the property. I hadn't heard anything since I'd been outside, but this conclusion meant nothing if she'd been taken and shoved into a vehicle during those ninety minutes. Although I saw no evidence whatsoever, I wanted to assume she'd been taken away on foot. I just didn't want to let myself believe that she'd been shoved into a vehicle and taken miles away.

This led me to my next questions: The road? Or the woods?

Once again, I had no clue. If Fields was conscious, she'd do her best to leave a trail. Dropping her .38 told me something bad had happened fast, but not so fast that she hadn't had time to unclip and hide the gun. But she *had*, and had done it so I could find it. She'd heard something, realized someone was after her, knew she couldn't get away and left the gun for me to find.

Why hadn't she used it? If she'd had time to take off the holster and place it on the stump, she would have had time to use it.

Had her assailant got the drop on her? Had there been more than one of them? If so, wouldn't they have seen her drop the gun? Wouldn't they have taken it from her?

The woods? Or the road?

Dragging someone through the woods against their will would not be easy. If they were on foot, they wouldn't want to risk being seen. If they knew about me or suspected I was aware Fields was missing, they'd assume I'd use a vehicle to track them down. I wouldn't be able to follow them by vehicle into the woods.

I veered off the road, into the overgrown yard, and stepped over a collapsed wooden fence. The woods sat about a hundred yards behind the house, extending so far into the darkness that nothing else was visible beyond that point.

As I kept moving, I switched to the flashlight, which cast a much larger and brighter halo. The weeds were just as thick here, but since this area was unfamiliar, I moved much more carefully so I wouldn't stumble. Several felled trees blocked my way. I sidestepped, avoiding broken limbs and crumbling deadfalls. I had to assume Fields wasn't able to leave a trail. If she was conscious, she'd be walking in front of her kidnappers and wouldn't be able to give herself away. If her hands were tied, her movements would be even more restricted. I had to keep moving and watch closely for signs.

I was about a hundred yards from the road when I heard the voices.

CHAPTER NINE

There were at least two of them, and they'd come out of the woods from the northeast and were moving in my direction.

I lowered myself into the waist-high weeds. Keeping low, I crawled over to a dead tree. Carefully I squeezed beneath the bottom section and lay amongst the underbrush, wedged under the stump and hidden by a large segment of deteriorating trunk. I lay on my left side, my legs straight out and directly beneath the deadfall, my back facing the approaching footsteps, my dark clothing and backpack blending in with the tree and the surrounding darkness.

Gripping the Ruger, I kept its barrel pointed at the ground. The safety was off, the gun ready to fire. My left hand shielded the gun from view. It was vital to keep the shiny finish of the silver barrel out of sight; any reflection from a flashlight beam would be disastrous.

The rustling noises grew louder. As they increased in volume, I realized they were everywhere. I had no idea how many of them there were. I'd originally thought there were two, but the increased rustling coming from both directions suggested more.

My pulse thundered as I lay perfectly still.

Someone stopped moving about twenty feet away, directly behind me. Seconds later, someone else stopped a little closer—about ten feet from the stump. More rustling continued a few yards toward my right as one of them circled the area. Finally it also stopped. The dead silence enabled me to hear the heavy thumping of my heart.

There were four of them. I was surrounded.

"Don't see nothin'," said a soft voice directly to my left. It sounded like the voice of a young man in his late teens, or early twenties. I heard the clicking of a flashlight.

"Coulda swore I spotted somethin'," said a voice on my right, moving closer. This voice also sounded young.

The clicking of other flashlights lit up the ground around me. I still didn't move, but my pulse hammered even louder. I was afraid they could hear it.

"Who'd even be out here?" whispered a third young male voice. "Nothin' but corpses in these houses."

"What'd that new bitch say? Somethin' about her daddy bringin' her out here and leavin' her?"

"Who can tell? She's a doper. Couldn't even remember her own name."

Relief and dread washed through me at the same time. If they were talking about Fields, at least now I had some idea of what happened.

"Don't matter," said one of them a few yards on my left. "Chick sure is hot. Simon's gonna fuck her good. He likes 'em tall and skinny. And he don't mind doin' dopers if they're good-lookin' enough."

Yep, there were talking about Fields. A sudden rage made my limbs tremble. I felt my index finger unconsciously rubbing against the trigger. *No. It won't work. Not like this.* If I killed them all, I wouldn't be able to find out where they were keeping her.

But at least now I could piece some of it together. During her walk, she'd heard someone in the woods and guessed there were more than one. Since she didn't know exactly where they were, she knew she had no chance of shooting them all and decided to act stupid. She was obviously close to the stump we usually passed during our walks. She'd unclipped the holster, put it on the stump and continued walking. The brush growing near the stump would hide the gun, and if she managed to direct them away from it, they wouldn't even be suspicious. When they found her unarmed, they wouldn't consider her a threat. Otherwise, they might have killed her.

Fields had done basically the same thing in Breezewood, when I'd first stumbled on her in the filling station office. Her charade had worked with me; it had obviously worked with them as well.

But for how long?

The flashlight beams danced and hopped along the weeds just a few yards beyond my stump.

"Simon wants us to keep lookin' for this bastard, whoever he is. He wants 'im bad."

"I still can't figure how he did both Doc and James. Not at the same time."

"That's fucked up, man. James was in the military, knew how to hunt."

Doc and James ... They could be talking about Willis K. Simpson and his partner.

"Simon told me he saw a Silverado pickup parked near Doc's station wagon on Bakerstown-Culmerville Road."

"How'd he get away? Simon and Cal both brought their guns with 'em when they went lookin'. Simon was pissed. He woulda capped whoever done it."

"Simon didn't wanna stick around, said he smelled an ambush."

More bits of the picture formed in my head. Simon was obviously the driver of the compact. Doc and James were two members of their gang. They drove around the neighborhood, looking for places to ransack. This morning they hadn't been so lucky.

"Kinda hard to hide a Silverado."

"Simon said he and Cal lost 'im somewhere on Bakerstown-Culmerville Road, says the bastard can't be far. Doc and James weren't gone maybe an hour this mornin' when Simon heard the shots. Simon thinks whoever it is has gotta be livin' around here somewhere."

"Can't be too far from where Simon found the station wagon. Not if they were able to lose Simon so easy."

"Simon figures maybe a mile or two from the house."

"Guys, we gotta get back. Mush Mouth don't like waitin' too long in the truck. Dark gives 'im the shakes."

"He ain't gonna crap his pants again, is he?"

A chuckle. "Ya didn't bring along a diaper?"

"Ain't his momma, fuck you very much."

The flashlight beam moved away. "Fucker's *gotta* be around here somewheres. Simon says he and Cal found that chick in the woods across the road, on the other side of the fence."

"It's gettin' fuckin' late. Her daddy's got guns, he could be out there right now, lookin' for 'er. I don't wanna get shot, man."

"Don't think he cares about her anymore."

"Think she's just a drop-off? Like those two we found in Saxonburg?"

"*Sara* was a drop-off?"

"Where the fuck *you* been?"

"Prob'ly on one of our food runs. Simon's got me goin' out all the time now. Ever since he found us at the Center in Pittsburgh, he's got me lookin' for food."

"That's only 'cause you were stealin' food at the fuckin' Center, moron. Simon figures that's what you do. Fuck, you do it good, too, dude!"

"*You* stole food, too, asswipe!"

"Can't believe Sara was a drop-off. Damn ..."

"You don't remember comin' back and there she was? Where d'ya think she came from? The fuckin' sky?"

"Thought maybe Simon found her somewheres. She's cute, man."

"She's a fuckin' scatterbrain. Why d'ya think he ties her down every time he wants to fuck 'er?"

A giggle. "Always thought Simon liked gettin' his rocks off that way."

"You're an idiot. She freaks whenever she thinks someone's gonna touch 'er."

"All chicks are scatterbrains nowadays."

"So is most everyone else. I see 'em all the time when we drive into town. Like a fuckin' zombie movie. Can't even tell when they're dead anymore. You gotta swat 'em in the head, wait and see if they do anything."

A chuckle. "Bring your lunch!"

"Simon said they're droppin' off dopers like they used to dump dogs. Can't blame 'em none. Look at Mush Mouth. Fucker's brain's Swiss cheese. Simon would dump 'im in a heartbeat if Mush Mouth wasn't his brother."

"Don't matter none. I like Sara even if she is a scatterbrain."

"The other one? Rita? She only lasted a day or two."

"Sweet chick, but loony as a shithouse rat. Screamed like a banshee whenever ya touched 'er."

"Did Simon really have to take 'er out to the dump and shoot 'er?"

"Said she was losin' her bodily functions."

"She just didn't wanna fuck no more. Simon won't feed a chick that won't fuck, says it ain't practical. Says everything's gotta have a purpose."

"We got to go back. Simon might decide to let us have a crack at this new one."

"Where'd you hear that?"

"Cal."

"Dude, Cal bullshits a *lot*. Simon didn't even wanna bring 'im with us when he was done stealin' food and meds at the Juvie Center. Cal gave 'im all sorts of shit. Simon was in a hurry, didn't wanna listen to his shit. So be brought 'im out here with the rest of us."

"So what?" A giggle. "What if Cal's right this time? I'm in!"

"Me, too. I mean, *wow*, man ..."

"Don't get your hopes up. Simon's been pissed all fuckin' day about Doc and James."

"Doc was one weird asshole, collectin' those damn scalps. Fuckin' things smell *bad*."

"Fucker sure knew how to find drugs out here. Know how Simon gets when he can't get buzzed."

"C'mon, dudes. Gettin' chilly out here. Don't see nobody. We can start lookin' for that psycho again in the mornin'."

The flashlight clicked off and the comforting darkness returned. The rustling resumed and rapidly grew fainter.

I crawled out of my hiding space. Using the stump of the tree for cover, I peered around it and watched the four black figures disappearing into the darkness of the woods.

I waited about two minutes. Then, keeping low and still gripping the Ruger, I stayed behind the cover of the trees lining the path while following them into the awaiting fortress.

***

127

Once I'd reached the woods, I increased my pace. Then, using the trees and thick brush for cover, I stayed as close as possible to the foursome. Using my penlight was out of the question, so I had to be extra careful to watch my footing. I couldn't lose sight of them, and I couldn't risk injuring myself.

It took us about twenty minutes to reach the other end of the woods. Beyond it, a beat-up four-door pickup sat in the middle of the road, facing the top of the hill. The bed was stacked high with furniture and rolls of fencing, partially covered with sections of torn tarp hanging down and fastened to the side of the truck with bungee cords. The lights were off, but the engine was running, and I could see a shadow sitting behind the wheel.

I crawled out amongst the bushes and lay on the cold ground beside a thick, segmented deadfall, about forty yards down from the truck. Two of the boys were walking around the vehicle, their flashlight beams jumping around wildly. The other two stood about ten feet down from the open tailgate, their backs to the road as they urinated into the ditch. If they hadn't been standing there, I could have snuck over, climbed the bed and hid beneath the tarp.

One of the other two boys stepped onto the shoulder, turned his back and set about doing what the other two were doing. The fourth boy remained in the middle of the road, scanning the area with his flashlight beam. It swept over in my direction, stopping about ten feet short of my position. I flattened myself to the ground and buried my face in my arms. The bright silver halo stayed focused on the woods for about twenty seconds before shifting and moving in the opposite direction.

"Hurry up!" The driver stuck his head out the window and gestured. "Don't like it out here!"

"Hold your wad," one of them said. "We're tendin' to business!"

"Can't ... fool me," the driver said. "You're ... takin' a leak!"

"And you thought he was stupid," one of them said, chuckling.

"Silly me," his partner replied. "Mush Mouth's a private dick."

"You're half right."

The boy in front of the truck zipped up and rejoined his partner. Their flashlight beams lit up the woods about a hundred feet to my left. They were talking too softly for me to hear what they were saying.

I hadn't a prayer of following them on foot. Once they got in the truck, they'd be gone in thirty seconds and I'd have to guess where they went. It would take me close to half an hour, perhaps an hour, to get back to the farm, dig up the keys, unlock the garage door, get in the truck, drive back here and start looking again. In that time, they'd be able to cover at least twenty miles. Judging by what I'd heard earlier, they didn't live far, but that didn't make this any easier. There were dirt roads, turnoffs and isolated houses everywhere in this area. It would take me several days and nights to check out

129

every road and structure within a five- or ten-mile radius. I couldn't risk Fields being held captive by this dangerous brood for that long. I had to think of something fast.

My only chance was to somehow delay them from driving away and divert their attention. I had to find some way to sneak over to the truck, jump onto the bed and hitch a ride to their hideout. This meant sabotaging the truck, but only temporarily. My option in this case was to shoot out their front tire once they started moving. Like all guns, the Ruger was loud enough to be heard at quite a distance. The loud engine noise of the truck would absorb some of the explosion, but not as much as I'd need. The opened windows wouldn't help me at all. My only hope was that they'd think the blast was actually a blowout.

As they set about changing the tire, I could circle around, sneak up to the truck, climb in back and hide amongst the clutter during their drive back to their place. While they pulled off the main road, I could roll out of the bed and hide in the grass or bushes. Later on, when I was sure everyone was asleep, I could set about looking for Fields. As long as this crew didn't keep dogs, I'd be reasonably safe.

I didn't have much time. I had to ditch the backpack. It was bulky, and would slow me down. I still had the Ruger, the .38, the .22, and a sharp hunting knife. With the speed loaders and forty loose rounds of .22 mini mags in my ammo belt, I was carrying more than seventy rounds. I'd feel much better with extra mags in my pockets, but there wasn't time to rummage through the backpack. I had to work with what I had.

On the off-chance that I'd be able to return, I decided to hide the backpack so I could retrieve it later on. I squirmed out of it, placed it on the ground beside me and pushed large sections of broken bark on top of it. I gathered up some dead leaves and dropped them on it as well. I found a fairly straight stick and jammed it into the ground vertically beside the deadfall. This done, I lay down in the ditch, rested the barrel of the Ruger on my left forearm, and waited.

"C'mon, dammit!" the driver yelled. "You guys ... ain't ya done yet?"

"Naw, we like standin' out here with our schlongs hangin' out! The cool night air's givin' me a hard-on!"

"Shut your pie-hole, you dumb shit!"

"Get in the fuckin' truck, *all* of ya!"

The boys zipped up, approached the truck, opened the back doors and got in. The other two killed their flashlights and went back to the cab.

Moments later, the high-pitched grinding of gears signaled the departure of the truck. It eased forward. Seconds later, its headlights lit up the hill straight ahead.

Using my off-center vision to gauge my target, I inched the barrel of the Ruger toward my left. I knew I had I had only a few seconds to shoot before the truck gained speed. To make the situation worse, the truck had no sidelights, and the darkness made it nearly impossible to actually see my target. As I'd done many times while patrolling the Border, I was going to have to guess where the target actually was. The rifle round had a range of about a mile, but its rainbow pattern left too much to chance. There could be a discrepancy of six or eight inches between where I'd aimed and where the bullet landed. All hell would break loose if I hit the body of the truck above the tire. But I couldn't wait. I was going to have to risk the shot.

The truck began gaining speed as it lumbered up the hill.

Just as I was about to pull the trigger, a loud *crack*! reverberated in the area, and the truck jerked to a screeching stop.

CHAPTER TEN

I lay in the dirt, struggling to determine what I'd just heard. Was it a gunshot? Or had one of the tires blown out at that precise moment?

Things like that just didn't happen—not when or how you wanted them to, anyway. It was way too convenient. Too easy.

To make sure I wasn't hallucinating, I sniffed the barrel of the Ruger. It hadn't been fired. Of course it hadn't. I certainly would have noticed firing it, wouldn't I?

Maybe, maybe not. The Ruger didn't have a hair trigger, but was certainly easy enough to fire without applying excessive pressure. Any sort of cough or twinge would have been more than enough to cause me to squeeze off a round.

But since I *hadn't* coughed or even tensed up during that moment, this wasn't the issue. My nerves were on edge and my head had been teetering on thought overload for the last hour and a half. I was concentrating on the shot, the trajectory of the bullet, the distance, the darkness. I was worried about missing the tire and hitting the truck. I was wondering how I could sneak over to the truck after I'd flattened the tire ... and how I could climb in back, undetected ... and what I'd do once the truck started moving again ... and when we'd arrived at our destination ... and looking for Fields ... and finding her, bringing her back without getting us killed...

Too many things were rushing through my mind. I could have easily pressed the trigger without even noticing.

I had to stop trying to figure out what I did or didn't do and face what happened. Something that sounded very much like a gunshot had come from somewhere very close, and I was the one with the loaded gun in my hand when it happened. However, the barrel didn't reek of cordite, suggesting that I hadn't fired the weapon.

So ... what *did* happen?

And why had the truck stopped so suddenly?

In the midst of my confusion, the truck doors flew open and the five males jumped out, all chattering away hysterically as they flicked on their flashlights. The darkness exploded with harsh beams of white light leaping and jerking in every direction. Three of them crossed the road, moving carefully toward me. I heard the clicking of automatics.

Instinct told me to get up, dash back into the woods and hide. But I couldn't move. The odds were stacked against me. Although the boys were nearly a hundred yards from me, they'd see me in their flashlight beams as soon as I got up from the ground. There were three of them, they were armed, and the brilliant globes of white light coming toward me would immediately disorient me. As they drew closer, my only option was to close my eyes, guess their position, and empty the magazine.

Logically, I couldn't do that. Dead, they couldn't lead me to Fields, and once Simon found out five of his men hadn't returned, he'd send out more of his gang to investigate. The area would be swarming with armed psychos in no time. I'd be forced to go into hiding, perhaps for days.

I had no idea how many of these young killers I could be facing. Simon had apparently raided a Juvenile Center for drugs and food and then decided to bring a batch of kids back with him to do his errands. For all I knew, he might have a platoon living with him. If so, he could send out truckloads all day long. It wouldn't be long before they found me and killed me. Even if I was able to avoid them, it would seriously delay my hunt for Fields.

The threesome kept on coming. I closed my eyes, lowered my face to the cold dirt and braced the barrel of the Ruger on my forearm. Once I'd emptied the mag and dropped these three, I could use the .38 on the other two.

Just as I slid my index finger into the firing position, someone near the truck yelled, "Where the hell you dumbasses goin'? That shit happened on the *driver's* side!"

Silence. They all stopped.

One of them said, "Sure sounded like it came from over here!"

"Idiot. Don'tcha know sound echoes? It bounces all over the fuckin' place in these hills!"

"But..."

"Wanna see the fuckin' tire? It's on the passenger's side! That oughta be your first clue!"

"Sure sounded like a gunshot ..."

"Like I said, wanna see the tire?"

135

"Just sayin'..."

"Ya never heard a fuckin' tire blow out before?"

"Still, it sounded like a gunshot ..."

"That's why we're gonna go check to make sure, Einstein."

Several agonizing moments passed, and the blinding lights dimmed as the boys turned around and trotted back to the truck.

I sighed in relief. The woods on the other side of the road quickly exploded with bright silver lights dancing and jumping all over the trees and the steep hill running beyond it. As the boys disappeared in the brush, I crawled across the rough surface of the cool macadam and searched for a place to hide.

***

For the next twenty minutes, I lay in the ditch amongst high weeds just a few feet off the road, about forty feet from the open tailgate of the truck, wondering if I should climb into the loaded bed. All five young men were in the woods on the other side of the highway, trudging through the thick brush, looking for signs of anyone who might have shot out their front tire. They were making too much noise and would not be able to hear anything I did.

Even so, instinct told me to wait. I'd have a better chance of hitching a ride undetected once they'd changed the tire, got back inside the truck and started up the vehicle. I'd only have twenty seconds or so to make my move, but this would probably be my best opportunity. Otherwise, I ran the risk of someone getting too close to the truck bed when they came back. I had no idea where they kept their equipment. They might have it stowed away somewhere in the bed, amongst the trash. I knew better than take such a risk.

When they finally returned from the woods, one of them opened the metal toolbox directly behind the cab and removed an X-wrench, a jack, and a small toolbox, while another boy crawled underneath the truck to unscrew the spare tire from its housing unit. The driver got back in behind the wheel and flicked the headlights on. The fourth boy knelt in front of the flat while the fifth walked around in front of the truck, his flashlight scanning the hill as well as the woods on both sides of the road.

"Was *too* a fuckin' gunshot," said the boy carrying the tools to the front of the truck.

"Was not." The other boy snatched the X-wrench from him and immediately applied it to the flat.

"Was too."

"Not."

"What else could it have been?"

"Fuckin' blowout—what else?" said the boy standing in front of the truck.

"Too fuckin' loud for a blowout."

"Did we see anybody out there? Any sign of anyone?"

"That don't mean..."

"Did we?"

"Thought I did, farther on up that rise..."

137

"That was a fuckin' *dog*. Ever see a fuckin' *dog* shoot out a tire?"

"Coulda swore I saw somethin' else..."

"I didn't."

"Me either."

"It was a fuckin' *blowout*, moron. Suck it up."

"Slick, here, just wants to shoot somebody."

"Dude, these tires ain't that old. Simon took 'em from that garage in Tarentum when he found this truck. Took 'em right off the rack. Rack was marked *new*. Know what *new* means?"

"New," Mush Mouth said from the cab. "Means ain't old. Not used."

"Mush Mouth the fuckin' professor."

"Just 'cause a tire's new don't mean it ain't gonna have a blowout. Any dumbass could figure *that* one out."

"Sure am glad a dumbass like you pointed it out for me."

"Quit bein' a dick."

The boy beneath the truck had unscrewed the spare and let it drop. He crawled out, dragged out the spare, straightened and rolled it around to the front of the truck. The other boy had unscrewed the bolts on the flat and jacked up the truck a few inches. As soon as his friend brought over the spare, the first boy pulled off the flat and pushed it over to his friend. "Dump it."

"Where?"

"Over there in the bushes—where else?"

"In the *bushes*?"

138

"Afraid some cop's gonna see us and haul our asses in? Dump the fuckin' tire and quit bein' a shithead!"

"Whaddya want me to do first?"

"Idiot."

"Ain't no cops no more," muttered Mush Mouth.

"There are still cops, moron. They're just either dead or doped. If they're doped, they don't even know they're cops."

"I just thought we oughta bring it back, patch it up."

"What the hell for? Simon's got a stack sittin' outside the garage. Don'tcha remember? We picked 'em up coupla weeks ago."

"Guess I forgot." The boy rolled the flat into the ditch and let it fall in the bushes. Behind him, his friend used the jack to lower the truck, then tightened the nuts on the spare.

About a minute later, the boy circled the truck and dropped the jack and wrenches back into the toolbox. He opened the rear door behind the driver and climbed in. As soon as the others opened their doors and climbed in, I snuck up to the back of the truck and knelt beneath the lowered tailgate. Mush Mouth revved the ignition and slammed the truck into gear.

I rolled onto the tailgate. The truck began to move. I crawled into the bed and ducked beneath the loose flap of the tarp.

***

As the truck gained speed, I crawled beneath an old wooden table and a large rolled-up rug reeking of cigarettes, booze, and vomit. There was also a box filled with pots and pans shoved near the front, against the toolbox. A stack of old magazines two feet thick, bound with heavy twine, sat next to the wheel well on the driver's side. I dragged it closer and gently tipped it over. When it was where I wanted it, I sat directly behind it, facing the tailgate. If I was caught in heavy fire, the sturdy bundle would provide me with protection. Other than heavy armor-piercing stuff, I couldn't think of any round capable of penetrating a solid mass of paper twenty-four inches thick.

The truck began climbing the narrow, winding hill leading to Cherry Hill Road a couple of miles north. This area had always been sparsely populated, the houses few and far between and set far back from the winding country road. From the darkness of the tarp-covered bed, I couldn't see much of anything, but the slight reek of decay lingered along the stretch.

About fifteen minutes later, the truck began slowing down. The driver turned left, onto another bumpy road, which would take us even deeper into the woods. This road went on forever, giving the impression it had been cut into the side of a mountain and neglected ever since. The truck stumbled across potholes, dips, tossed debris and crumbling macadam. All I could see was the darkness we left behind, where the homes and other buildings had become block-like shapes of blackness interrupting the soft gray darkness of approaching night.

As we went down the deserted road, I saw no lights or other signs of life. Several dark masses lay in the road as we went past. Carcasses of small animals, as well as dead leaves, tossed bottles, and other pieces of garbage littered our path.

We went around a bend and passed several groups of trees. The truck slowed down. I shoved the Ruger into its shoulder holster, crawled out onto the tailgate and risked a peek just beyond the flapping edge of the tarp.

Distant flickering lights blinked beyond the pine trees. Situated at the end of a long, winding drive, a huge two-story building sat about half a mile from the main road, concealed partially by the trees and other heavy growth.

The truck slowed again and began turning.

I had to make a quick decision. I didn't know if this turnoff actually brought us to our destination. For all I knew, this road could go past the property for another long stretch before becoming a different road. If I jumped off too soon, I'd be stuck in the middle of nowhere and wouldn't have a clue how or where to follow them.

If the house was actually their destination, I'd face a much more dangerous dilemma. I couldn't be in the truck when they stopped and parked. I'd have no chance of getting out without being seen, and would be sitting right there if they decided right then to pull off the tarp. I'd be able to kill several of them, but since I didn't know the setup, I'd probably get Fields killed and would also die shortly afterward.

The flickering lights I'd seen through the pines could suggest that they'd reached the end of their journey. If Simon was in charge of all this, he'd prefer living in luxury. In this dark new world of base survival, enjoying life in a mansion would be the perfect choice.

The truck continued slowing down.

This is it!

I didn't know if that was my own voice convincing me or my gut instinct directing me. I only knew that I was reasonably certain this brood lived here. If I was right, Fields was being held here.

The truck turned onto the road that approached the hill leading to the mansion. As we neared the big metal mailbox at the corner, someone said, "Wanna stop and check for mail?"

A chuckle.

"Dumbass ... ya say that every fuckin' time we come back here."

"Wouldn't it be funny if there *was* mail?"

"Yeah, dude. Hilarious."

As soon as the truck's front tires tapped the brim of the private road, I slipped off the tailgate and landed in a crouch on the gravel. The truck continued down the road. I rolled across the gravel until I'd reached the ditch, and disappeared in a thicket of underbrush.

I waited a full minute, the Ruger aimed straight ahead. I visualized the truck stopping, the doors flying open, the boys jumping out and coming my way, their flashlights splashing the road as they searched for signs of whatever the driver had seen roll across the driveway.

My worries quickly evaporated. The truck continued down the road.

When the big vehicle was a safe distance away, I crawled out of the underbrush and lay on my belly in the ditch, watching the taillights intensify as the truck stopped in front of the huge detached garage beside the mansion.

My nerves quivered as I waited for the taillights to dim. About fifteen seconds later, they turned dark, and the distant sounds of doors slamming shut echoed down the drive. Flashlights hopped and skipped jerkily against the darkness as the boys made their way for the mansion.

***

With my penlight marking my path, I was careful to keep the tiny beam close in front of me. Mindful of the thick, uneven underbrush, I used the light to avoid deadfalls and relied on my night vision to veer around low branches and dangling vines.

The woods grew thick with towering pines. I focused on the small white halo leading me, and after trudging through several acres of thick, overgrown woods, I reached the tree line that ended approximately forty yards from the front yard of the property.

Exhausted from my efforts, I switched off the penlight, crouched behind a stump and surveyed the scene.

The place looked like it belonged to a car dealer. At least two dozen cars, pickups, vans, RVs and ATVs sat on the other side of the drive, in front of and beside the four-car garage. The beat-up pickup remained behind the compact that had been following Fields and me earlier that morning. The sight of it caused the muscles in my back to bunch up. My head and neck grew warm, and my finger unconsciously tapped the trigger of the Ruger.

I took a couple of deep breaths to clear my head. The tension gradually eased up, and I resumed my study of the premises.

Two home generator units sat at the corner of the house, humming softly. Three refrigerators, two washing machines, a dryer, an upright freezer, and a freezer chest huddled closely to one another on a slab. I couldn't see the backyard from my vantage point, but there was evidence of a swimming pool, chain-link fence, and more than a dozen bicycles perched on stands behind the side gate.

I crept over to the next tree and saw the dark outline of a smaller two-story building situated directly behind the mansion. It sat in a grove of trees down a short hill, about two hundred feet from the main house. Bushes and shrubbery surrounded the building. A couple of lights flickered in the windows on the ground floor.

It looked like a guest house. I wondered if they were keeping Fields in that building.

I crept back to the stump, crouched behind it and listened. Aside from the humming of the generators, I heard nothing. I saw no evidence of dogs. In the darkness, I couldn't see cameras or any other signs of surveillance in the front yard or bolted to the roof, windows or gables. There was no one walking around. I had no clue how many people were living in the main house or the guest house, where everyone was, or if anyone was keeping watch. Since I saw no guards or security equipment, I had to assume that the people living here didn't care if anyone was sneaking around their place. There weren't many people sneaking around anymore, but that was no reason to let your guard down. The incident outside my grandparents' house this morning reminded me how important it was to be on constant alert.

Using the trees as cover, I crept along the tree line that ran closer to the front yard. A huge pine tree towered over the others and stood directly in line with the eastern wall of the main building. The front door faced me less than a hundred feet away, behind a sloped, weed-ridden yard and remnants of a flower garden. A large bay window hid behind the weeds, about ten feet to the right of the front entrance. Light flickered weakly in the window. However, all the other windows facing the front were dark.

Where were the five young men who'd brought me here? Where was Simon? Was there a basement? An attic? A playroom?

Was Simon using the guest house as a playroom? Was he keeping Fields there?

It had been about an hour since the truck had brought me here. Had the fivesome gone to bed?

Why didn't I hear or see anyone?

There was only one way to find out.

The weeds would conceal me in my crawl over to the house, but from there I'd be on my own. The flickering light behind the bay window suggested someone could be in that room. I'd be a fool to try a break-in that way. If I fiddled with a dark window somewhere else, someone might be sleeping in that room.

If I made any noise forcing open the window, all would be lost.

My only option was the most direct and also the most dangerous. The front door. I had to force it open, and quickly. But doing it this way would be very difficult, if not impossible, without certain tools. A crowbar would certainly help. So would a screwdriver. Hell, a battering ram would make life much easier.

I had to face reality. To force open that door, I had to rely solely on the strength of my shoulder and any momentum I could muster up. I'd forced doors open before, but under very different circumstances. I was twenty at the time, and usually had a battering ram in my hands, an assault weapon slung over my shoulder and armed backup going in with me.

Yes, this was very different. However, one aspect of the situation would balance the scales:

Fields was being held inside, and because of that, I was prepared to risk everything, including my own life.

But what if she wasn't? What if she was being held in the guest house? What if I couldn't break through the front door? What if I broke through and found a dozen young psychos sleeping in the front room, all armed with assault weapons?

It didn't matter. Fields was here and I was going to find her.

Nonetheless, I found myself gazing at the door, considering the odds. Should I do it? Or should I try the back? Forget the main house entirely and go for the guest house? Did it matter which building I tried first?

Yes, because no matter which building I broke into, once I'd invaded their world, there was no turning back.

I'd already decided there would be no turning back until I'd found her and brought her back home. If this meant killing everyone who got in my way, that was how it had to be. I didn't even know for certain if she was still alive, but that didn't matter, either. I sensed that she was, could feel it in my bones. I refused to believe we'd come this far just to see it all end this way.

My head swam relentlessly as I stepped closer to the pine and prepared to crawl through the weeds.

Don't, a voice told me.

I stiffened. My gut talking to me again? Or was this something entirely different?

I didn't care; I was going in.

147

I slipped past the pine tree. At that same moment, as I raised my tennis shoe a few inches, I felt something catch my instep, and I nearly lost my balance. My heart skipped a beat; I fumbled for the penlight. Déjà vu slapped me in the back of the head. I knew what happened even before I shined the tiny beam of silver light on the ground at my feet.

A tripwire.

There *was* a security system after all.

Further thinking instantly dissolved. My reflexes kicked in, bringing me back flashes of the old days. I hit the ground and lay perfectly still in the tall grass.

PART TWO: LIGHT

CHAPTER ELEVEN

I lay on the cold ground, listening, but heard nothing.

I began wondering if the tripwire was merely a battery-powered motion sensor, alerting those inside the house. As far as I knew, no booby trap had been activated.

However, that wasn't the issue. Touching it set off the silent alarm. Now it was too late to retrace my steps, and the only option I faced at the moment was...

Someone's behind you, a strange voice inside me said.

Once again I was startled by this bizarre phenomenon. I realized this might be my gut communicating with me again, but the manner in which it had interrupted my thoughts alarmed me. It somehow felt like it did not belong to me, but someone else. If I didn't know better, I would've thought some unknown presence was trying to get my attention. I knew the concept was crazy, but that's how it felt.

Crazy. It hadn't occurred to me before, but now this reasoning somehow made sense. This whole day had been so stressful, it was a wonder I could still function. In fact...

They're now about twenty yards away, the voice said, interrupting my thoughts again.

I continued lying motionless on the cold ground. If that strange voice was right, any sort of movement would get me shot. I was unfamiliar with my surroundings, had no escape plan in the works, and didn't know where my stalker was. So I waited, my pulse racing wildly.

About thirty seconds later, leaves stirred among the trees twenty feet or so behind me.

I hoped the weeds would conceal me. The weeds and the darkness—as well as the element of surprise—were my only allies. If the stranger sneaking up on me knew where I was, the most dangerous thing I could do was let them know I was a threat. Even so, I knew I couldn't stay hidden in the weeds forever.

The tactic of playing dead had worked in many instances, and since I had no idea who was sneaking up on me, I had to stay right where I was. As I lay, the Ruger in my right hand on the ground beside me, I carefully eased the tiny .22 Bobcat from my pocket, took it off safety with my thumb, pulled back the hammer, and held the gun firmly in my left hand. I kept my hand palm-down in the weeds, close to my head. Then I waited.

More rustling. I suspected my stalker was only a few feet away.

He's on your right side, the voice in my head told me.

How far away? I found myself ask.

Ten feet.

Ten feet was a good practical range for the Bobcat. If I had the chance, I was going to try to shorten the distance for an even more effective shot.

The rustling stopped. The clicking of a gun hammer thundered in my ears, yet I remained still. Then I heard the voice.

"I see you ..."

It sounded like a young girl. I nearly choked when I heard it. But I knew better than move.

"You heard me. Get up, or I'll shoot."

This was not happening. A young *girl*? My God. Would the horrors of this new existence *ever* stop?

"I'm countin' to three. One..."

"All right." I raised my head. "I'm getting up."

"Leave the gun. Hands up."

I let go of the Ruger and pushed myself up into a kneeling position. Regaining my balance, I slowly raised both hands out to the sides and turned slightly to my right, keeping my left hand directly behind my torso. If she was going to shoot me, she would have already done it. She was probably supposed to bring me back to the house. This gave me the advantage.

As I turned to look at her, I noticed that the darkness of the woods behind her concealed her almost completely, but I could see that she was quite small and slender, probably not much taller than five feet. She held a pistol or revolver in her left hand, and it was aimed at me. In her right, she held a flashlight. The flashlight was pointed at the ground but wasn't turned on. I suspected she was waiting to shine it on my face once I'd straightened.

She'd apparently moved another foot or so closer, which shortened the range of the Bobcat. I wasn't wild about shooting a young girl but had no choice. If she was a member of Simon's brood, she was probably just as much of a psycho as the two this morning, or the group looking for me in the woods. Society's credo had become short and dangerously simple in the last few months: kill or be killed.

Just as I reached my full height, she said, "Whaddya doin' out here? This is private property."

Her cold, flat tone brought back the searing heat billowing within me, and suddenly I didn't care how small or young she was. I turned another couple of inches toward her and made sure the Bobcat was hidden from her view. "I was just in the neighborhood and thought I'd stop by."

She didn't say anything at first. Then she shook her head. "*Huh?*"

"Aren't you a little young to be pointing guns at people?"

"Fuck you. You ain't s'posed to be here, dude. Besides, I'm good with this fucker."

"Really? It's bigger than you are."

"Fuck you, asshole. Maybe Simon'll let me use you for target practice." She clicked the flashlight on and started to bring it up.

They've got Fields ... these psychos have got Fields ...

The rage slammed through me. They'd taken Fields, and this arrogant little bitch was a member of the group responsible. I couldn't let her blind me with that flashlight.

Just as the glaring beam reached my waist, I brought my left arm across my chest and emptied all eight rounds into the small, skinny body. She managed to get one off, but it was low and slapped the ground a foot or so to my left. The flashlight leaped out of her hand and splashed the woods and the dark, starry night in a wide, wavy arc before thumping to the ground and forming a lopsided halo in the weeds. She fell quietly to the ground and lay still.

I retrieved the Ruger and went over to where she lay. I grabbed my own pocket flashlight and shined it at her face. Nausea made me gag. I'd killed a young *boy*, and he looked no older than eleven or twelve.

"Jesus ..." My heart raced; I grew nauseous. "I just killed a damned..."

Later, the voice in my head said. *There are more of them.*

My temples pounded deafeningly as I scrambled into the brush.

***

I stuck to the other side of the tree line, keeping low, while the growing beams of silver light waved in my direction. I counted eight beams, and guessed they were no more than a hundred yards away. They were spread out in a long, choppy line spanning the center of the woods, each several yards from one

153

another, aiming their light at everything in their path as they moved toward me. I estimated I had no more than a couple of minutes before they reached me.

Another beam appeared, this one quite far on my left, and began closing in on the others. Moments later another one coming over from the right, on the far side of the tree line, jumped toward me. Directly behind me, two more beams of light coming from the front yard of the house hopped around in the tall grass.

A knot of cold fear grew heavy in the pit of my stomach. I was surrounded. I had the Ruger ready, its mag filled to capacity. The Bobcat, however, was empty, and I didn't have time to reload. And the .38 held only six. Way too many odds against me. It was dark, my aggressors had lights, and there were entirely too many of them. Unless they were poor shots, they'd get me before I could pick off more than one or two of them. I hadn't a prayer.

But I had to find some way of getting through this. Fields depended on me.

Straight ahead, the voice in my head told me.

What?

Straight ahead, about fifteen feet. Three trees down, you'll see a log.

Without hesitation I holstered the Ruger, dropped to my knees and crawled toward the dead log. As I moved, the flashlights continued drifting across the uneven brush toward me, jumping up into the trees and then sliding back down to the ground. I reached the log. The deadfall had once been a huge tree where a large section of bark had slid off,

154

forming a crude cover between it and the dead limbs leaning against the pine tree a few feet from it. I found a depression in the ground directly behind the bark. Some sort of den an animal had once used, obviously. I couldn't risk flicking on the flashlight and hoped the space was large enough to accommodate me. I also hoped it was vacant.

I squeezed into it and, lying on my left side, pulled the leaves carefully over me, until I was completely covered. To prevent dirt, leaves and twigs from getting in my eyes, nose and mouth, I grabbed the front of my jacket and covered my face.

The crunching of leaves grew louder. Footsteps smashed dead branches and crushed leaves directly behind me, and I could soon tell by the increasing vibrations in the ground that they were just a few feet in front of me. One of them jumped over my log and landed heavily on the ground a foot or so to my right. He stayed there for long, tense moments, shifting his weight as he moved his flashlight beam around. Then he stepped away.

I lowered my jacket about an inch below the level of my eyes and pushed a couple of dead leaves aside. Someone came into my sight, and then someone else, and finally two others. The foursome reached the tree line and stopped moving. Through my mask of dead leaves I could see them moving their beams toward the front yard then turning around and aiming the brightness directly into the woods. They were all slender—some tall, others short. Although I couldn't see their faces in the dark, I could distinguish holsters dangling over skinny legs and rifles perched atop narrow shoulders. They were all young—probably around the same age as the one I'd just killed. The memory of that unfortunate incident forced the cold knot in my gut to grow into a heavy block of ice.

A blinding whiteness slammed into my hiding place. I closed my eyes, nudged the jacket back up over them and remained completely still. The light stayed on me, and I was certain I'd been spotted ... but I knew better than move.

They can't see you, the voice told me.

It didn't matter; I did what my gut, as well as my training, told me. *Relax, don't move, breathe slowly, and become one with your environment. Become the ground, the tree, the dirt. Above all else, survive ...*

After a couple of long, excruciatingly-tense minutes, the blinding white beam finally shifted, and the comforting darkness that had become my only ally rushed back to console me.

"Jackie's dead!" whispered one of them harshly.

"Fucker got *Jackie*?"

"*Told* ya I heard eight shots. Sounded like a fuckin' twenty-two."

"Fuck!"

"Shit!"

"Simon's gonna be pissed, man ... really and truly, man ..."

"He's got weed for days. He'll be all right."

"He's got a little crank for tomorrow, too ..."

"What about the stuff he got from Doc's wagon?"

"Doc only likes Zanax and Vicodin when he really wants to get fucked up. Took Zanax this mornin', when he found out Doc and James got capped. Doc had enough weed for a coupla weeks in the wagon, but you know Simon ..."

"Yeah, he likes to have a month's supply on hand for parties. And now *we* gotta find the stuff for 'im."

"Yeah. Doc ain't around no more ..."

"*Damn*. Gotta find that stupid fuck ..."

"That's why we're here, bitch ..."

"Where the fuck *is* he?"

"Fucker's gotta be here *some*where ..."

Silence.

"Think maybe he circled back?"

"Fucker could be anywhere ..."

"Dammit, Jackie, you stupid asshole ..."

"Spread out, we'll go back in and come out the other way. First one sees 'im, shoot the flare. 'Member, Simon wants this fucker alive!"

The lights scattered, and the boys rushed back into the woods.

I held my breath as two of them shuffled back, stopped about three feet in front of the pile of leaves covering me and slammed my area once again with a trio of blinding fireballs from their flashlights. Then they split up and went back to their hunt.

I didn't start breathing normally again until the comforting silence told me they'd gone.

***

157

After a couple of minutes of heavy silence, I decided it was safe to leave my little nook. The hunting party would be looking for me at the other end of the woods. I had time to circle the property and find a way back through the back yard. If Fields was being held in the guest house, I had to get her out without alerting anyone in the main building. If she wasn't there, I had to find someone who could give me answers. I didn't have much time, and would have to resort to crude interrogation tactics. The thoughts of torturing a kid disturbed me, but I reminded myself that they were armed and dangerous, out of control and beyond hope. In this new world, everyone was doomed, especially children.

I pushed away my blanket of dead leaves and crawled out from behind the sheet of bark. I spent another minute or so listening to the silence before moving away from my sanctuary. When I was sure the silence indicated no immediate threat, I crawled over to the tree line. Once I reached the boundary of the property, I ran over to the chain-link fence.

I no sooner got to my feet when I noticed a flurry of blinding flashlights emerging from behind the trees in the distance, coming my way again. I counted ten of them; they were moving quickly through the woods.

I sprinted over to the end of the property and scrambled down the short hill that emptied onto the narrow one-lane dirt road cutting through the residences. As I crossed the road I found myself waist-high in weeds. The silvery haze of a flickering flashlight beam grew steadily as it came down the road. A kid on a bike searched for me as he rode, moving the flashlight in wide, wavy arcs along the road and into the hilly terrain on both sides of the narrow path.

I flattened myself in the bushes and waited as the intense beam swept over me. It immediately shifted, moving in the opposite direction. Just as the cyclist turned away, I dashed out of the bushes, ran over and pushed him off his bike. He went down easily, the bike slamming to the ground, the boy landing with a surprised gasp. The flashlight flew, slapping the dirt and rolling toward the ditch, its haze spilling onto the hilly knoll beyond it.

I leaped on him, and we clutched at one another while rolling across the dirt road. I climbed on top of him and tried sitting on his arms, but he went for his gun before I could pin him. His leg came up, his knee catching me in the tailbone. A heavy spike of sizzling pain sliced up my spine. Gasping, I forced myself to ignore the pain while grabbing his right arm and pinning it beneath my knee. He tried slamming his knee into my back again. I grabbed his throat and squeezed. He choked and his leg went limp. When I let go of his throat, he tried throwing me off by twisting his pelvis and bringing up his legs again. Reaching behind me, I slapped him in the crotch. He howled and doubled up. Then I punched him in the jaw and he went slack.

As he lay there, gasping, I reached behind me and pulled his gun from its holster. It was a .45 Desert Eagle. A heavy, powerful weapon, especially for a kid. This boy appeared to be about eighteen and went around one-forty or so. I wondered if he'd ever fired the damned thing. But it didn't matter; the fact that he was carrying such a formidable weapon and would have used it was enough to encourage me to be extremely cautious.

I slapped him sharply on both cheeks. His eyes shot open and narrowed when he saw me, and he grunted and tried bucking me off him again. I cocked the hammer of the Eagle and pressed the slab barrel into the soft part of his neck, just above the Adam's apple. He immediately stopped resisting.

"I'll make this short and simple. Give me the right answers and I'll let you go. Fuck with me, and I'll blow your head off. Understand?"

A nod.

"Good. Now ... where do you keep the women?"

He blinked. "Huh?"

"The women. You idiots just brought one back a couple of hours ago."

"*Huh*?"

"Deer Creek Road. Don't act stupid. I saw five of you morons wandering around in a beat-up pickup."

He did something that didn't help his situation; he laughed.

I whacked him sharply on the jaw with the barrel. He squealed. His body tensed up.

"I guess I should've told you this before, but I thought it was obvious. Apparently it wasn't, so now I'm going to spell it out. I'm not in the mood for any shit right now, and I don't consider any of this funny. Get it?"

A nod. His eyes narrowed, and he swallowed. "Who the fuck *are* you, dude?"

"I'm the dude asking you questions. I'm also the dude with the gun. Now ... where is she?"

The boy smiled sheepishly. Apparently he didn't believe just how serious I was about this.

Without taking my eyes off him, I grabbed the little finger of his right hand. Then, placing it between my thumb and index finger, I snapped the finger like a twig. He opened his mouth to scream, but I shoved the barrel down his throat, and he gagged and began choking.

"One last time. Where is she?" I pulled the barrel out of his mouth and reapplied it to his throat.

He began sobbing. "H-*Hurts,* man! Hurts like a *mother...*"

"Just be glad you haven't pissed me off yet."

He sniffed and turned to gawk at his hand.

I grabbed his second finger. "You've got nine left. Consider yourself lucky you only have to answer one question."

He began whimpering. Rage suddenly showed in his glossy eyes. "They're ... comin' here, man ... they'll be here in ... in less than..."

"As you already know, it only takes me a second to break a finger. So let's just up the ante." I let go of the finger and grabbed his index finger. "If I break this one, you'll have to learn how to shoot

161

with your other hand. But that won't work because I'll probably decide to break the other one as well."

"Man, don't! Please? C'mon, now, I didn't *do* nothin' ..."

"Where is she?"

"I ... dunno. I think Simon has 'er in the house out back."

"Why there?"

He shrugged. "She's a doper, man. He ... he keeps the dopers there."

"Why?"

"When he brings one back, he finds out what they can do. The ones that look good but can't do nothin', he keeps whenever he needs a good fuck. If they don't fuck, he sends 'em back to the guest house."

The back of my neck heated up. "Then what happens?"

"Simon won't fuck no female that's doped 'less she's a babe."

"So he just keeps the doped women in the guest house?"

"Yeah, man, but not for very long. The ones that piss 'im off get taken away right off."

I swallowed a lump in my throat. "Taken away?"

"Tomorrow mornin' we gotta take 'er the dump. He don't want no female he can't fuck..."

"Wouldn't want *that*, would we?"

"Hey man, don't break any more of my fingers, *please*?"

"Where's this dump you keep talking about?"

162

"Just up the road."

"How far?"

"Mile, maybe two. It used to be a farm, got an old well out in back. Ol' man used to live there. Simon and a bunch of us went there for supplies one day, seen 'im sittin' there on his front porch, mumblin'. We went in the house and took a bunch of good shit—food, even some meds. While we were loadin' up the truck, ol' man started cryin', pissed off Simon. Simon wasn't in the mood to hear an ol' man cryin', so he took the ol' dude out back and pushed 'im down the well."

"Why?"

"Simon don't like nobody sufferin', 'specially an ol' man. No sense in that, right?"

"I guess not." It was getting extremely difficult to keep from pulling the trigger.

"Anyway, whenever Simon wants someone dead, we jus' take 'em in the truck and drop 'em down the well. Simon don't like smellin' dead bodies, says it ain't sanitary, makes 'im crazy. When Simon gets crazy..."

I cracked him hard on the back of the skull with the Eagle and rolled him back into the ditch. Then I tossed the Eagle into the high weeds. I wanted to keep it, but its weight would inhibit my movements.

At least now I knew what was going on. I was glad Fields had been able to keep Simon from raping her, but now I had to make sure I found her before these monsters could dump her. I just hoped she was alive when they brought her out here.

I went over and picked up the bike. As soon as I situated my butt on the seat, clusters of bright lights exploded from the darkness about half a mile behind me.

Grabbing my flashlight and gripping it in my left hand, I began pedaling vigorously down the narrow dirt road.

CHAPTER TWELVE

I stayed on the dirt road for the next mile or so before heading west at the turnoff. I had no idea how far I should go before stopping to rest. I had to find the abandoned farm the boy was talking about. I sincerely hoped he hadn't been lying when he'd told me it was just a couple of miles up the road. I saw no reason to doubt him. He was a stupid, misguided kid. He lacked the strong emotional discipline necessary to withstand someone breaking his fingers while the slab barrel of a Desert Eagle was shoved down his throat.

On the bike, I could cover sufficient ground, but I'd already begun to get tired and hungry, and had to find food and rest for a few hours. I couldn't be tired or hungry when I faced them again.

I had to assume they'd already found their friend. It would delay them for a few minutes but would also force them to continue with the hunt. The boy had probably been a scout. Since I'd already killed three others of this brood, Simon would consider me a major threat and send out his entire pack in the morning, when it was easier to see. I had to be fully rested and alert when this happened.

The area was woody, hilly and desolate, the houses considerable distances from one another. The bike would help, but I had no idea how long it would take to find food and shelter. I'd already cursed myself for ditching the backpack. It had been necessary, but now I badly needed some of its contents.

I had to stay focused. Otherwise, I'd run the risk of losing my concentration, and knew from experience that such an oversight always turned deadly.

Once I'd found food and had some rest, my next step was to find the abandoned farm, locate the well, and fashion some booby traps that would give me the edge I needed to rescue Fields.

I turned at the corner and went down a private dirt lane. Three homes sat in complete darkness in the distance. I saw no signs of life. The first place I came to, an old one-story ranch, sat in the middle of a small, neglected yard. A dying flower garden spanned the front of the house. Bushes and weeds had taken over, strangling most of the grass. Climbing ivy had choked off both trellises, their tentacles reaching out and covering the window shutters. A gazebo sat off to the western end of the front yard, its paint peeling, one of its walls leaning toward the ground. The red wooden mailbox had toppled over and lay across the cobblestone walk leading to the front porch.

I got off the bike, applied the kickstand, and bent to pick up the mailbox. I don't know why I bothered; no one was around to notice. I thought it undignified, lying there like that. It looked like someone had been proud of it at one time.

I stuck the bottom end of the post back into the hole in the dirt. I didn't have any tools to work with, so I pushed some dirt back into the hole with my tennis shoes and patted it down. It swayed a little, so I let it rest against the picket fence beside it. Then I went back to the bike and brought it through the entrance. Tall weeds had engulfed the fence just beyond the gate, which had fallen over and nearly touched the ground. One rusty hinge kept it from falling altogether. Two large plastic garbage bins sat beside one another inside the fence. I shoved the bike behind them, among the weeds. Then I turned around and noticed a dark figure sitting in a rocker, watching me.

He was about seventy or so, with curly gray hair and a full gray beard. He wore overalls and a long-sleeve shirt. He didn't move. I couldn't tell if he was alive or dead. If he was alive, he was doped, and probably wouldn't move much at all. I hated going inside the man's house and making myself at home, but I couldn't be picky right now. I'd done this same thing several times before, but that didn't make it easier, nor did it make me feel better about myself or the situation in general. I thought of Reed once again, and a cold feeling of depression swept through me.

I could not take advantage of this poor man. All I wanted was something to eat, a glass of water, and a chair to relax in for an hour or so. If I was lucky, I might find some bottled water and a can of tuna or vegetables in the house. If not, I'd just leave and look elsewhere.

"Hello, sir." I waved as I started up the walk.

He didn't acknowledge me, but as I drew closer, his head turned very slowly to his left, toward the road.

I turned to my right and stiffened.

Flashlights flickered about a block down the road. In the darkness I could make out shadows of boys on bikes. They slowed down while turning the corner at the end of the street.

***

I grabbed the Ruger and hurried back to the garbage bins. Squeezing in among the weeds, I crouched down and let the darkness swallow me up.

There were four of them, and they all had flashlights. They stopped outside the open gate and parked their bikes while shining their lights on the old man, who still hadn't moved. The lights jumped across the front yard, over to the garbage bins and across the road, before returning to the front porch.

"Hey, dude! What's happenin'?"

No reply.

"Knew he was a doper," one of them muttered with a chuckle.

"Let's check out what he's got."

"Yeah. Geezer might have some good shit stashed inside."

They swaggered up the walk, their flashlights leaping across the yard, returning to the porch and shining the glaring beams on the man's blank face. From my vantage point, I could tell by their slim, narrow builds that they were about the same age as the thug I'd left in the ditch. They were dressed in lightweight jackets and jeans. Their tennis shoes

168

made no sounds on the cobblestones. They all wore ammo belts and holsters, and the guns hanging down to their knees looked large. I had no doubt that, like their friend, they were carrying Desert Eagles.

"Anyone drop by out here lately?"

The old man didn't reply.

Two of them climbed the three rickety steps and flanked the old man's rocker. He still hadn't moved. I'd expected him to look in my direction, but he seemed to be staring down, at the steps. I was relieved he wasn't able to give away my position. In his mental state, he'd probably already forgotten about me.

"There's this fucker out here, somewhere..."

"Jus' killed a buddy of ours," his friend threw in.

"Bashed his head in," added the third one at the foot of the steps, tossing his beam at the end of the street.

"Fucker's crazy, dude..."

Silence.

"Got any munchies, pops?"

One of them aimed his beam at the front door. He walked up to it, kicked it open and aimed the bright orange halo at the open doorway. Then he stepped inside. One of the two on the front walk rushed up the steps and followed him in. A few moments later, the one standing on the old man's right followed suit.

The fourth stayed out on the walk. He glanced at the old man then turned sharply and sprayed the front yard with his flashlight. Some of the haze hit the garbage bin in front of me before edging back into the weeds. The boy then turned and aimed the blinding light directly at the old man's face.

I wanted to shoot him but knew what would happen if I missed. If they were carrying heavy-caliber guns, my .22 Ruger couldn't possibly stack up—not in these conditions, where my aim would be less than perfect in the darkness. I could try using the .38, but I couldn't get to the pancake holster without making sufficient noise in the weeds.

"Wanna be careful, livin' out here by yourself, ol' man." The boy flicked off the flashlight. "Fucker we're talkin' about? He's one badass, he'll kill ya, he sees ya sittin' out here like this—know what I mean?"

The old man didn't reply.

"Ol' dude like yourself? You're a sittin' duck, 'specially with a serious badass like him out here. Shoulda seen what he done to our buddy back there. Bashed 'is head in, broke all his fingers..."

The others came out of the house. One carried what looked like candy bars, while the other two nibbled on what sounded like crackers or pretzels, from a small bag. One of them said, "Don't have too much in there, ol' man. Need to take a trip to the local market for supplies. We might be passin' by again, soon. We get hungry—know what I'm sayin'?"

The boys chuckled.

"Never know, stores might run out one of these days."

A giggle.

"Yeah, ain't much left in there now. You're gonna be chewin' your nails in a couple days."

They were all nibbling as they shuffled down the walk, retrieved their bikes and got back on them. The one who'd stayed out on the porch said, "'Member what I said, ol' man. Fuckin' dangerous, sittin' out here."

The foursome rode away, giggling.

I stood up and forced myself to shove the Ruger back into the shoulder holster. I didn't want to chance a firefight—not with the old man sitting there.

But I decided not to go inside. I couldn't possibly take anything from this poor man, especially after those jerks had done the same thing. I pulled my bike out from amongst the weeds. Before I got on it and rode away, I turned and waved again. "I hope you'll be okay, sir," I said. "I wish I could've stopped them from doing what they did, but I didn't want to get you killed." Then I turned back to the road.

"Hungry?"

The soft, high-pitched voice startled me. I turned sharply around and saw right off that the old man was staring straight at me.

"Did you ... just say something?"

"You look hungry and tired." The old man got up from his rocker. He jabbed a thumb at the door. "C'mon inside."

I couldn't believe this. Was it really happening? Or was I just imagining it?

"C'mon, now. Hide that bike quick. Those assholes might come back in a few minutes."

***

Inside, the old man lit a small kerosene lamp. The area glowed, sprinkling the large, cluttered living room with hazy shadows. After closing and locking the door, he left the room for a few moments and came back carrying another kerosene lamp. He moved fairly well for his age. He was about my height and, except for some excess flab around his middle, fairly slender.

"You sure had me fooled," I said.

In the haze of the lamp, his deep-blue eyes twinkled like tiny gems. "You have to act like that if you wanna sit out in your rocker at night and watch the stars." He placed the second lamp on an end table next to the large L-shaped sofa facing the front door. The other lamp stood in the center of a round cocktail table, between the sofa and a large overstuffed armchair.

"You've got a point there," I said.

"So here we are now, just a few of us left, and we can't even sit outside on our own front porch without a gang of nutcases comin' over and helpin' themselves to whatever they want." He gestured to the armchair. I let myself fall into it and instantly felt my body relax. Only then did I realize how long I'd been running on adrenaline.

He shook his head. "Twenty years ago? I would've shot those bastards. Now?" A shrug. "Kinda hard, dealing with shit like that when you're

172

eighty and your eyesight's not so good anymore. Drink?"

"I'd love one. But don't feel so bad. There were four of them, and they all had guns. I'll bet they're all pretty good with them."

"Wouldn't surprise me. Every so often I hear gunshots out in the woods a ways off. It's probably those idiots having fun with strays." He grabbed one of the lamps and left the room. I saw the light dance in the open doorway next to the living room wall and guessed it was probably the kitchen. I noticed that the curtains and blinds were closed and pulled tight in both living room windows, keeping light from trickling outside, which would be seen by looters or other vandals wandering around.

He came back carrying a bottle and two glasses. He put the lamp on the end table, placed the glasses on the table between us and poured at least three inches into each. "Scotch all right for you?"

"Scotch will definitely be all right."

He handed me a glass. I drank and immediately felt the strong stuff warming my insides. He plopped down on the couch and sipped some from his own glass. "Walter," he said.

"Moss."

"Moss?"

"Alan, but everyone calls me Moss."

He held out his glass. We clinked. "To better days."

"That wouldn't take much."

"By the way, thanks for doing what you did with the mailbox. I thought about doing it myself, but I don't want anyone seeing me. You never know when these little bastards'll pass by on their bikes. I don't want 'em knowing I'm not doped."

"I can't blame you. Acting normal can be deadly these days."

"I've seen a beat-up pickup go by a few times, and also one of those electric compacts a dozen times in the last few weeks."

"I've seen them, too. They belong to a man named Simon."

"Simon?"

"These boys live with him."

"Where'd they come from?"

"From what I heard, a Juvenile Center in Pittsburgh. Simon went there to raid the pharmacy for drugs and supplies and decided to bring some of the kids back with him and use them to run errands for him."

"Nice."

"He's got a huge mansion on Cherry Hill Road. He probably just took it over and moved right in. Apparently he's set himself up as their leader or something."

"Shit, that's only a coupla miles down the road. And you say those idiots live with him?"

"There are women, too. Drop-offs, apparently. Sounds like he's got some sort of harem operation going on."

He blinked. "Drop-offs?"

"I heard the boys say the normal people are dropping off the doped."

"Like dogs?"

"Exactly."

The old man shook his head. "Keeps on getting better and better, don't it?"

"As long as there are people still walking around, things will always be bad."

"Ever seen this Simon character?"

"Not yet, but I plan to."

Walter sipped more Scotch. "Why'd you do it, Moss? Make the mailbox right?"

"I didn't like seeing it lying there like that. To me, it looked like it wanted to stand up again. We don't have any use for mail anymore, but it bothered me. It's hard to explain. I guess you could say it saddened me. Is that why you invited me in?"

He put his glass down. "The wife helped me put it up. Forty-seven years ago, I believe it was. We'd just bought the house. It wasn't a good time to buy a house back then. The industry was in the worst recession we'd ever seen, probably because our Government was in the worst stage of corruption most of us had ever seen. But Madge and I had only been married three years and wanted our own place. We had a little money saved, and we always liked this area, so we took out a mortgage, cashed in our Government bonds and moved right in. Raised two kids, sent 'em both through college, shared a lot of memories—some good, some bad." He laughed. "That mailbox saw more than a dozen coats of paint. It survived its share of idiot postal workers running into it, as well as power company trucks and other folks trying their best to knock it down ... but it always managed to hold its ground."

"When did it fall over?"

He rubbed the back of his neck. "I buried Madge about four months ago. She started getting bad, forgetting things, having headaches all the time, until one morning she didn't wake up. Anyway, it wasn't too long after that when the damned thing started leaning. Then it fell some time in the night, and when I woke the next morning and saw it lying there on the walk, it hit me hard. It was almost like it just gave up when Madge died. And when it collapsed, I felt as if my life I knew it was gone. I had a quiet cry, said a prayer for Madge and never looked at it again."

Four months ago. About the same time Fields, Reed and I were burying Uncle Joe, this poor man was burying his beloved wife of nearly fifty years. "Sorry, Walter."

He nodded, and in the haze of the lamp I saw his eyes glistening. "What you did—when you picked it back up, it was a very nice moment ... very special for me. It felt like someone had just dropped by to say hi—not just to me, but also to Madge. The neighbors did that not too long ago. Back in the day, they stopped by once in a while. Sometimes one of our friends would bring us a dozen ears of corn, other times fruit or tomatoes. A lot of good folks died in the last year or so, Moss."

"I know." I thought of my mother and Uncle Joe. And, of course, Reed.

"I buried Madge in the back yard, near her flower garden. It took me all day. Hell, I'm an old man, Moss. I had to stop every fifteen minutes or so, catch my breath. Shovels stopped being my favorite things fifty years ago. But it had to be done. Madge had to have a place to..." He waved it aside. "Long story short, no one stopped by that day. Everyone was already dead, or as close to it as you can get."

"I can see why I brought it all back."

"But that wasn't the whole story. I liked what you said before you tried to leave. About you wanting to stop them doing what they did. I ... really liked hearing that."

"The only reason I didn't do it was because I didn't want you getting caught in the crossfire. I thought you were doped, and if you were, you wouldn't be able to get out of the way fast enough."

He smiled. "I appreciate the thought, Moss."

I drained my drink, picked up the bottle and poured a couple of inches into my glass and another couple of inches into Walter's glass.

He picked it up and swirled it. "I never thought something like that would happen again—not in my lifetime, anyway. I guess I thought ... well, when you live alone, and everyone else is dead, dying or crazy, you don't expect to meet anyone decent. Know what I mean?"

"Unfortunately."

"Then someone drops by, says something nice and actually does something nice for you." He held out his glass again. "It's been a really good day, my friend."

I picked up my glass and we clinked again.

"That a Ruger I saw in your hand out in the front yard?"

I pulled it out and handed it over. He examined it. "Sweet. Had one just like it, years ago." He reached underneath the cocktail table and placed what looked like a Glock on its surface. He obviously had a holster Velcroed or stapled to the underside of the table. "I spent twenty years in the Air Force as a pilot. At least that's what I did before they started up those drone programs to spy on everyone. Then they didn't need me up there anymore, and stuck me behind a desk in one of their recruiting centers. How 'bout you?"

"Army. Three years. Riot control then border patrol."

"Nasty duty." He grimaced and had another sip of Scotch. "Are you the man those punks were talking about? The one killing folks?"

"That's me."

He sat back and stared at me for a few moments. "Care to tell me why?"

"Simon took my girlfriend. I'm getting her back, one way or the other. I don't care how many of them I have to kill to do it."

Walter frowned. "He ... took your girlfriend?"

"She was taking a walk in our back yard. A couple of them came onto the property, grabbed her and took her away."

"Just like that?"

"Just like that."

"Can't say as I blame you. If it was me, this Simon bastard would already be dead." He replaced the Glock underneath the table.

"He will be, as soon as I get her back."

"There are prob'ly a lot of them."

"I don't care."

"I admire your determination, son, but if ya don't mind my saying so, you look tired and hungry. You're gonna need some food and rest."

I couldn't even think of asking him to share what little food he had left. I could try to find something in one of the other houses down the street. I had to get going. I forced myself out of the comfortable chair. "It's all right. I saw what they took from you. You can't spare much, so I think I'll be going. It was very nice..."

"Sit back down, young fella."

"But..."

"You didn't see what they *didn't* take." He got down on his knees and pulled up the bottom of the couch cover. Then, grabbing a sash handle, he yanked a large drawer out from beneath the sofa. The kerosene lamp was kind of dim, but I could see stacks of canned foods, jerky, bottled water, and jars of olives, pickles, and a bunch of other things.

I sat back down. "Wow."

He grunted. "I've got food and supplies hidden all over this place. I keep a small supply of snacks on the kitchen counter for emergencies, like what happened earlier. I've got a small home generator hooked up behind the house. The freezer and two small refrigerators are hidden behind a secret wall in the basement."

"I'm impressed."

He pulled out a couple of cans and put them on the table. He grabbed a can opener and placed it on the table beside the cans. "Tuna all right? If you want a regular meal, it'll take me a little while to heat up the..."

"Tuna's just fine." My stomach growled as I picked up the can opener and opened a can. Walter produced a fork and napkins and placed them on the table. I had a tasty mouthful of the moist, water-packed meat, and watched in delight as he placed a paper plate on the table, found a pack of salted crackers and a small brick of cheese, and arranged them on the plate. He dropped a cracker on the floor, picked it up, blew on it and put it on the plate. He saw me watching him. "Sorry about the manners. I don't get visitors much anymore."

I laughed. And for the first time since before breakfast, I actually had the feeling things might turn out.

CHAPTER THIRTEEN

Later, after I'd devoured a can of tuna, a small plate of crackers and cheese, and a large chunk of beef jerky, Walter told me to relax on the sofa. I wanted to protest, but my tired body strongly suggested otherwise. I lay back and immediately felt the tension leave my limbs.

Walter picked up the garbage, grabbed one of the lamps and shuffled off.

I lay amongst the soft cushions and listened as he ran water from the tap in the kitchen. I closed my eyes and imagined Fields bustling about in my grandmother's kitchen, washing the dishes and putting them in the drainer. I imagined her coming into the living room to join me on the couch. I could practically smell the vanilla scent in her hair as she sat down next to me, and could feel it brush my face as it slid across her shoulder.

I opened my eyes, and when I saw the strange shadows flickering in the light from the lamp, I realized this wasn't our home. Fields wasn't here. Someone had taken her from me. I didn't know exactly where she was, but that didn't matter. She was my friend, my partner and the love of my life, and I was going to find her and bring her back.

I tried to relax, to let the food I'd just consumed strengthen me, settle my nerves. It was just enough to keep me going for the next few hours, and I was confident it would give me the stamina I needed. But I couldn't stop thinking about Fields. I couldn't stop worrying about her—wondering where she was, what she was going through, what they'd done to her.

Once again the rage within me erupted, but this time my struggle to keep it contained was less successful. I obviously didn't want to fight it anymore. I wanted it right there, ready to go when the time was right. I'd be taking no prisoners and would see only payback when I finally faced the demons that had ripped my world apart.

I'm coming to get you, Fields.

I hoped she'd hear me. I knew that even if she didn't, she'd know I was out there, and that it would not be long before I rescued her. She'd know because she knew me. And in the last few months, she'd grown to know me better than anyone else ever had.

Walter came back and lowered his butt onto the cushion of the armchair. The lamp provided a fluttering orange haze onto the table between us, but I could barely see his face, and I was sure he could barely see mine. "You're thinking about her again."

"How could you tell?"

He chuckled softly. "Even in the dark, I can see that you look like a coiled spring."

I didn't reply; he was pretty perceptive.

"Try to relax, my friend. You need to be rested and ready to kick ass when you leave here."

"I'm ready to kick ass right now."

"I can tell. I'd probably feel the same way if someone had taken Madge away from me."

"Every time I think of that, I want to..."

"Relax."

I took a deep breath and lay back. It helped, so I closed my eyes and thought of other things. Despite my anger, my eagerness to jump up from the couch and rush outside to find her, I felt my exhausted body surrendering to the couch.

"How many others do you think there are?" Walter asked after a short silence.

"Like us?"

"Yeah."

"Hopefully, more than we think."

"I can't help wondering where they are. If some of them have found one another and decided to stick together. Maybe a batch of them has decided to try and start things up again."

"That would be too much to hope for. People like us are probably doing exactly what we're doing."

"Hiding?"

"It's safer this way. Otherwise..."

"Yeah. You never know anymore. I've learned only one thing about people in my life, and that hasn't changed in all these years. I learned it a long time ago, when I was a kid. They're totally unpredictable."

"That's right. You never know what they're gonna do." I remembered a cooler filled with human penises, and a box crammed with human scalps. "For all we know, this Simon guy might have been a respectable business owner before all this happened."

Walter stared at me for a few moments before he spoke. "My friend, people don't change—not really. I've been around a long time. I've seen a lot of things—some good, some bad. Mostly bad, because people always tend to do the wrong thing when the pressure gets too much. This thing with Simon and his brood isn't new. You know that as well as I do. Folks walking around with a few loose screws always look for ways to set themselves up above everyone else. Just about every administration I ever saw since I was a kid was guilty of that. It happened everywhere else, too. I was in grade school when this pint-sized character from the wrong side of the tracks—can't recall the sick bastard's name—made the news by starting up his own clan and sending his women to rob and murder innocent people. That happened in California, where they didn't believe in killing murderers or psychos, so this nut job spent the rest of his days in prison."

I knew what Walter was getting at. Fields practically said the same thing this morning, when we were going through the contents of the station wagon.

Besides, if what that kid had told me was true, the bastard had robbed a helpless old man, then pushed him down an abandoned well. Whatever he'd been before this no longer mattered.

"You're right. It doesn't matter what anyone used to be. What matters is what's happening now."

"People are either born good or bad. If they're good, they're gonna stay that way, no matter what.

Otherwise, they're gonna show their true colors at the first opportunity. I know this thing that killed off mostly everyone was bad—hell, it was horrible. But one thing it did do: it brought out everyone's true nature."

"A catastrophe usually does."

"I don't care if this Simon bastard was the damn pope. He's a bad seed, and that ain't gonna change. Look what he did with your lady. He went onto your place and took her. Not only is he a kidnapper, but he's also a damn killer. He's no different from that nut job in California. You send people out to do your killing for you, it makes you even guiltier than they are."

Killer. I'd been called that many times before. And I *was* a killer. I'd been trained to kill, and for three years, I killed for my country. But the killing hadn't stopped.

I had no idea who Simon was, where he was from, or if he had been trained to kill. All I knew was that he killed people he didn't want around, people he didn't need anymore. He killed people who could no longer satisfy or gratify him.

I killed only for survival. Even if Walter was right, wasn't the end result all that mattered? Was there any real difference between Simon and myself?

"So am I," I finally said.

"You're different, my friend." He sat forward in the chair. "Whaddya think would've happened if those punks knew I wasn't doped?"

185

Once again he was right. If they'd known Walter was rational, they would have considered him a threat and killed him.

"Don't compare yourself to lowlifes like them," Walter said. "You're good. You're decent. You put our mailbox back where it belonged. You knew it didn't belong there, lying on the walk like that, so you picked it up and put it back. No one asked you to do that—you just did it. And you treated an old man you never even saw before with respect—don't ever forget that. You didn't know if I had a brain cell in my head that was still working, but that didn't stop you from being a gentleman. You spoke kindly to me, the way gents talked to one another in the old days. Maybe you've killed people, but that don't make you a killer—not deep-down. You're a good man, and every once in a while you've got to do what's necessary to survive. Sometimes that means killing someone. You're not a killer, you're a survivor."

***

My eyes shot open.

That in itself was strange, because I couldn't remember closing them. My thoughts reeled for a few moments as I struggled to piece together what might have happened. Then I remembered.

After talking with Walter, I'd lay back down, closed my eyes and tried to shut everything off, but all I could think about was getting back on the bike and looking for that abandoned farm. I knew I had to look for a place to hide while they brought Fields over to the well. And I had to find some way of killing them all without endangering Fields.

I wanted to leave, but my exhausted body kept telling me to lie there. I needed rest. Fields needed me to be rested when I went to find her. She knew I'd be of no use to her—or to myself—if I let the rage take hold of me. I needed to have a clear head and a clear state of mind.

My fatigue finally won out. It felt so wonderful to just lie there, so I didn't move. The turmoil thrashing through me gradually vanished, and I surrendered to the exhaustion.

Sleep came quickly.

I sat bolt upright and gawked at the darkness engulfing me. The unfamiliar surroundings and smells drove me into an instant panic, but as my eyes adjusted, and I could distinguish the man sitting in the armchair facing me, my anxiety lessened. Consciousness drifted back, and with it, the last few hours. I sighed as the waves of panic within me ebbed back into nothingness.

"Walter?"

A snort. "Huh?" He shifted in the chair and pushed himself forward. He looked around the room, stared at me for a moment and yawned. "Guess I drifted off, too." I heard the flick of a match. The haze from the kerosene lamp slowly added a soft orange haze flowing up from the table. The flickering shadows behind Walter could have been eerie figures lurking in the darkness.

I pushed my legs over the edge of the sofa and rubbed my eyes. "What time is it?"

187

Walter grunted into a standing position, hobbled over to the drapes and peered outside. "It's still dark." Yawning, he hobbled back to the chair and sank back into the cushions. "You were only asleep a couple hours. Go back and catch a few more winks. I'll..."

"No." I needed to be out there, hunting. I wasn't sure if I'd heard a voice in my dream, if the voice belonged to Fields or if it was just my anxiety taking over. Whatever it was, I didn't want to leave anything to chance. Bad things happened when you left things to chance. Bad things had already happened; I didn't want them to worsen. "I've got to get out there. They could be bringing her out here to dump her somewhere right now."

"Like I said, son, it's still dark. They'll probably wait till it's light..."

"I can't take that chance." The more I thought about it, the more I could feel the panic struggling back. Even if I hadn't actually heard a voice in my dream, I knew I hadn't much time. Simon and his band of young thugs could already be on the road with Fields.

I picked up the Ruger and shoulder holster from the table and squeezed back into it. Then I slipped the .38 back in Fields' pancake holster and slid the .22 Bobcat down my pants pocket. A bottle of water sat on the table, about a foot from the kerosene lamp. It was nearly half full. I took a healthy sip, then spilled some onto my opened palm and used it to splash my face. It did the trick, and I was instantly awake.

"I've got to find that farm. Do you have any idea if there's a farm out here anywhere?"

"There are three or four of 'em—at least, there used to be. Dairy farms, mostly. All are abandoned and run-down, of course. I haven't seen or heard anyone out there—at least, not the few times I snuck out in the evenings, looking for a place to dump trash."

"This one would have a well."

"They all have wells, son."

His statement slammed the reality home. This was the country. Every residence out here had a well. The only thing different about this one was that the opening would have to be accessible. And since Simon had been using it to dump bodies, it would have to be deep.

How would I find it?

I suddenly realized I could be going about this the wrong way. I already knew where they lived— why was I wasting my time and energy trying to figure out how I could find their dump spot out here in the woods?

I wanted to slap myself for not considering this sooner.

I had to get back to their compound and work from there. But this time, I couldn't get caught. I'd already snuck into their place and killed one of them before getting away. Now that they knew I was too dangerous to approach, they wouldn't bother trying to bring me in alive.

I was seriously outnumbered. I'd seen at least a dozen of them but suspected there were even more living there. My saving grace was my military training, and that I'd been using it almost constantly the last six months. My reflexes were still good, my aim still excellent, and my gut just as reliable as ever.

Even so, I had to consider the fact that my only means of escape was a bike. In a truck, they could hunt me down in seconds. And if I tried following their truck to the well, they could lose me in even less time.

If only I could get to Uncle Joe's truck.

Even that option came with its own double-edged sword. The truck was big, noisy, and difficult to maneuver on these bumpy, winding roads. Unlike the bike, they'd spot it in a heartbeat and start shooting. I wouldn't be able to shoot back for fear of Fields getting caught in the crossfire. Even if they didn't shoot me, they'd surely damage the truck. I'd be on foot, out in the middle of nowhere, and the gang could easily hunt me down...

"Moss?"

"Yeah?"

"You're not gonna lie back down, are ya?"

"Too much on my mind."

"I figured as much. So, as long as you ain't going back to sleep, tell me your plans."

"You know my plans."

"You want her back, but you can't get at her, and you're wondering how you can do it."

"That's about it."

He sat back in his chair. In the dim haze of the lamp I could see him staring at the ceiling.

"Talk to me, Walter."

"I'm thinking of Madge."

"What about her?"

"I'm thinking of what *I'd* do to get her back."

"What *would* you do?"

He shrugged. "Just about anything."

"Yes, but what does this tell me..."

"It might not tell you what you really need to know—not in black and white ... but it should tell you what's at stake. You know, it really doesn't matter what you need to do to get her back, just so long as you do get her back. If it was me, I'd damn well do whatever it took, and if I had to kill every damn one of those bastards to get her, I'd make damn sure I had my guns loaded and ready."

"But I can't risk shooting them all without putting her in danger."

"Sounds to me like you're being a tad cautious about all this."

"I have to be cautious. Otherwise..."

"Tell me about her, son."

"Walter, I don't have time to sit here and..."

"From what you already told me, this lady of yours sounds pretty fine."

"She's the best woman any man could hope to have."

"She'd have to be, wouldn't she?"

"How's that?"

"For you to wanna risk everything."

For me, Fields *was* everything. She was all I cared about. And this was why I wanted to be so careful. I couldn't bear it if she was hurt because of something I'd done. "She's everything to me, Walter. She saved my life. She's had my back ever since we hooked up. I'd be dead if I wasn't for her."

"Then I'd say you're underestimating her, son."

"How's that?"

"If she's all you say, then she's smart enough to know you and how you work. She'll know you're coming to get her, and she'll probably know how you'll go about doing it. Most of all, she's probably smart enough to know to duck at the right time— wouldn't you say?"

I hadn't thought about it that way, but as soon as he'd said it, I realized he was absolutely right. Fields had survived an attack by three roving TABs. She'd got the drop on me ... and overtook a female TAB ... and helped us get out of that underground facility.

And she'd saved my life this morning.

"You're right, Walter. I *have* been underestimating her. She's tough, and can be a real badass when the chips are down."

"She'd have to be. She's just like you, ain't she?"

"We're a team. It doesn't get any better than that." I got up from the sofa. "I have to get back to Simon's place before they take her anywhere. I'm going there, and I'm taking out as many as I can, and if I know Fields as well as I think I do, she'll be right there, taking out a few of them on her own."

Walter grunted out of the armchair. "I guess you know what you're doing, then."

192

"Walter, I've got to make this short." I held out my hand. "It's been nice, and I'm really glad we met."

"You're going back there on that bike?"

"It's the fastest way I know."

Walter scratched the back of his neck and grinned. "I think I might have something that'll get you there a little faster."

Before I could reply, he'd already picked up the kerosene lamp, turned and led the way through the cluttered kitchen.

CHAPTER FOURTEEN

A stack of large boxes piled six feet high stood against the wall at the other end of the long, cluttered room. Walter easily pushed them a couple of feet to the right. A door appeared where the pile had once been. He eased it open and extended his arm. The light from the kerosene lamp spread straight ahead, casting eerie shadows into the garage.

A sleek, metallic-blue classic Chevy sat in the single stall, gleaming in the hazy light. Judging by its impeccable paint job and glittering glass, it had obviously been cared for over the years.

"Wow ..." I couldn't take my eyes off it.

Walter chuckled at my reaction. "It's a '68 Chevy Nova SS, with a 396 engine," he said proudly. "A beauty, ain't it?"

"It looks almost ... new."

"It belonged to my son. George bought it years ago. He'd flunked out of college and enlisted in the Marines. He saw it when he was stationed at Parris Island. He saved up all his money, borrowed some from Madge and me, and bought it. After Boot Camp, he had a week's furlough before they were gonna send him to California. He drove it here. He told us ... he'd be back to claim it when he came home."

Walter had used the word "belonged." "He ... never came back?"

Walter didn't reply.

"I can't possibly take this, Walter." The thought of taking it away from its home made me feel evil. This was the man's prized possession. His son's pride and joy.

"George would want you to. This baby really flies. Three hundred and seventy-five horses. Handles fairly easy, too. You'll need it if you wanna get where you need to be before it turns light."

I wanted to speak, but the words caught in my throat. A man I'd only known a few hours was offering me a classic car his son had left him, and I had no way of thanking him or paying him back. I couldn't even promise him I could take proper care of the car.

"I feel really funny about this."

"I'm offering it to you."

The sincerity in his eyes touched me deeply. I still couldn't accept the fact that I'd met someone like him in this cold, frightening world of death. He was like an older version of Reed.

"I really can't, Walter. Your son ... it was his. I'd feel like..."

"Just get in, fire her up, and go find your lady. Then bring it back if ya can."

"When was the last time it was driven?"

"I've been keeping it going for the last several years. George asked me to make sure it was ready to go when he came back to get it. It was no problem for me, since I'd always loved old cars, and it quickly became a hobby, then an obsession. It was ... the only way I had of keeping close to my son while he was away. I've kept her here in the garage, and every week or so I'd take her out, drive her a mile or so down the road, turn around and bring her back. Last year, before all this happened, I took her out on Route 8 once a week and on I-79 once or twice a month, to open her up. Then folks started dropping, and the others turned crazy, so taking her out turned out to be too dangerous. Then I lost Madge and, well..." He sighed.

"I don't know about this, Walter."

"She's going to waste, son. She needs to be driven."

I didn't think he understood what was likely to happen. "Walter, I'm going after a bunch of armed crazies. I might get shot, and even if I don't, I can't guarantee..."

"There's a lot of 'em out there. I'd feel much better if this helped you even the odds a little."

"This can't possibly turn out well."

"Son, I couldn't live with myself if I didn't do something to help you. You were a military man, too. George would have liked you. You're a lot like him, ya know. Sincere, honest, and not afraid to stand up for what ya believe in. Now get going. You don't have much time. Take the car, get your lady away from them and bring her back in it. I'd like to meet her."

"But I can't..."

He held out the keys.

"Walter, this is..."

"Like I said, you don't have much time."

In spite of the cold fear weighing me down, I watched my hand reach out, and stood there in

196

awkward silence as Walter dropped the keys in my palm. I wanted to shake his hand, thank him and tell him I'd try my best to be careful with the car, but he'd already shuffled down the narrow aisle to the door, bent over and pulled it open. The darkness of the evening rushed right in, bringing with it the coolness of the night and mixed scents of mildew and distant lingering death. Without a word, Walter moved over to the side of the garage and waited.

My legs weighed a ton, but I managed to approach the car. I yanked open the heavy passenger door, got in, pulled it shut, slid over and situated myself behind the wheel. The inside smelled a little musty. The pine tree freshener hanging from the radio knob had stopped radiating its scent long ago. I adjusted the bench seat and strapped myself in. Then, with shaky fingers, I slipped the key into the ignition and started it up. It roared to life, like a lion being disturbed from a long nap, and I could feel the walls of the garage vibrate.

My body trembled as I put it into reverse and backed out slowly, testing the brakes as I did so. They were a little sticky, but they worked. As I eased past Walter, I could see the smile on his face, and also the tears in his eyes glistening in the dark.

"I'll be here when you get back, son."

My heart filled my mouth when I said, "I'll be as quick as I can."

"Does your lady drink?"

I smiled, remembering the times we'd sat on the front porch at night with a glass of bourbon, watching the stars. "She likes to keep up with me."

"I'll have the glasses ready, then."

Snapping back to the present, I backed down the short drive that ended on the other side of the picket fence, among the weeds in the vacant lot next door. Walter had already gone back inside and, closing the garage door, let the house be swallowed up by the darkness of the night. Using only my parking lights, I slipped it into low gear, got onto the main road and cruised down the straightaway.

I'd gone only two or three miles when I saw the flickering headlights in the rearview mirror. They drew closer, and suddenly they turned into high beams, nearly blinding me. I pushed the front of the mirror toward the floor to kill the glare and mashed my foot down on the gas. The Nova roared, nearly leaping in the air, and the speedometer registered ninety in just seconds.

I flicked on my low beams just in time to see more lights dancing around the next bend. There were four of them, and they were standing about two feet from one another, forming a flimsy roadblock. The two young men in the center shined their flashlights directly in my eyes while the two on either end crouched down on one knee, aiming their rifles at the car.

***

My heart raced as the cold reality sliced through me. They'd obviously been hunting for me all the time I was with Walter. They'd been watching the roads and were waiting, and in this night of absolute silence and stillness, any sound would draw them out.

198

In such a heavily-wooded area, the task of watching the roads was simple, but would require a number of people. There were four of them facing me and a vehicle following me. If there were two of them in the vehicle, that meant six of them were about to capture me.

Even with those odds, I wasn't about to give up.

I pushed down the visor to soften the glare of their flashlights and rammed my foot down on the gas. The only way to break up the roadblock was to plow through it. The speedometer needle scooted over to 100 mph as the Nova hurled its sleek body with full force into the foursome. The boys at each end pulled in their rifles and scattered. The two in the middle weren't able to get out of the way. A high-pitched scream stopped abruptly as the right front panel of the Nova slammed one of them squarely in the chest, tossing him like a rag doll. The force of impact sent him flying over the car.

At that same moment, the Nova caught the second boy just as he'd twisted to his right. Another blood-chilling scream penetrated the night air as the car crushed his legs at the knees. The force of impact rolled his broken body off the road and into the brush.

I glanced in the rearview as a shadow dropped onto the road nearly a hundred feet behind me. It was probably the limp form of the first boy. The vehicle following me—the truck that had taken me to Simon's compound several hours earlier—swerved to miss the obstacle.

My sense of triumph didn't last long. Apparently one of the riflemen had recovered quickly enough to reposition himself in the brush and sight me in. A shot rang out, and a bullet whizzed angrily past my open window. I heard another shot, and the mirror on the passenger side disintegrated. Splinters of glass and metal penetrated the darkness; a jagged piece of metal and more glass chunks skittered across the windshield. I thought of Walter, hoping I'd survive long enough to apologize to him for damaging his son's car.

I mashed my foot down to the floor; the needle jerked to 120. I figured I was already out of range of their rifles. All I had to worry about now was losing the truck. The next bend loomed about a hundred yards straight ahead. To negotiate it safely, I'd have to slam on the brakes or risk skidding into the woods and wrapping the classic ride around a tree. The truck could move fast but wouldn't be able to handle the turns as well as the Nova. And after I'd rounded the bend, I could accelerate and lose them on the next straightaway.

But just as I pulled my foot off the gas, several more shots rang out in the night. A loud *thud*! followed by a *ping*! hit the rear of the car. Something slapped the back of the bench seat. My heart skipped a couple of beats when I realized one of the bullets had punched its way into the car body and exited through the trunk and then the back seat, hitting my seat and, catching a spring, stopping short of my flesh by inches.

A burst of warm relief swept through me. The truck remained a safe distance behind me, and I easily made the curve. With luck, the Nova would enable me to gain distance once I'd negotiated the turn.

I rounded the bend, glanced at the dash and instantly felt my blood turn to ice. The rapidly sinking gas gauge told me the absolute worst. A slug had punctured the tank.

All was lost; I was sunk. I was fortunate the shot hadn't sparked the gas, but the fact that it had hit the tank ended any attempt to outrun them. I kept my foot stuck to the floor, hoping to squeeze out one last burst of speed that would afford me enough distance to bail, but just as I reached the straightaway, the car died. I veered off into the brush and let it coast, until it stopped in a cluster of high weeds.

I didn't have time to feel sorry for myself. Just as I pushed open the door, the bright headlights behind me grew, shining directly on me. I heard the screeching of brakes and realized at once that the truck had stopped in the middle of the road less than a hundred yards away. Then I heard the creaking of doors opening.

Even without turning around, I could tell they were getting me in their sights. Instinct told me to stay in the car. Getting out would be bad. It meant exposing myself. But I couldn't just sit here and let them kill me.

Just as I ducked back inside, a rain of bullets pounded the inside panel of the door. The rear window shattered, and glass sprayed the seats.

Keeping low, I crawled across the bench seat, pushed open the passenger door, and leaped into the thick underbrush as another burst of gunfire slammed into the door.

**

Although the thick foliage of the woods provided sufficient cover, heavy gunfire sprayed the bushes just beyond the passenger door of the Nova and the trees directly above me. I crawled awkwardly through the wooded terrain, remembering my old riot control days, when I'd dodged heavy gunfire almost daily. Those were dark, dismal days, but this was much worse. I now faced death by a bunch of kids who should be getting ready for school, who should be living with their parents—not some cold-blooded psycho.

"C'mon out, motherfucker!" The high-pitched voice snapped me out of it.

"Spread out—he can't get away!"

"We got 'im now!"

"Fucker's worm-food!"

Four different voices. At least four of them had been in the pickup. The riflemen back at the roadblock were probably already on their way, and would be hunting me along with the others in no time. That made it six against one. I had years of experience over them, but their sheer number—plus the fact that they were about to surround me—gave them the advantage. I had to somehow get them to circle me. If I could find a good spot to draw them out, they ran the risk of shooting one another. Right now, my only prayer was to find a safe place to set up. I had to get my guns out and ready.

Just as I began to crawl, I glanced upward and cringed. The first signs of daylight peeked through the branches of the pines like shards of smudged glass. My luck had finally turned on me. Morning would be here much too soon. I had no choice but keep as close to the ground as possible, using the thick brush as camouflage to gain distance.

Two shots ricocheted deafeningly among the trees. One round slammed into a pine tree fifty feet ahead of me, the other into a bush about ten yards to my left. Once the silence returned, I heard nothing. This told me they were listening, hoping I'd make some noise.

I didn't move.

More silence, then: "Hey, asshole! We know you're in there!"

Their ages didn't matter. They all had guns and knew how to use them. Right now they were firing blindly. I had to assume at least one of them would hit me if they had any idea where I was. I could tell by the sounds the slugs made slamming into the trees that most of them were heavy calibers. The round hitting the pine tree had sounded like a .45, or .357. Either caliber would kill or severely wound me, no matter where it hit me.

"C'mon out!" This boy's somewhat mature voice sounded like he could be in his early twenties. "You gotta pay for Jackie and Sam!"

"What about Niles and Booger? Ran 'em right over, like road kill!"

"You're surrounded, asswipe!"

A chuckle.

"I get dibs on his guns," one of them said, and a shot slapped a pine tree twenty feet on my left.

"I get dibs, too."

"Dream on, dorks," replied one of the others. "Simon wants 'em for his collection, said we can have one of the bitches. Irene, maybe."

"She's a doper. Nobody wants her. Smells, too."

"I want the one Simon's takin' to the well. Skinny brunette. Nice ..."

"Like I said, dream on, dickweed. Bitch won't be around no more."

While they were talking, I crawled over to the giant pine tree and sat with my back against the thick trunk. I pulled the Ruger from my shoulder holster, placed it on my thigh and took out the .38. I left the Bobcat in my pants pocket. I wouldn't need it right now. There were ten rounds in the Ruger, six in the .38, and eight in the Bobcat. If I could get at least two of the boys in my sights, it would demoralize the others and enable me to gain some distance while they figured out their next move.

"C'mon out, asshole! We're wastin' time!"

"Fucker can't get away ..."

I peered around the tree. I only saw two of them, but they were spaced much too widely apart for me to get clear shots. They'd already crossed the road and entered the woods. One boy veered off to the left and disappeared behind some brush while the other came in my direction. He moved slowly, careful of his footing as he stepped over deadfalls and fallen branches. He wore loose jeans and a baggy sweat shirt, and his light-brown hair hung over his shoulders beneath the black baseball cap he wore low on his forehead. He was fairly tall and slender, and not much older than eighteen. But the huge automatic pistol he gripped in his right hand, possibly a Desert Eagle, made his tender age irrelevant.

The odds were painfully obvious. Since I couldn't see the others, shooting just one of them would alert the others of my position. But I didn't have much of a choice. He was less than thirty feet away, coming straight toward me. He'd be walking past my tree any time now. I was just going to have to get it over with. I couldn't very well shoot him and keep myself in plain sight while I sighted in the others. I'd have to disappear as quickly as possible, which meant ducking into the brush and crawling away as soon as I shot the boy.

Using my knee for balance, I kept the slab barrel of the Ruger pressed against the side of the tree to help steady my shot. The boy stopped for a moment and turned to his right. He'd obviously heard something and was tilting his head, listening. About ten seconds later he resumed his quiet journey toward me. I was tempted to glance to my left to see what had caught his attention but knew that would make me miss my chance. I pressed the trigger and got him in the forehead, directly beneath the brim of his cap. He gasped and fell backward, his pistol leaping from his hand.

Five seconds of silence, then:

"*Motherfucker*!"

"Asshole just shot *Anderson*!"

"Andy? *Andy*! *Fuck*, he got *Andy*, dammit ..."

An explosion of gunfire punched into the pine tree, the brush, and the area around me. I flattened myself into the heavy growth and began crawling away. I didn't get ten feet before something hot slammed into my right arm. I collapsed in a pile of dead leaves. Still gripping the Ruger and the .38, I lay there, breathing heavily, my arm quickly turning numb, my heart pounding like an amplified tomtom. I carefully holstered the .38, brought my hand over and gingerly felt my right bicep. I knew what had happened before I even felt the blood and the warm, swollen flesh of my arm. You never forget what happens when you're shot. One of them had hit me, and the slug had gone deep into the bicep muscle.

The gunfire stopped.

"*Got* 'im!" yelled a high-pitched voice several yards to my right. "*Got* the fucker! *Whoopee*!"

"Get 'im, Marlon?"

"Got 'im! Got the fucker!"

"Lucky shot! Lucky shot!"

I began breathing again and waited for more gunshots, but all I heard was the crunching of dead leaves and branches somewhere off to my right, growing louder quickly. I wanted to shoot but didn't have the strength to raise my arm. I couldn't switch

206

hands without making noise in the brush and giving away my position. I also couldn't move as quickly as I'd have to, so I lay perfectly still. Besides, I suspected he was still aiming his gun at me.

The crunching abruptly stopped. Deafening silence followed. I could feel the boy standing over me, staring at his prize. He was probably wondering what to do. Should he finish me off? Wait for his friends to join him? What were their instructions? Take me alive? Dead? Judging by his voice, he sounded very young. I wondered if I was his first victim. In normal conditions, that would seem likely. But these conditions were hardly normal. I wouldn't have been surprised at all to find this boy had killed before.

But none of this mattered. The only thing I cared about was that they had Fields. And right now they were probably taking her to an abandoned well ...

The rage, the determination, and the will to live came thundering back. Simon had taken Fields from me, and I was going to get her back. I couldn't do it right now because this little bastard had just shot me and was about to finish me off...

No. He *wouldn't* finish me off. I wouldn't let him. I had the Ruger in my hand, and both the gun and my hand were concealed beneath the brush. And I still had the Bobcat and the .38. Granted, I'd just shoved the Bobcat into my pants pocket, and the .38 sat snugly in its pancake holster under my jacket ... but they were still there. I'd have to distract the boy somehow if I wanted to get at either of them, and since I'd just been shot, my movements would be as quick or as precise as they needed to be.

But I had to do it. And I would. I'd done it before. As long as I was still alive and had breath left in me, I was going to survive this and find Fields.

Just then, I heard the voice. I could tell the boy was standing just a few feet to my right. It was the same voice I'd heard a minute ago, right after the bullet had penetrated my arm. It was the voice of a child.

"I gotcha, motherfucker. Gotcha good."

I slowly raised my head.

A boy in his early teens stood less than five feet away, holding a small black long-barreled revolver in his right hand. The tiny black hole aimed at my face told me it was a .22. Small calibers weren't nearly as devastating as larger, heavier guns, but could do more damage due to the pinball effect of the tiny round. But it didn't matter. When a gun was pointed at your face, you realized at once that its caliber was the least of your problems.

The boy's large blue eyes were wide-open and glazed. Drool had gathered on his lower lip as he kept the barrel of his gun pointed dead-steady at my face.

CHAPTER FIFTEEN

As I stared at the gun pointing at my face, I thought not of my own mortality, but of Fields. Because of me, the woman I loved was going to die.

I'd also failed Walter. He'd given me his dead son's beautiful classic car, and I hadn't gone three miles with it before letting this pack of armed killers tear it apart with gunfire.

As I lay bleeding in the brush, I trembled with rage. It was all I could do to keep from raising my wounded arm and emptying the mag into the little idiot who'd just shot me.

This nightmare was difficult to accept. It was bad enough the terrorists and the superpowers of the world had destroyed society. But even though the worst of it seemed to be over, the survivors weren't able to pick up the pieces and do what they could to start afresh. The nightmare continued, moving into an even darker and more frightening phase, one that paralleled the bleakness of Hell itself. What was left were zombie-like souls shuffling around aimlessly while others ran around like a pack of wild dogs, killing and taking what they wanted.

"Got 'im, dudes!" This boy was around five-six and probably tipped the scales at slightly over a hundred pounds. He stood there in his baggy black jeans, turquoise baseball cap, blue tee shirt and scuffed tennies. His gun belt was much too big for him; the rawhide strips dangling from the bottom of the holster nearly touched the ground. In the old world, a boy his age would be permanently fixed to a couch, sitting through endless video games, or texting illiterate nonsense to other members of his species.

"How old are you?" I could barely get the words out.

"What's it to ya?" The kid's large, glazed blue eyes stayed on me. "Old enough to drop ya." The gun in his hand didn't waver. On such a small, slender hand, the effect was terrifying.

"Yeah. You dropped me, all right."

"We're comin', Marlon!" shouted one of his friends as the three drew nearer. "Hang tight!"

"No problem, dudes! Take your time! He moves, he's *so* dead!" He tilted his head. "Hear me, pops? You move, you're *so* dead."

"I heard you." Despite the circumstances, I found my growing anger difficult to contain. "And I'm definitely not your daddy."

"Lotta blood there." The kid seemed fascinated.

"That usually happens with a bullet wound, brainiac."

"Bet it hurts like a mother, too." He kept staring. I couldn't tell if that was amazement or pride showing in his eyes. Neither quality made me feel any better.

"Keep 'im covered, Marlon! Simon wants 'im in one piece when we take 'im down to the basement."

The "basement." It sounded like something out of a horror flick.

"Andy was my bud." The glazed eyes, mixed with the grin, disturbed me even more than the gun in his hand. "You fragged 'im, you bastard. Wasn't for Simon, I'd frag *your* ass. Right here, right now."

Frag. I hadn't heard that term in over twenty years. I never expected to hear a kid use it.

"Frag?"

"Yeah." A shrug. "Never heard that one before? Gotta frag the enemy. Those are the rules."

"I heard it once or twice before, thanks."

Frag. Enemy. Rules. When it finally dawned on me, I realized just how bleak this situation really was. An opportunistic survivor named Simon had taken in these kids and made them useful to him by turning them into soldiers, thieves and killers. They'd been living a fantasy existence ever since. It wasn't their fault. The big shots running the world had made life and death an epic video game. Reality hadn't died, it had been replaced. Only this giant deathmatch remained.

"So what happens now?"

The boy shrugged. "We take your ass back to the house and hand you over to Simon."

"Who's Simon?"

The glazed eyes beamed. "Simon's the Dude. The Man. Enough bullshit. Toss that piece over here."

"Piece?"

"Don't be a retard. Fucker's right there, in your hand. Hand it over *easy*."

211

"Everything okay, Marlon?" shouted one of the others, and I could tell by the crunching of leaves that they'd come closer.

"Fuckin' A, Jake!" Marlon's glazed eyes remained steady. "C'mon, dude." The gun in his hand hadn't wavered. "Toss it. Don't have all day."

I had no choice. I had to do something before the others got here. I figured I had less than a minute to do it.

"I can't ... raise my arm ..."

"I'm gonna fuckin' cap your ass." The boy's cold eyes remained fixed on me. I could see the quiet rage in them and was confident he'd shoot me without batting an eye.

I realized in that one frightening moment that the figure standing before me was a stone-cold sociopath trapped in the body of a teenage boy. A killing machine in the body of a child who believed life was nothing more than a game. The young Muslims I'd faced in my military days all had that same icy darkness in their eyes. But unlike them, this boy was not killing in the name of religion, but because reality had become very simple, and life had been reduced to killing those who didn't suit your purpose.

"Simon wants you brought in alive. See, he wants to do some cool shit to ya before he wastes your ass. But you pissed me off when you fragged Andy, so I really wanna frag you right here. Simon'll understand. He frags dudes all the time. But I'll give ya one last chance. You toss that piece by the time I count to five and I won't put another fuckin' hole in ya."

"Give me a second to..."

"One ..." The barrel moved slightly to his left and pointed to my right thigh. If I didn't soon move, I wouldn't be able to do much of anything anymore.

I couldn't let it end like this. I wouldn't let them kill Fields—not as long as I was still alive.

"Two ..."

My wounded arm felt as if it had been dipped in hot wax, but I managed to raise the elbow a couple of inches from the ground. I gritted my teeth while raising my arm, which felt even heavier because the Ruger suddenly weighed a ton. As I raised it, I snatched up a large clump of dirt and dead leaves in my left hand. I kept raising the Ruger while focusing on thinking through the red-hot waves surging through my wounded arm. *Fight it. You've been through this before. You know you can do again.*

"Three ..."

The boy was watching my right hand. All I had to do was raise the gun a few more inches and toss it toward him. While he bent to reach for it, I'd toss the dirt and leaves at his face. If I could pull the Bobcat from my pocket quickly enough, I might be able to put a round or two in his chest before he got the dirt and leaves out of his eyes.

"Four ..."

As I raised the gun the last few inches, I kept my left arm close to my side and out of sight. I grabbed as much dirt and leaves as my grip would allow, squeezed it into a ball and...

"Five..."

The deafening explosion came from a considerable distance behind the boy. The slug slammed into his back, forcing out a fistful of blood, bone fragments and tissue through the center of his skinny chest. The boy's gun flew to the ground; his legs collapsed under him, and he was propelled three feet forward. He landed face-down in the dirt just a few feet from me, and did not move.

Ten seconds of silence.

"M-Marlon?" came a voice about fifty feet to my right.

More silence.

"*Marlon*?"

"What the fuck *happened*, Jake?"

"Marlon! What happened? Still there? Still got 'im?"

"What'd he do, Marlon? What'd that fucker do?"

"That sure was one helluva fuckin' blast!"

Silence.

"Fucker fr-fragged *Marlon*, Jake ..."

"No way! Impossible! Marlon said he *got* the bastard. Had 'im cold."

"Why ain't he sayin' nothing, then?"

"Why ain'tcha sayin' nothin', Marlon?"

More silence.

"Jake? Didn't Marlon say he had 'im?"

"Marlon?"

214

"Motherfuckin' *asshole*! You're fuckin' *dead*!"

A gunshot thumped into the tree next to me ... then another, into the bushes.

Ignoring the searing pain in my pulsating arm, I pushed myself up, retrieved the Ruger and scrambled deeper into the brush just as more gunfire slapped the foliage and trees around me.

***

I didn't have time to analyze what just happened. As I reached the next rise and slid carefully down the steep, heavily wooded decline, I had more important things to worry about. The pain from my wound had increased. I gritted my teeth as I slid down the bumpy slope, keeping my bad arm cradled against my body while covering the bloody wound with my free hand. My entire arm throbbed steadily. I had to dress the wound and stop the bleeding as soon as possible. It would have helped immensely if it had been a clean shot, but I wasn't optimistic. Most small calibers tended to splinter, and it often took a painfully thorough examination to locate all the pieces. But I couldn't worry about that now.

A large pyramid of dead trees lay in a huge cluster at the bottom of the hill, a hundred feet or so in front of a narrow, winding creek. I reached the bottom without further injury. Keeping low, I dragged myself through the tall brush. It was slow going. I was careful to keep most of my weight on my left side, forcing my left arm to do most of the work. I used my wounded arm primarily for balance and to hold the Ruger.

As I crawled toward the wooden fortress, ignoring the sudden stabs of pain from protruding branches and sticks, I began wondering once again what had happened.

I was fairly certain one of the riflemen from the roadblock had come back to finish me off. He was no doubt angry that I'd not only escaped, but had also killed two of his buddies and nearly him as well. He could have lost his patience when he'd seen me, and took a quick shot, hitting Marlon instead.

Further thought suggested that unlikely. For one thing, both riflemen were skilled shooters. One or both of them had managed to hit the side mirror, gas tank, and back seat of a car moving away from them at a hundred miles an hour, in the peak of darkness.

Something else told me why this couldn't have happened. A skilled shooter wouldn't risk taking such a wild shot. Our location had been too dense and uneven, and nearly invisible from the road. The terrain—as well as the overgrown brush—concealed me almost completely. No one standing more than ten feet behind Marlon could have seen me. Even if they'd been able to, they would have seen that Marlon had the drop on me and would consider such a risky shot unnecessary.

It didn't make sense that the same capable shooters who'd disabled Walter's Nova had mistakenly hit Marlon squarely in the back while I lay on the ground just a few feet from him.

This reasoning brought me to one and only conclusion: The shooter had Marlon in his sights.

With all families, there would be rivalry, peer pressure and, given their young ages, temper tantrums. Favoritism would enter into the equation, as well as the constant need for approval by Simon, their patriarch. The overwhelming obsession to become leader of the pack could be a common priority with these punks.

Was that the reason? Had Marlon made a lethal enemy amongst this dysfunctional brood of killers?

Or was this merely an accident? A simple case of a misfire?

Several more shots whizzed above my head as I crawled toward the massive stack of fallen limbs and tangled branches. A slug slapped the pile a couple of feet on my right. Another spray of gunfire came at me from my left. A moment later, when two large-caliber slugs slammed into the enormous dead pine lying at a 60-degree angle on my right, I knew then that they'd surrounded me.

My fortress sprawled just fifteen feet straight ahead. By this time, my left arm was aching from the massive effort of supporting and dragging nearly two hundred pounds over rugged terrain, but I forced myself to keep going, staying low in the weeds.

I finally reached the massive pile. I scrambled over a thick log and dropped behind it just as three successive slugs thumped into its side. I crawled along the length of it, where it supported a cluster of knotted limbs at the end. I soon saw some bushes moving around near the top of the hill, about eighty yards away. Gingerly raising my wounded arm, I aimed the Ruger at the center of the brush and got off three quick shots.

Immediate silence followed.

Just as I lowered my arm, a shot came from the right, ricocheting off a log a few yards in front of me. Staying behind the jagged wall of gnarled branches, I peered through a narrow opening on my right and saw some bushes twitching unnaturally a few feet from a group of pines. I grabbed Fields' .38. Using my left hand and bracing my elbow on my left thigh, I popped off three rounds. "That's for you, Brooke," I whispered. A scream echoed down the hill. Someone yelled, "*Motherfucker!*" Instinct told me to get down. Seconds later, a torrent of gunfire slammed into my barricade from three different directions.

I balanced my weight on a small pile of torn branches, between two logs and beneath a large, broken limb, and listened. Silence. Taking advantage of the break, I tried examining my wound, but my sanctuary was too dark and I had to work by feel. I could tell the blood had already started clotting. If I was careful, and didn't do anything to re-injure it, I could wrap it. I needed a little time to take off my jacket and shred my shirt. I cursed myself once again for ditching my backpack. The first-aid kit sure would come in handy right now. The alcohol could at least sterilize the wound. Even if I couldn't get to the kit, I could douse the wound with the whiskey from the flask in the pack. The last thing I needed right now was an infection.

Six more shots punched into my barricade. Silence followed for about a minute, and then three more shots ripped into the logs, vibrating the limbs and sending chunks of bark and dirt flying.

"C'mon out, asshole! You're surrounded!" The voice drifting down the hill sounded like the same boy who'd been communicating with Marlon earlier.

A few seconds later, another voice, this one on my right, yelled: "You don't have a chance, dickhead!"

Then, on my left: "Come out now! Maybe we'll letcha have a crack at that skinny bitch before Simon dumps 'er!"

That perked me right up, but I knew they were baiting me. Kids seemed to know about such tactics at a very early age. I'd known quite a few sociopathic children during my school days. They always seemed to be on the defensive and were always looking for ways to hurt or shock others. When such a kid was allowed to turn into a predatory killer, human decency vanished and was replaced by cunning and a natural skill in manipulating his victims. Killer instinct came with the territory, serving as a powerful force.

My survival instinct came from practical experience. I'd been in similar tense situations, probably more than this wild pack would ever see. Even if they were keeping Fields somewhere close, they'd never let me get near her.

219

A couple of minutes later, the sound of a truck echoed through the trees. The screeching of brakes tore through the wooded area, and I knew right then that the number of my hunters had increased. Doors slammed shut; distant voices penetrated the air.

About a minute later, a high-pitched voice swept down from the top of the wooded knoll. "Hey, dirtbag! We're gonna take you down!"

Laughter followed, and the woods exploded in gunfire.

I dove down deep into my cocoon of felled logs and felt the vibrations as slug after slug pounded into the deteriorating wood. I didn't know how many more of them had come, but it sounded like there were at least a dozen or more perched at the top of the hill, shooting at me. I could also tell by the increased volume of the blasts that they were moving down the hill as they fired into my shelter.

I realized then that I couldn't save Fields. Even if I knew where she was, I couldn't possibly get to her in time. I couldn't do anything right now—not with this pack shooting at me.

But I had to do *something*. I couldn't let them pin me down like this, and I sure as hell couldn't let them dump Fields down a well while I hid in a stack of fallen trees, cradling my wounded arm.

Crawl through to the other side.

Once again, that same strange voice disrupted my thoughts.

I couldn't tell if it was my own mind or my imagination inventing some unrealistic escape plan. Or maybe it was indeed that strange voice I'd been

220

hearing erratically for the last several hours. Whatever it was, I felt I should listen to it. I figured I had no choice, and no other options. In fifteen minutes, they'd have reached the bottom of the hill, would have me surrounded, and would fire endlessly into the stack of timber until there was nothing left.

I crawled through a heavy mass of fallen branches and limbs. As soon as I began making headway, the gunfire started up again. I lowered myself closer to the ground and waited for the heavy assault to stop. It went on for what seemed forever, but I knew they'd eventually have to take time to reload.

After maybe a minute or so, the bursts trickled off, and a heavy silence followed.

I took advantage of the lull and resumed crawling through the narrow, twisted trail, squeezing between limbs and forcing my exhausted body through intertwined branches, vines and weeds. I trudged on, careful to shield my bad arm while consciously gripping the Ruger. After slithering through the endless trail, bright shards of daylight glittered at the other end.

I cautiously stuck my head out among the dangling vines and peered to my left, then my right. I saw no one, nor did I hear the crunching of leaves, the snapping of twigs or the clicking of a gun hammer. A sudden gunshot thumped into my fortress several yards behind me, but I heard nothing else. The creek awaited me straight ahead. Just beyond it, the heavy growth of pines and scrubs would provide concealment to enable me to get away. I might even have time to circle around and steal one of their vehicles.

I listened for a minute or so, waiting for the gunfire to resume. More shots rang out, one of them buzzing wildly into the brush. I still didn't see movement in the woods or brush on the other side. They probably hadn't had time to circle me yet, and were still easing down the hill and getting into position. I knew better than to waste any more time.

Keeping my bad arm free of the heavy vines and brush, I crawled out of my barricade. Just as I pushed myself up, I caught movement out of the corner of my eye. I turned and froze.

A slender figure dressed in camouflage pants, black tee shirt, and a pale green baseball cap emerged from one of the bushes about twenty feet away. He held what looked like an M16 rifle in his hands and had it aimed directly at me.

"Smile, dipstick!" he said, and pulled the trigger.

CHAPTER SIXTEEN

Two simultaneous explosions echoed up and down the hilly terrain. The kid's rifle blast flew wild, narrowly missing my head the moment I dropped to the ground.

A large hole appeared in the boy's chest as blood and tissue spewed out of him, splattering the ground. The boy arched his back. His head jerked back violently, as if someone had slammed his spine with a sledgehammer. His arms flew out to his sides and his rifle leaped from his grasp, landing in the bush ten feet in front of him. He fell face-forward onto the hard ground and did not move.

Once again I was perplexed and unable to analyze what had just happened. A fresh volley of gunfire had exploded from the other side of the hill, spitting into the timber and the wild brush around me. I sunk down even further into the shoulder-high weeds and began dragging my tired body awkwardly toward the creek.

Veer to the right, the inner voice inside me said, and once again I chose to obey it.

Duck!

I immediately hit the dirt. A bullet whizzed by me, slapping into one of the pine trees just beyond the creek. I lay motionless in the weeds, my heart pounding.

The sudden silence told me they were probably reloading again. That usually took them thirty seconds. I had to take the gamble.

Using my good arm, I pushed myself back up. Keeping low, I began duck-walking again, but as soon as I crossed the creek, I heard rustling in the bushes directly ahead. My pulse sputtering, I dove face-down into the dirt, rolled into the bushes and came back up on one knee, the Ruger braced in both hands, its barrel aimed straight ahead.

Don't shoot! the inner voice yelled.

I wanted to squeeze the trigger but found that I couldn't. My hand had gone numb. After tense moments, feeling returned, and my finger eased off the trigger and backed away from the guard.

Strange. One of them was hiding in the brush, twenty feet away. He was probably the second rifleman. If I was right, he was going to finish me off, and I should do him before he did me. So why would the inner voice tell me not to shoot? Why shouldn't I shoot someone who was obviously trying to kill me?

The more I agonized over this, the less sense it made. First Marlon, then the other kid. What was happening out here? Who shot Marlon? Who shot the boy with the rifle? Was the same person responsible for nailing both of them?

The brush rustled again. My back grew warm; every muscle in my body began tingling. Should I or shouldn't I shoot? Who was hiding in the brush? Was this the same person who'd killed the boy? The same person who had also killed Marlon? Judging by the sheer size and power of the massive wounds that killed both boys, I was pretty certain the same weapon had been used. But I didn't think either of the riflemen at the roadblock had used such a powerful weapon when they were shooting at me. A .30-06 would have penetrated the trunk of the Nova as well as the back seat, but would have also torn through the front seat, slammed into me, then pounded into the dash before losing its punch. I'd only had a glimpse of their weapons, so I really couldn't tell. Even if I did know what weapons were being used, it wouldn't tell me why two such skilled shooters had killed two members of their own gang.

So who was hiding in the bushes? And why would he be wandering around in the woods, picking off gang members at crucial moments?

None of this made any sense, and as I'd learned early on, if something made no sense, there was a damned good reason for it. The world I'd once known had died. No cavalry existed anymore. There were no more cops. No good guys. No communications or help network. I no longer had a cell phone, and if I did, it wouldn't work. Even if it did work, a call to 911 or anyone else would be fruitless. It was just me and a wild pack of psycho kids who'd kidnapped the love of my life and were now coming after me. Whoever was hiding in that brush was one of them. He was either a terrible shot or a very good one. Either way, he was someone with his own sick agenda, and he was walking around carrying a very powerful weapon.

In either case, I wasn't about to give him a chance to kill me at such a close range. Still gripping the Ruger, I brought my finger back to its proper place in front of the trigger, aimed the gun and prepared to empty the magazine into the center of the bush twenty feet straight ahead.

"I'm a friend."

This voice was real. It wasn't in my head, and it was the voice of a grown man. It also sounded like it had come from the bush.

A *friend. I'm a friend.*

What did that mean? Did I know him? Or did he mean *ally*?

Or was this merely another hallucination?

Confused and frightened, I finally noticed my arms, which still held the Ruger at arm's length. They weighed a ton and had been shaking so much, I couldn't get a clean shot even at a distance of twenty feet. Heavy waves of exhaustion had been thrashing into me more than ever; it wouldn't be long before I collapsed. I'd been running on pure adrenaline the last few hours, but now my reserves were dangerously close to depletion and would soon shut down. The exhaustion was showing itself in many ways. Now, besides that "inner" voice, I was hearing another, and this one sounded more genuine than anything I'd ever heard. *Fight it. Ignore it.* I kept the Ruger pointed toward the bush.

More shots broke out. One of them slammed into the pine tree just a few feet behind me.

I dove into the bush again and huddled there, ignoring the intense throbbing in my arm while struggling to decide on my options. Despite my efforts, I could not grasp the reality of all this, nor could I think of a solution. Because of the increasing pain in my arm, I was having more and

226

more difficulty concentrating. Hallucination or not, something inside me told me not to fire at the bush, and as I cautiously pushed some of the foliage away with my good arm, I saw someone moving around behind it.

Then I finally made a decision. I didn't know if it was due to the exhaustion, my growing sense of helplessness or the pressure of being constantly fired upon. Whatever it was, it told me to trust the voice. And my instincts. I was looking at a man— not a hallucination. And if this man had wanted me dead, I would already be dead.

I lowered my arm.

Seconds later, a face appeared from behind the bush.

"Over here, Moss," he whispered harshly. "And for Christ's sake, keep down!"

***

The back of my skull buzzed.

Moss. He'd called me Moss. Yes, that was my name, but in this situation, it didn't make sense. How did a man I'd never seen before know my name? What in heaven's name was going on?

More gunfire exploded in the woods. A heavy barrage splintered into the group of pines around us. The gang had apparently continued down the hill and come much closer. I crawled over to the brush and rolled to the other side, until I was directly behind the pine tree. Then I came face to face with the man kneeling in the brush.

He looked to be around my age, and was dressed in camouflage pants, shirt and cap. The brim of the cap was pushed down, so I could barely see his eyes. He wore an ammo belt; a canteen hung by a thick strap over his left shoulder. The canteen caught my attention, and for the first time since I'd escaped the bullet-ridden Nova, I realized how dehydrated I was.

But fresh water wasn't the most crucial thing weighing on my mind. I couldn't stop wondering who this man was, how he knew my name. If he knew anything about me, he'd have to be one of them. So what was his next move? A bullet to my head? Was that why he'd coaxed me out of the bushes? So he could get me close enough to do the deed without making a mess of it again?

No. The inner voice had guided me here. Despite my instincts, my fears, I felt compelled to listen to it. And because of this reasoning, I had to trust this man, whoever he was.

My suspicions came thundering back, smothering every other thought and emotion in a heavy darkness.

He knew my name.

How was this possible? Had Fields told him?

This would mean he *was* one of them. If so, he'd no doubt talked to her, asked her questions. Knowing Fields as I did, and assuming she'd been playing possum all this time, they would have been forced to revert to extreme measures to get her to talk. Torture, perhaps? Sense deprivation? Threats? They'd had her nearly twelve hours, now. Twelve hours, in my experience, afforded kidnappers more than enough time to find out whatever they wanted

228

to know from their victim. From what I'd seen during my Pakistani Brighton tour, a terrorist could find out anything he wanted to know in just a few minutes.

Would Fields be able to stand the pressure for this long? Or would she cave? Would she tell them about me? My military training? My background? How I functioned?

My guts twisted, and my exhaustion began trickling away. The throbbing in my wounded arm even eased up. If this bastard was actually Simon or a member of his gang, I was going to find out very quickly. And if I discovered that he'd hurt her in any way, he was going to die a very painful death.

He knelt on his right knee, his left side against the pine tree. His right side faced me, but the bush separating us concealed his weapon from view. He was watching the area to our right, just beyond my former sanctuary. He actually appeared to be watching our attackers. Logic told me that if he'd been gunning for me, he would have already shot and killed me by now.

My suspicions remained strong. Gritting my teeth and summoning what strength I had left, I transferred the Ruger from my right hand to my left. My left arm wasn't in much better shape than my right from all the abuse I'd subjected it to, but it wasn't numb with pain, and could still function. I wasn't quite as proficient with my left arm, but the target was only a few feet away, and even though the pistol grip was designed for the right hand, I could manage the shot.

All I had to do was ask the question. If I didn't get the right answer, I'd put a round in his kneecap. That would disable him long enough for me to take his weapon, get him on the ground and repeat my question. A second round would shatter his other kneecap, and the elbows would be next. If he still didn't talk, I'd simply finish him off and hunt for a way out of the woods. I was pretty much a physical wreck at this point, but that didn't matter. I was going to find Fields if it was the last thing I ever did. If I didn't, or if I found her too late, I had no desire to continue my existence in this chilling nightmare world.

I gripped the Ruger more firmly in my hand and cleared my throat. My heart was in my mouth and my nerves were tingling, but I managed to get the words out nonetheless. "I've got a question to ask you."

He turned to face me, shifting a little amongst the bushes, and I saw the weapon resting on his thigh. It looked like a Desert Tactical Arms Stealth Recon Scout sniper rifle, with a telescopic sight. The same model the military had used more than thirty years ago, in Iraq and Afghanistan. At the time, it was used strictly for military personnel. By the time I enlisted in the military a decade later, they'd stopped using them, and it was almost impossible to find one. The fact that this man had one, for some inexplicable reason, comforted me. This strange feeling somehow told me that he wasn't Simon, or even a member of Simon's gang. Like many off-the-wall ideas, this one didn't come with an explanation. The only thing I knew was that I no longer felt as tense or as uneasy as I did moments earlier.

"Is that ... a Scout?" I asked.

He nodded.

"I haven't seen one of those in years. What caliber is it?"

".338 Lapua Magnum."

A nasty, heavy load. No wonder Marlon and the other guy had gone down so hard. The round used by the Scout was designed to penetrate body armor at nearly eleven hundred yards. Once again, I found myself wondering what the hell was going on, how this strange guy who apparently knew my name had just come from out of the blue and saved my ass twice in the last couple of hours ...

More gunfire slapped the ground just a few yards away. The gang was getting closer. He motioned for me to get down, and we moved another twenty yards farther into the woods. Once I found a good spot, he crawled over to the pine and peered around it. Then he raised the Scout, peered into the sight and popped off a couple of heavy rounds into the hill on the other side of the valley. The gunfire stopped immediately.

He turned back to me and stared at my bloody arm. Then, resting the butt of the rifle on the ground between his feet, he reached into his jacket. He seemed concerned. "How bad?"

"Not bad. I need to clean it up."

"Is the bullet still inside?"

"It was a .22, so yeah, probably."

"Bummer." He produced a silver flask. Another shot rang out, smacking a tree just beyond us. He barely flinched. I had the feeling he was a seasoned soldier. "Pour some over the wound and have a slug or two."

I rested the Ruger on the ground in front of me.

He frowned. "You're using a .22?"

I took the flask. "I needed something light to carry around. These assholes have been chasing me all night. I'm using mini mags."

"Is that all you've got?"

"I'm also carrying a .38 Ladysmith in a pancake holster behind my back, and a .22 Beretta in my pocket."

He shook his head. "I'm surprised you've only been hit once."

"I guess you could say it's my lucky day."

He got back into his kneeling position, raised the Scout, sighted in again and emptied the mag into the countryside. He pulled out the empty, pocketed it, removed a fresh 5-shot box mag from his belt, slammed it in, bolted it action-ready, sighted it in and got off two more shots. An ear-splitting shriek echoed across the woods. He set the rifle back down and reached into his jacket pocket again.

I carefully spilled a steady trickle of whiskey directly onto the bloody wound. It burned like the blazes. I clenched my jaw and held my breath until it had soaked through and the stinging died down. Then I had a swallow. The whiskey burned all the way down and its tingling perked me right up.

I snapped the flask shut and held it out. He motioned for me to keep it. Not wanting to argue, I slid it into the inner pocket of my jacket. He found something else in his jacket and pulled it out. He offered me a bandage wrap.

I just gawked at it. I must have looked really stupid right then, but I still couldn't believe any of this was actually happening.

"Take it. Wrap it as best you can. We'll fix it later."

Later? That meant ... well, it meant later, as in the future.

Didn't it? Of course it did. It also meant hope. And that meant I was somehow getting out of this.

I wanted to shake his hand ... to thank him for showing up ... for saving my life—not once, but twice.

But I knew better. This wasn't the time for pleasantries. The gang was still out there, shooting at us. But since I'd just been told we might actually be able to do something "later," maybe then we'd have time to share the rest of the flask. But Fields would have to be with us for the celebration to have any real meaning for me. And that meant we still had a lot to do once we got out of here.

I took the bandage. "Thanks. I really..."

"We gotta get out of here. I just spotted two of those little bastards crawling around behind those dead trees."

***

Staying behind the trees, my companion and I backed away from our nest amongst the bushes and snuck over to the hill about forty yards behind us. The rise was overrun with trees and brush, ascending at a forty-five-degree angle for more than a hundred yards. A long, arduous climb, but obviously our only escape. If my new friend was right, the armed gang would be crossing the creek in just a few minutes. Being here to meet them would be very bad for everyone.

I stayed about ten feet behind him, watching him closely and stepping in his tracks as we squeezed through the thick trails of wild brush and vines. Without losing step, I removed the magazine from the Ruger and shoved the gun into its shoulder holster beneath my left arm. I opened the flap of my ammo pouch, grabbed a handful of .22 mini mags and dropped six of them into my palm. While I remained focused on the man in front of me, I worked by feel to carefully load the magazine. My nerves were shot and I was exhausted. Even though the shot of whiskey helped me stay alert, I felt myself succumbing to the fatigue. I even zoned out once or twice, and recovered only after I'd stumbled on exposed roots. Fortunately, my instinct and sense of survival remained in high gear, and I managed to maintain my footing. I kept a firm grip on the magazine and kept myself from dropping the ammo.

By the time we were about twenty yards from the top of the hill, I'd finished loading the mag. An exhilarating feeling overwhelmed my exhaustion, and I soon discovered that I felt much better than I did when we'd begun our climb. The pounding in my wounded arm had even eased up. I pulled out the Ruger, slammed the fully-loaded mag back into it, and jacked one into the chamber. As a precaution, I turned and scanned the wooded drop behind us. I saw nothing.

"They're probably spreading out after they cross the creek," my friend said. "It won't be long before they figure out we're not there anymore. Then they'll decide to make the climb."

"I don't think they're good trackers. It takes years to become a decent tracker."

"They're just a bunch of whacko kids playing war games with real guns."

"Unfortunately, some of them really know how to shoot."

"Maybe, but they know nothing about tactics. We were both in the military. We both know that if you weren't wounded and had a rifle, we could've stayed down there and picked them off, one by one, in fifteen minutes or less."

We were both in the military.

How the hell did he know *that*?

My suspicions trickled back. A man I'd never seen before knew not only my name, but also the fact that I'd been in the military.

Did I know him? I tried to remember if I'd seen his face before, but he didn't look familiar. I definitely had to find out what was going on, who this guy was. But this wasn't the right time. Once we got out of here, I could ask my questions.

"Keep moving," he said. "We don't have much time, and I don't want to give them the opportunity to see where we are."

He was right; they were down there on this side of the creek and were probably already checking out the area. The gunfire had trickled off, but every so often a stray shot came from the general direction of the valley. Some of them were crouched behind the trees while the others who had crossed the creek searched the woods.

A couple of minutes later, we reached the top of the hill. Tired, sweaty and out of breath, my limbs heavy and tingling, I swayed a little and forced myself to stay on my feet. But my discomfort faded away when I peered down the steep slope that led to the winding country road.

A dark gray SUV sat half-hidden in heavy brush about ten feet off the road at the bottom of the hill.

The sight made me want to leap with joy. A moment later, I caught myself wondering if I was hallucinating. It was, after all, a strong possibility. I was exhausted, thirsty and ready to collapse, with the bullet wound in my arm. All this, as well as the loss of blood, was making me delirious. But there was one way to find out. I slowly brought up my free hand and gently rubbed my eyes. When I opened them again, I fully expected to see no vehicle parked among the bushes. In fact, I fully expected the man beside me to disappear as well.

I took a deep breath and opened my eyes.

The vehicle remained there. And the man who'd saved my life was still standing beside me.

Even so, I was convinced I might be dreaming.

"Is that an actual vehicle down there?" I asked. "Or am I seeing things?"

"You're not seeing things."

I still found myself skeptical. I knew how the imagination worked, how it took over when the mind and body were tired and most vulnerable to suggestion. "Is it ... yours?"

"Yeah."

Relief swept through me in heavy tremors, making me light-headed. For the first time since Walter and I had shared that first glass of Scotch, I actually felt like I might survive this nightmare.

"Think you can make it?"

The growing exhaustion had been weighing heavily on my shoulders ever since I'd reached the top of the hill. I forced it away. I wasn't quite ready to lie down. I still had a couple of things to do before calling it a day. I reminded myself that if I could climb a steep hill like this one, going down the other side would not be nearly as difficult. "I know I can."

He was staring at my wound again. "You look pretty well done-in. If you want me to help you down this drop, tell me now. We'll give it helluva try if you want, but it'll definitely slow us down ..."

I frowned. I knew he was just being considerate, but I wasn't in the mood to hear something like that. I intended to see this through, and I'd do it on my own two feet.

"Don't worry, I'll keep up." I holstered the Ruger and zipped up my jacket. Then I began squeezing through the heavy brush just as a sudden

burst of gunfire slammed into the crest of the hill a
hundred feet behind us.

CHAPTER SEVENTEEN

It took us about five minutes to get to the bottom of the hill. I lost my footing several times, stumbling and nearly falling, but grabbed some exposed roots to keep the momentum from pulling me down the hill. My friend stopped during my first mishap and took a few steps back up the hill to help me, but I motioned for him to keep going. Reluctantly he turned back around and continued his descent. The widening gap between us inspired me to get right back up. My light-headedness drifted back a few times, but I focused on Fields, and in no time I was alert and in control of myself again.

Just when I thought my legs would give out, we'd reached the bottom of the hill.

The Desert Scout held straight out, my friend scanned the road and the woods as he hurried across the road. I could barely keep up with him, but it didn't matter; I knew where he was going. My limbs had become concrete pillars, and my hips screamed in agony with each step. My wounded arm burned like hot coals, stabbing me with each beat of my heart. I clenched my jaw and forced myself to keep moving. Each step brought me closer to Fields; I kept reminding myself how far I'd come, how much closer I was to finding her. We needed one another, and even though I was exhausted and bleeding and barely able to stand, none of it mattered because I was convinced we'd be together again.

I finally made it to the other side of the road. The light-headedness returned as I stepped into the brush and trudged through the tall weeds hiding the big vehicle from view. Once again I ignored my discomfort and focused on reaching the truck. It was an effort to pull open the door, as well as to climb in, but I'd come much too far to give up. Grabbing the door handle and armrest, I pulled myself up. It took a mighty effort to slide my pitiful butt into the seat, but as soon as I did, my body melted, and I experienced a sensation of ecstasy I'd never realized existed.

My friend had already climbed in and situated himself behind the wheel. He'd laid the Desert Scout on the back seat, placed a Colt .45 auto on the console between our seats, and reached into his pants pocket. My pulse hammered as I watched him pull out a ring of keys, select one and jam it into the ignition. I was certain the big machine wouldn't start. The key would be the wrong one, and he'd have to take a very long time to find the right one. There were probably a dozen other keys on the ring, and by the time he was able to start up the truck, Simon's gang would drive by in their truck and kill us.

My fears were quickly proven wrong. The SUV started right up. It took only a second or two for him to shift gears and ease the big vehicle through the thick grass, over the hilly shoulder and onto the road.

I found myself staring numbly at the road as he accelerated to 60, then 65, in no time at all. Then I glanced at the .45 on the console and thought of Fields. I thought of the previous night, just a few short hours ago, when I'd found her .38 in the woods. In that same instant, just as I found myself growing angry again, I noticed that I wasn't holding the Ruger. My neck grew warm and my heart sputtered. Forcing myself not to panic, I pressed my left arm firmly against my side and felt the hard bulky shape hanging there. Relieved but still not convinced, I opened my jacket. There it was, resting in its holster under my left arm.

"Still there?" my friend asked.

I nodded.

"I saw you holster it at the top of the hill. Good move."

It was a good thing I'd been thinking clearly back there. Otherwise, I would have probably fallen down the hill and lost it in the weeds.

I pulled it out. As I placed it in my lap, I glanced out the side window, expecting to see the distant figures of two riflemen appearing in the middle of the road, kneeling, aiming, sighting us in ...

The road was deserted.

I sat back in my seat, fastened the harness and fought off more waves of dizziness. I couldn't let go. Not now. There were more urgent matters to tend to. I had to tell this man about Fields while I was still conscious. Once I collapsed, he wouldn't have any idea why I was even out there. He'd take me to wherever his place was and would bandage me up, but this wouldn't help Fields. This wasn't

241

the time for me to slip away. I had to tell this man what we had to do, where we had to go.

"You oughta be tending to that wound," he said. "I'd do it, but we've got to..."

"Listen ... I've got to tell you about..."

"They almost killed you back there."

"I don't care about that. I have to..."

"You're barely able to stay awake, Moss. What's so damned important that you don't even care if that wound gets infected?"

I took a deep breath and blurted it out. "Those psychotic assholes took my girlfriend. The man in charge ... he ... they're out here somewhere."

"I know."

He knew. He knew about Fields. This stranger somehow knew about Fields. I couldn't grasp the concept. Was I already losing it? Imagining all this? Slipping into deliria?

What the hell was going on?

I suddenly felt as if I'd just turned on the TV in time to watch the tail end of a good story. This stranger knew my name. He knew I was former military. He even knew where I was. But most incredible of all, he *knew about Fields*.

"Did you just say what I thought you said?"

"Moss, you don't look so good. You need to rest. Lie back and..."

"Answer me, dammit. Did you or did you not say you know about my girlfriend?"

"Yeah. I did. Now lie back and relax."

What the hell was going on? Any dizziness that had been flickering around me had just fled into the darkness. And the throbbing in my wounded arm had eased up. This was a good thing, because right now I didn't have time for dizziness or to worry about the hot throbbing in my arm. I was pretty angry and confused right now, and wasn't about to let minor distractions take over. I had to find out who this man was and how he knew about me and Fields.

"Who the hell *are* you? And how do you know I was in the military?"

"The name's Shaw. Harry Shaw. You can call me Harry..."

"Listen, Shaw. I really appreciate what you did back there, and I'm indebted to you for getting me out of there and all, but my lady is out here somewhere, and..."

"We'll find her, Moss. We have a pretty good idea where they are."

"He's got a regular car lot behind his house out on Cherry Hill Road. I don't even know what vehicle he's..." I stopped talking when the chills drifted slowly down my spine. *We*. He'd said *we*. "Did you just say *we*?"

"Settle back in your seat. We'll be there in just a few minutes."

This was too much. I was afraid I really was hallucinating. In fact, I suddenly had the sinking feeling that I'd actually died somewhere back there—possibly when Marlon was holding his gun on me. I was beginning to suspect Marlon *wasn't* the one who was shot. I might have this all wrong. Maybe *I* was the one who'd been shot. When I died,

243

my spirit got everything mixed up the moment I entered the other side and started sniffing around.

I gazed at the Ruger in my lap. Touched it, picked it up. Held it in my hand. Put it back down. Felt the wrap Shaw had given me back there. Then I tapped my pocket where I kept the flask he'd given me. Everything was there.

This situation was real. I was real. The seat I was sitting in was real. The vehicle we were riding in was real. The man sitting beside me was real.

And he'd just said "we." Not "we," as in the two of us, but "we," as in he and someone else. *We have a pretty good idea where they are.* I couldn't get much of anything else out of that statement. The only thing that made sense was that I was real, Shaw was real, and there was someone else, someone Shaw had just mentioned.

I only hoped this other person was also real.

"What the hell's going on?" I couldn't believe the words had left my throat in a coherent flow. Couldn't believe I'd been able to ask the question at all.

"Trust me, okay?"

"I don't know what's going on, Shaw. I don't even know if I'm still alive. If you're actually sitting there. I want to believe I'm alive, but none of this is making any..."

"You're still alive, Moss. If you're doubtful, just slap yourself on the arm."

I wasn't *that* irrational—not yet, anyway.

"Listen to me, now. We know about Simon, and we know where he's taking Miss Fields. Just

244

settle down and try to relax. We'll be there in about ten minutes. Think you can hold on until then?"

"What the hell do *you* think?"

***

Shaw mashed his foot down and got the SUV doing 75 on the narrow country road. I sat back in the seat and immediately felt my tense limbs relaxing. Due to the crumbling pavement and frequent turns, Shaw struggled to keep the SUV from going off into the ditch, and we screeched around the hairpin curves, thumping the bumpy shoulder several times. For some reason, it didn't bother me. At the moment, all I cared about was the comfortable seat and the calming sensation of the inside of my eyelids. And this man had just said he knew where Fields was.

I heard Shaw mumbling a little later, and figured he might be trying to explain what he'd meant before, when he'd used the word "we." My curiosity got the better of me, and I decided this would be the time to find out what was going on. I opened my eyes, but he'd already stopped talking. He stared straight ahead as he drove, gripping the wheel with his right hand. His left hand soon joined his right. I thought I saw it come out of his jacket pocket, but I couldn't be sure.

"Did you say something?" I asked.

He shook his head and kept driving.

"I thought I heard you say something."

"You're tired, Moss. Relax."

He was only half right—I was more than tired. I closed my eyes and let my tortured body melt into the seat. The steady humming of the SUV gradually dimmed, my limbs quit aching and my arm stopped hurting. My world grew dark and soft, almost dreamlike. The darkness dimmed and turned gray, then silver, as if a heavy fog had just lifted. Shapes appeared in the fog. They gradually darkened, and as they drew nearer, they grew more distinct.

A long, thin black figure approached, growing lighter and more distinct, and finally turning into Fields. She was dressed in jeans, tennis shoes and her red tee shirt—the one with the tiny silver stars that I liked so much—and her hair was full and shiny. She stopped just a couple of feet away and bent over me. Her hair brushed against my face. It felt like a warm summer breeze had kissed me, and my body tingled all over.

Then she kissed me on the forehead, and when her face was just inches away, she whispered, "Why did it take you so long to get here, Moss?" But she was smiling, playing with me, and I knew things would be okay, and we'd never be separated again.

I wanted to say something equally glib and cute. The first thing that came to mind was, "Traffic was heavy," but when I opened my mouth, I found that I couldn't talk. A large lump had filled my throat. The excitement of being with her again had no doubt turned my brain into overload, and my body wasn't able to function properly. Or maybe I was more exhausted than I thought. Whatever the reason, she understood. Her smile still lit up her face, and she continued stroking my hair. Then she whispered, "It's all right, Moss, everything will be just fine once you get up."

I knew exactly what she meant. We had to return to the farm and continue living our lives. It was vital to put this nasty nightmare behind us and go on, somehow, living day by day, as before. But we couldn't do anything until I got up and took her back to my grandparents' farm.

I tried getting up but quickly discovered that I couldn't. I was stuck to the ground, and no matter how much I struggled, something held me down.

She watched me patiently, and after a few moments held out her arms. She spoke again, but this time her voice sounded different.

"Get up, Moss."

Her voice had lowered in pitch, turning into a man's voice, one that sounded very familiar. In fact, as I tried analyzing it, I realized that it sounded like *Reed*.

That was impossible. Reed was dead. He couldn't possibly come back from the dead and talk to me like this.

Could he?

Reed? Is that you? Am I dead? Or did you come back to...?

"Moss, get up. We're here."

Someone was tapping my arm. I opened my eyes. A gray dashboard. My Ruger sat in my lap. A harness kept me fastened to the seat. My jeans were covered with dirt and leaves and stickers. My hands were filthy, and blood streaked my right forearm. A blood-soaked bandage covered my right bicep.

247

I was sitting in someone's SUV. It wasn't Fields sitting beside me, it was Shaw, and he was nudging me. His door was wide open behind him. "C'mon, Moss. We're here. Get up. We've got things to do."

I turned and stared straight ahead, at the frighteningly-familiar view just beyond the windshield. About a hundred feet beyond us, at the top of the gravel drive...

My grandparents' barn.

We'd come back home.

Shaw hadn't taken me to an abandoned farm out in the boonies. He'd brought me back home ... to my grandparents' farm.

Confused, overwhelmed and suddenly painfully alert, I gawked helplessly at the bizarre sight. Then, when the harsh realization slammed through me, I saw something else that struck me as very strange.

Parked farther up the drive, about fifty feet from the barn's huge sliding door, sat two vehicles. One was a gray Ford pickup, the other the light-blue electric compact that had followed Fields and me the day before.

Simon's car.

The bastard had found out where we lived and had brought his gang back to my grandparents' farm.

CHAPTER EIGHTEEN

Enraged, I scrambled with the seat harness and the door handle at the same time. My mind had gone berserk. Simon had found out about my home and came to take whatever he could find. While his gang of armed psychos had been hunting me all night long, he'd come here to invade my home.

Had he brought Fields with him? Had he threatened her to bring him here?

I was going to find out.

As soon as I began struggling, an avalanche of hot, screaming pain danced up my arms and down my sides. I quickly grew light-headed, and sank back in the seat.

"Easy," Shaw said. "Don't pass out on us now."

"I'm fine." I knew that was a lie, and I was sure Shaw knew it too, but it didn't matter because I'd come this far and wasn't about to stop because of a little queasiness. But as I waited for the waves of dizziness to subside, something began nagging at me.

Shaw had just said "us." What did *that* mean? The two of us? Was it just a figure of speech? Or another reference to what he'd said earlier, when he'd used the word "we"?

This was something I was going to figure out later, after I'd confronted Simon and forced him to tell me what he'd done with Fields. Right now I had to concentrate on more important matters, such as staying alert. I couldn't pass out; I refused to. "That bastard's here, isn't he?" I asked, my voice unsteady. "He's here, and God only knows what he's doing or what he's done."

Shaw had already got out and climbed down. He held his .45 in his right hand. With his left, he pointed to the barn, then eased the door quietly shut.

It registered immediately: Simon was in the barn. That was what brought me back: the cold, harsh reality that Simon had come to my place and gone into the barn. His reasoning didn't matter. Neither did half a dozen questions that came with this scenario. The only thing that did matter was that the same bastard responsible for taking away the love of my love, for sending two killers onto our property, had come back, and now that he did, I was going to end this right here and now.

My adrenaline thundered right back, and I went right back and tackled the seat harness. This time I was successful, snapping it open on the first try. I grabbed the Ruger, kicked open the door and slid out of the truck. The bottoms of my feet smacked the gravel, sending a torrent of hot tingling pain scurrying up my legs. I nearly collapsed, grabbing the door handle for balance. My legs would eventually work. They'd been through much more than this. All they needed to do was carry me up that hill.

Once the tingling subsided, a heavy gush of heat flowed down my legs. It felt like I'd been lowered into a tub of warm water. Good. It was safe to start moving again. Shaw was already halfway up the hill, but I knew better than try and catch up with him. I gripped the Ruger tightly as I forced myself forward.

About half a minute later, just as we were twenty yards or so from the barn, we heard a gunshot. It sounded like it had come from inside the barn.

Shaw and I both stopped cold, and for several tense moments we listened to the silence. My head grew hot and my pulse pounded. My imagination ran wild, and once again I wondered who'd come with Simon in that truck. And why Simon was in the barn. And who'd fired that shot.

Just then, Shaw took off in a dead run, heading straight for the barn.

Another fresh batch of adrenaline shot through me. I veered off to the right, into the thick grass, toward the overgrown path that led to the lower floor of the barn that faced the road. This section contained the horse stalls, access to the silo, and the long row of stalls where Uncle Joe kept the cows when the farm was fully operational many years ago. I trudged through the weeds, the Ruger held straight out in front of me.

When I was about twenty feet from the far corner of the barn, someone staggered outside. It was a man, and he held a gun in his hand.

I froze.

He turned toward me and I saw a large dark circle of blood growing in the center of his white sweatshirt. His arm hung loosely at his side, the barrel of the gun pointed at the ground.

He looked strangely familiar—about my age and bulky, with a receding hairline and a scraggly brown beard. He looked like he'd once been muscular but had let himself go. He was a couple of inches taller than me, but at least twenty pounds heavier.

It only took me a few moments to remember him. He was a year ahead of me in high school—a member of the football team and captain of the basketball team. He'd been voted Most Popular as a senior, made good grades, was popular with girls and had been offered several athletic scholarships. Last I'd heard, he'd studied Phys Ed at Carnegie-Mellon and had taught at one of the local high schools.

Like most jocks, he'd been an arrogant bully, but hadn't been known for causing trouble. Apparently he'd decided to spend the rest of his days in charge of a psychotic gang of killers preying on what was left of the neighborhood.

"Simon Ettinger." I couldn't believe this.

He took a breath and blinked, squinting, trying to remember. His eyes were glossy and seemed out of focus. His nose was running as well. "Moss?"

"Yeah."

A cough. "Figured it was you."

It was time to end this. "Where is she?"

He lowered his head and coughed again, wetly.

I could barely contain myself. It didn't matter who this bastard was or if I once knew him. He'd taken the woman I loved from me, and now he was going to die.

The strength in my numb right arm had mysteriously returned, and I found no difficulty raising the Ruger. My hand trembled a little at first before turning deadly still. I took a breath and aimed the barrel at Ettinger's right eye. "Did you ... kill her?"

He raised his head and blinked, and I caught the beginnings of a smile.

A *smile*? Was this maniac kidding? *You asked for it, you bastard.* But just as my index finger began applying pressure to the trigger, Ettinger coughed up phlegm mixed with blood. Slobber covered his lower lip and chin. His voice was a throaty whisper when he said, "That's ... a laugh." Then his head fell forward. His gun dropped to the ground and he collapsed in the grass.

Another figure emerged from the barn.

It was Fields. She was wearing the same outfit she'd had on the night before, but her jeans were dirty and smudged, and her hair was mussed. Long, matted strands fell in front of her face. She held a long-barrel revolver in her right hand and stood looking down at Simon, her gun aimed at his motionless body. She slowly raised her head, but her hair blocked her view. With her free hand, she pulled it back. When she saw me, her jaw dropped, and she gawked at me as if she didn't believe her eyes. She let her gun drop in the grass.

I quickly discovered I could not move. I wanted to run to her, wrap my arms around her and hold her, but my legs had gone numb again. *Of all the damned luck ...* I tried to say something but my voice was gone as well. I'd turned comatose, and once again the fear that I'd died came drifting back. This had to be death. It certainly was hell, or as close to damnation as I could imagine. I'd finally been reunited with Fields, but all I could do was stand there like a zombie, gawking at her.

She rushed toward me.

A moment later, someone else appeared behind her—another man. He was large and broad-shouldered. Like Shaw, he was dressed in camouflage slacks and matching jacket. His arms hung at his sides. A gun extended from his right hand. He approached Simon cautiously, knelt and felt for a pulse. Then he straightened and watched Fields and me. He holstered his gun, reached into his jacket pocket and pulled something out of it. He brought it up and placed it next to his ear.

It was a *cell phone*.

My eyes glazed over. A cell phone. Right. Why, of course. In this world of death, corpses and walking zombies, no electricity, satellites or any other power sources, there had to be *some* miracle that defied all rational explanation.

Roaches and cell phones would always survive a holocaust.

When Fields was only a couple of yards away, I tried raising my arms. Like my legs, they'd gone numb. The Ruger was still in my hand. I no longer needed it, and let it drop. I figured that without its weight, I could raise my hands and wrap my arms around her.

But a heavy curtain of blackness dropped over me, and I collapsed beneath it.

***

Fields sat on a chair beside the bed, applying a fresh wrap to my arm.

Just a few minutes earlier, when I opened my eyes and saw her, I thought I'd died and gone to Heaven. But when she touched me, kissed me lightly on the lips and told me I'd been asleep for nearly forty-eight hours, I realized we were both still alive, had survived the nightmare and had made it safely back home. It wasn't exactly Heaven, but it seemed as close to it as one could get in this horribly dark, frightening world.

"How'd I make it up the stairs?" I asked. "I don't remember anything once I blacked out."

"I carried you."

My expression must have been classic. She laughed. "Two big, strong guys happened to be walking around at the time. They came over and asked if I needed help. They didn't seem to have anything better to do, so I asked them to lend me a hand."

"Nice of them."

She was silent for a few moments. Her smile vanished, and she told me how sorry she was.

"For what?"

"For causing all this. For feeling so sorry for myself that I left the house alone at night and let myself get picked up by a bunch of crazy jerks."

"It happened on our property. It wasn't your fault."

255

"But it wouldn't have if I hadn't just left the house half-cocked. Or if I'd just stayed closer to the house. Or just went over to the stoop, sat down and brooded right there."

"You were upset. You needed time by yourself. You didn't deserve anything that happened out there."

"But it happened. To make it even worse, it happened just hours after I'd chastised you for leaving the house that morning without telling me."

She was right, but I didn't feel this was the time for an I-told-you-so. She was already punishing herself. "That was different."

"I nearly got us both killed. That's going to be hard to live with."

"Like I said, it wasn't your fault. You'd had a really close call earlier that day and it freaked you out. Actually, it had been a horrendous day on several different levels. You needed time to sort things out."

"You didn't want me to go for that walk. I should have listened to you." A shadow had drifted across her face. I figured she'd just gone back to relive some unpleasant memories. I wanted to know where she was, what exactly had happened. I wasn't sure if I could handle it, and told myself I should ask about this later, when I felt better. Right now I was weak and tired, and didn't want to deal with violent emotions. I wanted only to bathe myself in her wonderful presence.

She noticed my inner turmoil almost at once. "You want to know what happened that night? After they picked me up?"

I just sighed.

"I promise it won't upset you."

"How can you promise something like that?"

She shrugged. "Nothing really bad happened."

"Nothing?"

"Nothing as bad as what you're probably thinking."

I suddenly realized that I could no longer stand the suspense. In spite of my instincts, my fears, I said, "Then tell me what happened."

"It's dark at night in the woods, but it's also very quiet. When I reached the clearing on the other side of the pine trees, I could hear rustling coming from three different directions, so I knew right then that I wasn't alone, that there were several of them coming toward me, and that I'd be surrounded before I could do anything to prevent it. I knew they weren't very far away, so I didn't have much time. I obviously couldn't outrun them or stand a chance of getting them all with my gun, so I unclipped the holster and placed it on a stump along the trail we'd used several times before. I knew that if they saw the gun, they'd consider me a threat and would kill me and take my gun, or rape me first, then kill me and take the gun. But if they found me unarmed and thought I was doped, they might leave me alone, or just check me out to see what I had on me and go away. But they didn't. They walked me through the woods, to the road on the other side of the farm. A car was parked there, on Deer Creek Road. They shoved me in the back and took me to Simon's place out there in the boonies."

"They didn't hurt you, then?"

"Aside from getting a little wild when they were patting me down, no, they didn't hurt me. They just kept pushing me to the car. Simon turned out to be a different story. He wanted to rape me as soon as they brought me into the house. He grabbed me and pulled me into his den and started to undress me, but quickly changed his mind."

"Where does the part come when I won't be upset? You obviously haven't gotten there yet."

She smiled. "Like I said, he changed his mind even before he tried getting my top off. It was the way I was acting that turned him off. He didn't know how to deal with me."

"I'd heard his boys say that he didn't like messing around with doped women."

"I didn't try acting doped. I wasn't sure how well I could pull that off, so I tried something else. I'd worked with the mentally disturbed during my nursing years, and remembered how they acted, spoke and moved. Not too many guys are anxious to get physical with a handicapped woman, so that's what I did."

"It obviously worked, then."

"Simon helped quite a bit, surprisingly. He'd taken something just a few minutes before I was brought into the house. I think it might have been a popper, so he was pretty buzzed. Just a minute or so after he took me into his den and began tugging on my top, I cried like a little girl. That turned him right off, so I figured I might as well make my performance even more convincing. I told him all about you. I said you were my daddy and that you were crazy, always scaring me and pushing me around and locking me in the basement at night. I told him you'd tried to kill me that morning. You were cleaning a gun after breakfast and when I walked by, I accidentally knocked over your whiskey glass and you got so mad, you picked up your gun and tried to shoot me, but the gun jammed. This made you even madder, so you told me you were going to kill me as soon as you got another gun. I ran out of the house and hid in the woods. I heard gunshots and thought you were shooting at me, but after a while I heard your truck and saw you loading two bodies onto the back of it. That's when I ran back into the woods and hid there all day."

"Good thinking. How'd he deal with it?"

"Like I said, he was pretty buzzed, but when I told him that, he got really angry, and kicked the door. He went over to his desk, opened a drawer, took out some powder and poured some on the blotter."

"Coke?"

"No doubt. He was babbling about his friends Doc and James, and how he was going to kill you for killing them. He did two lines, slumped over the desk and went to sleep. I didn't know what to do. I knew I could probably sneak out through the window, but since I'd seen people running around all over the place, I knew someone would see me and wake him. There were people in the house, too, but no one would come in the den. They seemed to avoid it, and whenever they came down the hall, they veered away, keeping as far away as possible.

"I just stayed in the room and waited for him to come to. I knew I could probably find a decent hiding place, but something told me not to. Some of those guys living there looked like they'd nail anything, and I didn't want to give them any ideas. They wouldn't have touched me because I was with Simon, and there was a strong, unwritten policy about who they could and couldn't mess with. I just didn't want to take a chance. Besides, I knew I wouldn't be there long. I figured you were looking for me and had already found the gun and holster, so I wasn't worried. I just bided my time."

"How many were living there?"

"There were at least a dozen of them in the main house. I didn't get to learn anything about the guest house, but I could tell several of them were living there as well. Most of them living on the ground floor of the main house were women, all around twenty-five or thirty. I saw a few in their early teens. A few were doped, but most were functioning fairly well. The pretty ones acting normal were dressed in shorts, two-piece bikinis or slips. I even saw a tall blond woman around thirty walking around in a leather outfit. It was really bizarre. Not many of the boys were walking around, just two or three of the older ones. They were in their mid- or late twenties, I guess. I imagine the others were living in the basement. From what I learned, they had video games and other things to keep them busy when they weren't doing errands for Simon."

"He came a long way from being the classic high school jock."

"You knew him?"

"Not very well. He was a year ahead of me."

"Good thing I never told him your name. He wouldn't have believed you were my father."

"How'd you get him to bring you back here?"

"I told him I wanted him to come here and take your guns so you couldn't try and shoot me anymore."

"That's all it took?"

She smiled. "I told him a few other things. They were mostly lies, but given the circumstances, I didn't think you'd mind."

"What else did you tell him?"

"I told him you had hundreds of guns. He really liked that. I also told him you had canisters of ammo in every room in the house."

"I guess that would turn him on."

"It did, but then I told him a few other things to encourage him to bring me here. Like I said, he was pretty upset over Doc and James. At first he wanted to take me somewhere and dump me. I overheard him talking about it when he left the den. I realized I needed some sort of bait to use to get him to bring me back. The gun and ammo thing just didn't seem quite enough. When he came back in the den, I told him about the special refrigerator you kept in the barn. As soon as I mentioned that, his entire demeanor changed. His eyes grew and his face seemed to glow."

"Special refrigerator?" This was getting interesting.

"I told him you came back from some hospital or clinic one night a few weeks ago with a carload of boxes of medical supplies you'd found in their drug cabinets. I had to help him carry them into the barn."

"Smart."

"I just figured that since he was constantly buzzed, he'd want to get his hands on anything he could, and wouldn't care how he got it."

"I overheard some of his boys talking about the same thing. Doc and James drove all around the county, looking for drugs. They made sure Simon always had enough drugs on hand. When we killed them, it ended his constant supply, and he was forced to rely on a few of the other boys to make the trips. That was really good thinking on your part."

"I remembered what we'd found in the station wagon, so it was really a no-brainer. Anyway, I told him you kept the refrigerator in the barn and had it hooked up to the home generator to keep the stuff fresh. He asked me if I knew what any of it was. I said I didn't know, but that you'd sampled some of it and went on a trip, and when you came back, you told me you'd seen God."

I laughed. "That was cruel. I'm impressed."

"Like I said, he was hooked. That's when he ordered almost all the boys to go out looking for you. He wanted to drive right to the barn and steal everything, but when word got back that you'd killed three or four of them, he got really upset, and knew it would probably be much better if he brought me back with him so he could find everything quickly, before you came back."

"Among his other faults, he was a stone coward."

"It worked out perfectly. I figured that since we've got everything booby-trapped here, it was my best chance. I led him into the barn and we went down the stairs. I told him the refrigerator was hidden in one of the horse's stalls, behind stacks of hay."

"Did he find the tripwire I rigged across that sixth step?"

"He found it right off and landed pretty hard on the concrete slab. I barely had enough time to get out of his way. It took him several minutes to recover. By that time, I'd already grabbed the revolver you'd hidden behind that loose board in the overhead rafters."

I was so proud of her. I would have taken her in my arms if I'd had the energy. "He obviously had no idea who he was dealing with."

"Neither did you when we first met in Breezewood." She bent over and kissed me again.

I raised my good arm and placed my hand over hers. Then I noticed the bandages. My left hand was nearly covered in dressing, and my left forearm was similarly wrapped, all the way to the elbow. "What happened to my hand and forearm?"

"Oh, aside from serious bruising, more than a dozen cuts and scrapes, and a very large gash on your forearm, you also had a swollen ankle, and your thighs were sliced in more than twenty different places by what I can only guess were thorns or sharp branches. And don't get me started on all those stickers I found imbedded in your skin."

I assumed the bruising was the result of my using my hand to drag me across the field. My adrenaline had no doubt kept my mind free of distractions such as pain. "I hadn't noticed much of anything else at the time."

She frowned. "I found more than twenty stickers on your face alone."

"You got them all?"

"I think so. I needed tweezers, of course, and Harry gave me a magnifying glass."

"I owe you, big-time."

"It was the least I could do for what you did, silly." Her beautiful green eyes glistened in the late morning light coming in through the window. Her face was inches away. Once again I wanted to take her in my arms, but she picked up a pair of scissors from the end table and went back to work on my bandage.

My arm throbbed, but it didn't hurt nearly as much. She'd apparently gotten the infection under control.

"Were you able to get the bullet out?"

"It fragmented in two pieces. The first chunk had already come out, judging by the hole. I found the other piece without too much trouble. It was pretty close to the surface, lodged in your bicep muscle. I cleaned it out and stitched you up. Harry and Vaughn helped. They had all the medical supplies we needed in their trucks."

"Vaughn?"

"Vaughn Gresch. He got here right after Simon and I pulled up the drive. I heard a truck right after Simon tripped on the step. I'm sure Vaughn would've shot him if I hadn't already done it."

Once again I was curious about the two men. I wanted to ask her, but she kissed me again and pulled the sheets up to my neck. "You'd better rest. They want to talk to us when you're feeling a little better."

"About what?"

"They wouldn't tell me."

I didn't like the sound of that. I also didn't like Fields' expression. She was obviously holding something back. "Would you tell me if you knew?"

"They really want you to rest first. They've got a ton of questions to ask you."

"Good. I've got a ton to ask them."

I lay back and wondered if I should tell her what had happened right after I'd blacked out in the grass near the barn.

"Something wrong?"

I just sighed.

"Tell me."

"I ... saw Reed."

She sat there, watching me. She didn't speak for the longest time, just sat there, looking puzzled. "When?"

"Right after I blacked out."

"Did he say anything?"

"It was kind of fuzzy. I didn't expect to see him standing over me like that, so I thought I must be dead, too. I asked him what was going on, and he told me that he'd been guiding me when I was looking for you."

"Was he?"

"When I first went into the woods, I heard a voice. It hadn't occurred to me what was happening at the time, but I guess I did suspect it was him all along. Now that it's all over, and I can see things more objectively, I honestly believe Reed was actually out there with me, and that he saved my life."

Fields was silent as she bent over and kissed me again. Her face was just inches away. "I think it was him, too."

I could tell she meant it, and hadn't said it just to humor me. I knew then that I should tell her about something else Reed had said. "He said something else before I..."

"You need rest," she whispered. "Get lots of it. We've got a lot of catching up to do in here."

Despite my fatigue, her suggestion perked me right up. "What about those two guys who carried me up here? Where are they?"

"They're around, somewhere. But don't worry, I've seen your work." She smiled and winked. "I honestly don't think you'll need their help."

"That's not what I meant."

"This room's got a door, doesn't it?"

266

"Yeah ..."

"And there's even a lock on it, if you feel the need."

I smiled. "I see your point."

"Good. Now rest up. This lady isn't gonna wait *that* long, you know." Then she kissed me one more time, stroked my hair and left the room.

Exhaustion set in as soon as I heard her walking down the steps. I closed my eyes and thought about what Reed had said when I'd asked him about the glittering star. He told me he'd wanted to get my attention, and that was the best way he knew to do it.

I decided to tell Fields about it when I awoke, if I remembered. Right now it didn't matter. Right now I didn't want to do anything but lie there and relax. I was much too tired to explain anything to anyone right now.

All I wanted was a few more hours of deep, uninterrupted sleep.

CHAPTER NINETEEN

When I awoke again, the clock on the table beside the bed said it was 10:55 the following morning. Fields was lying beside me in the bed, in her red shorts and black tank top. The sight, of course, immediately brought me around, but I quickly discovered that I still felt weak and sluggish. I could only lie there and enjoy the sensation as she leaned on one elbow and kissed me—first on the cheek, then the lips.

Although the experience was far from unpleasant, I wanted to reciprocate, but knew deep down that I wasn't ready. After what I'd been through, I needed more time. I'd been through this same recovery process before, and although I'd been much younger then, I hadn't forgotten how the body stuck to its own schedule. I'd also learned the hard way what happened when you refused to listen to it.

I slept the rest of the day, waking only a couple of times to stagger into the bathroom. Fields joined me later on, waking me as she slipped into bed and put her arm around my waist. I remained in the same position, on my left side, my back to her, moving only my hand to hold hers as I drifted off again.

However, the next morning I knew right off that all the sleep and rest had hastened my recovery. When I awoke, I felt strong, alert, and very much alive. I immediately awoke Fields, taking her in my arms and kissing her passionately. We made love, and I knew then that things would be all right from that day on. We were together, and nothing would ever separate us again.

***

Twenty minutes later, I eased carefully out of bed and after a few awkward steps, made a trip to the bathroom. My wounded arm continued to tingle, but I'd been shot before and knew the unpleasantness would gradually ebb and become less and less noticeable in a few weeks.

After covering my bandages with Saran wrap and fastening them with rubber bands, I took a long, stimulating shower. It invigorated me, and I felt much better. I wanted to get back in bed with Fields and stay there for the rest of the day. But I remembered that we had to deal with the two men staying with us downstairs. Since I was now well-rested and ready to go, I decided this morning would be the perfect time to find out who they were and what they wanted.

Fields had already dressed by the time I came out of the bathroom. She'd put on her short-sleeved turquoise tee shirt and jeans, and was sitting at my mother's antique vanity, brushing her hair. The delicious sight stirred me up again, and I wanted to pull off that shirt, hike down those jeans, and carry her back to the bed.

"There are two men downstairs," she said without losing a stroke with the hairbrush.

I sometimes found it irritating that she could read my mind so easily. This was one of those times.

"That didn't stop us before."

She didn't reply, just kept brushing her hair.

"The door's closed, too. That helps, doesn't it? Besides, you don't scream *that* much. I could put my hand over your mouth if you're self-conscious. I've done that before. You even said you liked it ..."

The brushing stopped suddenly. "I don't want them staying here with us. Do you?"

"No." I couldn't stop staring at the fluttering pulse in her slender neck.

She put the brush down onto the mirrored surface. "I mean, they did save our lives and all, and they've been very helpful and polite the last few days ... but enough's enough, right?"

"Right."

"In other words, I'd really like to find out why they're still here and what they want. Wouldn't you?"

"Good point."

"Breakfast would be a good time for that, don't you think?"

"Sounds good to me."

She turned around and kissed me lightly on the lips, then stood up before I could kiss her back or put my arms around her. Despite my growing urges, I knew she was right. Certain questions had to be answered before our lives could return to how they'd once been.

We left the bedroom and slowly descended the stairs. I held on to the banister, and we made it down to the landing without incident. The two men were asleep in the living room. Shaw, covered with an afghan, dozed rather noisily in Uncle Joe's vintage armchair while Gresch sprawled beneath another afghan on my grandparents' old sofa.

Fields and I began making breakfast, and in just a few minutes the two men staggered in and took chairs at the kitchen table. Shaw nodded to me as I tended to the bacon and eggs on the griddle. He sat at the table and finished buttoning the sleeves of his shirt. Fields placed the pot on the table. Shaw thanked her and poured some into the cup in front of him. "How's the arm?" he asked.

"I'll live."

"You were lucky. Those slugs shatter like glass when they hit something."

I brought over the bacon and eggs and placed the large dish in the center of the table. "Well, this one didn't. Thanks for the help."

"No problem." Gresch took his coffee black. He drank some, put the cup down, grabbed the spatula and dished out some scrambled eggs onto his plate. "We had to come here anyway, so while we were here ..."

"Tell me something." I sat down across from him. I wasn't exactly in the mood for levity. Fields and I had just been through hell, and these two strangers appeared from out of nowhere, like mythical heroes in a board game, armed with weapons and even a cell phone. Fields had said they had questions. I intended to beat them to the punch. No matter what they had to ask, my questions were far more important.

"Ask away." Shaw picked up a slice of toast and buttered it. His gaze immediately drifted over to Gresch, making me even more suspicious.

"How the hell did you two find me?"

Shaw stopped buttering his toast and gave me the sort of look one gives someone who'd just asked the world's silliest question. "Your chip, of course."

Of course. I hadn't given the damned thing much thought. I'd even denied its existence for nearly twenty years, until Fields, Reed and I were caught and taken to the underground government facility months earlier, and I was told several very unpleasant facts by a man calling himself Colonel Hughes, who really wasn't a man at all.

Now that the subject had been brought up, it made perfect sense. But it also posed even more questions. It made me wonder who these men were and why they'd tracked me. And it made me wonder why they were still here. Most of all, it made me very suspicious, because I realized that someone else had obviously been behind all this.

"If you tracked me, both of you must know my next question."

Gresch put his coffee cup down. "For the last couple of months, we've been tracking every former military personnel showing up on file and looking for them individually to see who is still alive and still functional."

"File?" I found myself fighting this sudden feeling of *deja vu*. If this was the result of my abduction by the TABs, I certainly didn't want to sit still and listen to any more of it. This felt just like the interview Colonel Hughes gave me just before he and his two TABs led me through their facility to show me their New Order. "You're talking about computer files?"

Shaw had a forkful of scrambled egg. "They were able to get back into the system about a month ago."

They? The system? This was beginning to sound even more ominous. I knew how much of their equipment I'd actually destroyed, but not how much I hadn't. I'd been afraid at the time that I wouldn't be able to do enough damage to their programs. The facility had been much too huge and complex for the three of us to examine completely. Besides, we were much too focused on our escape, and didn't want to do anything that would extend our stay. We were all suffering from a morbid fear of being trapped in a solid stone facility hundreds of feet underground with a failing oxygen system and an ever-growing number of decaying bodies.

Now I had to face the unpleasant fact that I'd been correct in my suspicions that someone else would eventually track me down. I just hadn't expected it to be this soon.

And now I had to face the horrible fact that these two men couldn't leave this house alive.

The compact .380 Beretta Cheetah remained hidden under the large blue dishtowel on the sink counter, about two feet from the back door. It was the same weapon I'd picked up the morning I'd slipped outside in the middle of making breakfast to find Simon's friend Doc walking up our drive. All I had to do was get up from the table, move over to the door, push the towel aside and grab the gun. But I had to do it without anyone noticing. Shaw and Gresch were pros. They'd be able to read my body language in a heartbeat.

I decided to get them talking again. In a few minutes I'd pick up a strip of bacon and choke on it. Then I'd get up and hurry to the sink to pour some water. Once I got my choking under control, I'd turn around and ask them another question. During their reply, I'd spill some water on myself. I'd then reach over and grab the towel with my left hand while I picked up the gun with my right.

I hated to do this. Shaw had saved my skin; I wouldn't be here if it weren't for him and his friend Gresch.

But I couldn't let them take us again.

"You just said 'they,'" I said to Shaw. "Who are you talking about?"

"Vaughn and I served with Colonel Hughes," Shaw said.

My hackles immediately went up. I picked up the bacon and shifted in my chair. "When?"

Gresch put down his fork and frowned. "Before their crazy clone thing got out of hand."

"*Before* the TAB program?"

"Harry and I had both been out of the military for two years. We were both living out our early

274

retirements in wonderful peace and quiet in the woods a safe distance from the D.C. area. I'd built a tiny five-hundred-square-foot hunter's cabin five or six years earlier, when I was working as an electrician for Cumberland Power. I'd just been divorced and wanted to be by myself for a while. Living by myself in the mountains sounded great at the time. Harry had a similar setup in the Virginia area. Then all this shit started and, like the two of you, we'd been hiding from what was left of civilization."

I put the bacon back down and had a slug of black coffee. "So what's going on? Why'd you two show up here?"

"We're getting the word out," Gresch said.

That phrase just didn't seem like it belonged in this conversation. "Getting the word out" usually meant contacting other people. Spreading the word only worked when there were others to spread it to. You couldn't get the word out to people when most of them were dead and many of the others were winding down like old generators.

"I don't understand."

"Neither do I." Fields was just as confused as I was.

"Like you, Vaughn and I were both tracked," Shaw said. "More folks have been chipped than you think. The chip program, like most other Government-funded programs, was around years longer than everyone thought. Ettinger also had a chip—which is how we found his location and

275

tracked him here after we discovered you were in the same area."

"Ettinger had a chip? He wasn't in the military, was he?"

"Hardly. Seems he had some trouble with the law a few years back," Gresch said. "There was something in his file about a traffic stop and a large amount of cocaine and amphetamines found in his possession."

"Makes sense," I said.

"Yes," Gresch replied. "Most people think the Government started implanting felons around thirty years ago. Actually, they started doing that nearly fifty years ago, although it was kept quiet until the process was perfected."

"Whatever it took for you to get here, I'm grateful you got here when you did," Fields said.

"I'd always considered myself unlucky for carrying around that chip," I said. "I can't remember how many times I'd considered looking for a doctor who'd find it and dig it out."

"I'm glad you didn't," Fields said.

"So am I. It's funny how life always manages to land you a sucker punch when you least expect it."

"I think it was more than a sucker punch." Fields drank some coffee.

"It made things easier for all of us," Shaw said.

"You said they tracked you two," I said to Shaw. "What happened then?"

"A small group of Marines I'd served with at Brighton showed up at my mountain retreat and asked if I was interested in starting it up again. I learned soon after that they'd already gotten hold of Vaughn."

I perked up. "You were at Brighton?"

He nodded. "I was Army, Vaughn a Marine. And yeah, we pulled the same duty you had. Riot control?"

"I went after veekays, mostly."

Gresch huffed. "Who'd you piss off?"

"My CO thought it would give me character."

"He was wrong." Fields smiled and winked.

Shaw said, "Horrible duty. While we were in, the mortality rate was slightly more than seventy-five percent."

"It was close to ninety during my tour."

My original plan with the .380 now a distant memory, I stared at the two men in a much different perspective. They'd done the same things I'd done, seen the same things, and suffered the same horrors. Most of all, they had my cynical attitude—which went pretty far with me. It told me they felt basically the same about this mess as I did.

But none of this explained why they were picked to track me down. Nor did it explain who'd ordered them to do it, or what they were told to do once they found me.

"What did you mean when you mentioned getting the word out?"

"So far, there are nearly eight hundred at the settlement already," Gresch said.

"Settlement?"

"That's what it is right now. I guess you could say it's roughly the same size as the average small town. But apparently it's not the only one, and according the daily reports we've been receiving, the numbers of these settlements have been growing."

"Eight hundred in this area alone?" Judging by what Fields and I had seen the last few months, I found that number unbelievable. "I take it there are a lot more still functioning than we'd realized."

"Definitely," Shaw said. "Even going by the original stats the Government came out with before the doping process took down many of the grids, a ninety percent hit rate, in a country of nearly half a billion people, leaves close to fifty million."

"That's roughly the equivalent of a California, or New York," Gresch added. "In other words, a lot more people than we'd originally estimated are still wandering around."

"Are you counting everyone?" Fields asked. "Don't forget, there are the doped, as well as the ones who weren't doped but went crazy, like Simon."

"We can't be certain of anything right now," Gresch said. "We're counting just those we've been able to track and who've shown up at the various settlements. Since the ones who've turned psychotic have also been chipped, we're monitoring them closely, but not including them in our figures. The doped, unfortunately, can't be monitored, and have to be discarded—at least, until we're better organized, and have more manpower to handle the new workload."

"That still leaves roughly fifty million to find and gather up," Shaw said.

"So ... where are they?" Fields asked.

"That's why we've got to find those who are chipped first. The more former military we can locate, the more we'll have on staff."

"What are you doing about the power?" I asked. "I thought most of it would already be down by now."

"Not by any means. It nearly went belly-up in most of the larger areas, but now there are enough professionals around like us to monitor the grids and keep some of them running."

"You did say you were an electrician."

"I've got twenty years' experience. Vaughn has just as many years as a computer hardware tech."

"How many places do you have access to right now?" Fields asked.

"We can't be certain. At this early stage, everyone's struggling, working mostly by feel. This effort will take a while. Meanwhile, the more normals we can find, the faster we can get the process working."

"Normals?"

"Those still functioning and capable of contributing. And the more professionals we can find and transport to the settlements, the easier this process will be."

"We're not unduly optimistic, believe me," Gresch said. "This undertaking is going to be enormous. It'll be years before we get everything up and running."

"These eight hundred people you mentioned. Just who are they?"

"So far, we've managed to find electricians, computer techs, doctors, nurses, a few plumbers, and a number of builders."

Shaw poured more coffee from the pot. "We can't guarantee everyone will be still functioning in six months, of course. The doping process can take as long as a year or two to become evident and run its course."

"I think you need to get these doctors together and work on some sort of antidote," I said. "If some of us do get hit with it later on, it would be really nice if someone had some idea how to control it, or even slowing it down until they can find a cure."

"For that," Fields said, "they'd have to find out more about our immune systems. I imagine they'll want to examine every one of us once we're brought in. Maybe by that time, they can finally figure out why some of us haven't succumbed to this."

"Right now," Shaw said, "we're working on getting the lights back on and everything hooked up and running."

"I can see why they'd want a nurse like Fields." I couldn't understand why they'd be interested in me. I had no intention of returning to active military status. "I ran a tiny auto detailing business. I'm not a mechanic, or anyone you'd actually need for something like this. And auto detailing isn't exactly what you'd call important nowadays."

"You're normal," Shaw said. "You were also military."

"I was honorably discharged. That didn't mean anything to Colonel Hughes or General Forbes when they abducted us and took us at gunpoint to their underground facility a few months ago. But it meant a lot to me, and it still does. Don't judge me by what you saw me doing in those woods. That was an extreme case. It was an entirely personal matter. I'd never re-enlist. Not in a million years."

"We're not talking about starting up another military," Gresch said. "We're talking about bringing society back, however way we can manage."

"You're saying you won't need a military once you get everything back into place?"

"We have no idea. I won't lie to you. We might, later on. And if the other countries are doing the same things we are, I'd say yes, we'll need our own military in a few years. But at the moment, things are too damned hectic to make any assumption."

"Right now, we need people," Shaw said. "Last we heard, they were gathering up as many abandoned trailers and modular homes as they could find in a hundred-mile diameter and hauling them to the settlement. The place is in a good location. Apparently it was once a very small town with a couple of hundred fairly-new homes already standing in a five-mile area. It's rural, of course, near fresh water and miles of open country. We're finding functioning farmers as well, so food

281

shouldn't be a problem. Once the satellites and the computers are all operational, you can sit at a desk and help us with our tracking program. Or you could volunteer for surveillance. It'll be your choice."

"That's all you'll want me to do?" It sounded too good to be true. I began feeling a con in the works.

"The most important thing right now," Gresch said, "is rounding up as many able-bodied people as we can find. We've got to take back this country, get it running again."

"That's what General Forbes told me just before he ordered one of his TABs to escort me…"

"Forget all that," Shaw said. "That idea's dead. It died with him. And his clone."

"Did it?"

Neither man replied.

"I know what this is all about," I said. "I can see it happening all over again. That's why the TABs were created. A New Order, as Colonel Hughes phrased it."

"Was it Colonel Hughes who actually wanted it?" asked Shaw. "Or his clone?"

"It was their idea, wasn't it?" Even after all these last few months, I found myself getting angry all over again. "I may not be the smartest guy on earth, but even I know that you just don't unleash something you can't control. That's exactly what they did. They created the TABs and had no idea what they'd done until their superhuman monsters did what they were supposed to do by taking over."

"Maybe it was the perfect idea during its initial stages," Shaw said. "But like all good ideas, it became corrupted as they worked on it and began developing the concept while adding their own individual preferences. That happens, you know."

"The better the idea," Gresch said, "the more fragile it is. But that's all in the past. Let's not get into something that's beyond our control."

"We really have to start looking ahead," Shaw added. "Everything is behind us."

"Is it?" Despite their arguments, I still had my doubts.

A brief silence.

"How about it, Moss? Miss Fields?" Gresch's expression was dead serious. "Do you really want to stay here and keep living like this? You're prisoners in your own home, and you know it. You know it because every time you leave the house, you have to have a gun in your hand. You have to run to get into your vehicle, knowing full well someone could be hiding behind a tree in your own backyard, aiming a rifle at you. You know that every time you hear the wind, a thump, or even a crack that could be the house settling, you have to go for your gun and investigate because you're afraid it could be someone sneaking around outside. Doesn't it seem much more sensible to come with us and help us get everything started all over again? You've heard of the safety-in-numbers concept. In this case, it means everything."

"You honestly think you can start everything up again?"

Shaw sighed. "We have to try. As long as there are still functioning survivors with the will to start over, we've got to find them and work together. We can't just vegetate and wait for the end, can we?"

"Look what's already happened to society. Modern technology brought us down, you know. Modern technology made it possible for a twelve-year-old computer wiz to hack into databases and corrupt the country's entire banking system. I don't know about you, but that kind of shit always made me, well, a little nervous and paranoid."

"You're not alone," Gresch said.

"So what's to prevent it from happening again?"

"Nothing," Gresch said.

"It's a new beginning," Shaw said. "We've got to look at it that way. We can't let ourselves give up."

"It bothers me," I said. "No matter how much I want to start all over, I can't forget any of this. The computer killed everything for us. It was probably the greatest invention ever, but it was also the most deadly. It brought us all down. Starting over ... to me, that means bringing it all back."

"Maybe you're right, but even if history repeats itself..."

"History always repeats itself."

"Even if it does, that's out of our hands."

"It usually is."

Shaw smiled sheepishly. "The point is, we're Americans. We're survivors, hell-raisers, troublemakers, dissenters—whatever history wants to call us. We always have been. It's in our blood. Otherwise, we would never have pulled away from England in the first place."

"We really don't have much of a choice now," Gresch added.

Fields' large, glittering green eyes bored into my head. I could tell what she was thinking. Everything that had happened to us in the last few days—her abduction, our encounter with the bikers, Don lying dead in the bedroom of his father's house, and the fact that I was nearly killed less than thirty feet outside this house—had made this decision easy for her.

We'd lived through entirely too much fear and terror since coming here. We'd never been able to leave the house unarmed. When we did leave the house, we were forced to turn off all the lights and lock and double-lock the doors and windows before sneaking up to the garage and getting in the truck. We hid and snuck around to avoid being shot and killed more times than I wanted to remember. We fashioned booby traps every night before bed. We hid keys and guns everywhere. We kept a gun within our reach at all times. I couldn't imagine us living like this the rest of our lives. I couldn't even imagine us surviving like this much longer.

But even though I could not find it in my heart to fully agree with what Gresch and Shaw were talking about, I had to think of Fields. How much more could she take before she'd had enough? She was a tough lady, but this harsh existence could take a toll on anyone. Hell, she'd nearly caused her own demise just a few days ago. I didn't want to subject her to this anymore, and as I thought about it more logically, I realized I didn't want to subject myself to it, either.

I stared at her beautiful troubled face and realized once again how much I loved her, how much I needed her, and how much I wanted to take care of her. She didn't sign on to play war games for the rest of her life. Neither had I, and I certainly didn't think either of us should—especially since it now looked like the time had finally come when we no longer had to.

I gave her a slight nod, and she smiled and took my hand and squeezed it. We both knew what we had to do.

But even though it now looked like the time had actually come for the sun to shine again, I knew what else it meant. We had to move away from my childhood home. I also knew that once we did, I'd probably never see it again. I could walk up the hill one more time to say goodbye to the graves where my mother, my uncle, and my best friend, Reed, lay in eternal peace. From then on, I'd see my grandparents' farm only in memory, and would no longer be able to occupy the same rooms or share the same space my family had shared the last hundred years. I could no longer wander the woods, as I'd done with my Uncle Joe those few precious weeks before I lost him, or stand outside on the front porch with Fields at night, holding her hand while we watched the stars and waited to see one or two of them sparkle.

But as I thought about this, I realized what else it could mean, and this strange feeling of warmth made me happier and more relieved than I'd been in a long time. We'd be free again, and would no longer have to live in fear and darkness. I knew at that moment that living in fear and darkness is the same thing as death.

Still holding her hand, I turned back to Gresch and Shaw. A soft wave of sadness drifted through my soul, but my heart fluttered with excitement at that same moment.

"Where exactly is this place?" I asked in a soft voice.

CHAPTER TWENTY

According to Shaw and Gresch, the new settlement sat in a wooded valley about a hundred miles north, half an hour south of Jamestown, New York.

Fields and I spent our final day on my grandparents' farm packing the van. I'd wanted to take the Silverado, but we had too much to bring along with us. This trip had to be practical, not sentimental. I didn't want to leave any of the guns or ammo, so I bundled up the guns in blankets and piled them next to the six metal ammo canisters I'd shoved in a neat row in the back. The clothing we'd accumulated in the last few months filled up the rest of the available space. I'd put as much of the food with us as I could fit in two large coolers. Shaw and Gresch told us there would be provisions where we were going, but anything we could bring would help the situation.

This, of course, brought everything into a frightening prospective. We were leaving the farm for good this time and would probably never be back to see it again.

The reality of it hit me hard, and I immediately zoned out. For the longest time I stood in the doorway of the kitchen, staring at the knickknacks my grandparents had collected over the years, when I was a boy. When I was finally able to pull my eyes away from the walls and shelves, I found my gaze fixed on the old gas stove. Then I noticed the peeling cabinets, the overhead light, and finally the kitchen table.

We'd all sat there—Fields, Uncle Joe, Reed and me—talking, laughing, eating, drinking and enjoying each other's company the short time we'd had together. When we'd first come into this house, Fields, Reed and I had sat at this table while Uncle Joe told me my mother had died. Later that night, after I'd visited her fresh grave, he fixed cold cuts for all of us and put coffee, beer and whiskey on the table. Just a few short weeks later, he came in for breakfast one morning, sat down at the head of this table and began spilling his food and slurring his words. Not long after that, he couldn't remember his own name. Then he was gone.

Years before, I'd sat at this same table with my mother many times. Mom was young and beautiful back then, always smiling and happy. Whenever we visited my grandparents, she acted like a little girl. It was strange—one of those many childhood mysteries I never really understood until I grew up and figured it out logically. But it will always remain among my fondest and clearest memories.

As I struggled through these shadows of the past, I sensed Fields nearby. Then I smelled her hair and her perfume, and everything else vanished. She pressed against me, and her touch made me return instantly. Her face drew closer and I could feel tendrils of her hair gently touching my arm. Her breath singed my flesh when she whispered, "Everything will be okay."

That ended my nostalgia. Fields had brought me back to the present, where I belonged, and I knew right then that we had to go forward with this.

The memories would come with us. The only problem with that was that the bad ones came right along with the good.

Leaving would be much harder this time than when I first arrived and learned that my childhood home next door had been burned to the ground. When we left this time, I'd be bringing along the afternoons I'd spent with Uncle Joe those few short weeks before he'd died. I'd be bringing along the days we'd spent with Reed. That cold afternoon when we'd buried Uncle Joe. That cold afternoon when we'd buried Reed. That horrible episode that started the morning I'd sensed someone wandering around outside.

Once I finally decided to start moving again, I followed Fields through the kitchen and out of the house. I closed the back door, but didn't lock or bolt it. I forced myself to turn away and not look back or even take a moment to say good-bye. For us, the future lay in a different place. There was no sense looking back at all the things that had once been a large part of me, the things we'd be leaving behind. I took her hand and we went down the walk, climbed the steps to the gravel drive and ascended the hill. We walked over to the buckeye tree and stood there a few moments, staring at the three graves. I closed my eyes, thought of my mother, my uncle, and Reed, and somehow sensed that they'd be watching over us, no matter where we ended up.

The van sat outside the garage, packed and ready. We climbed in and buckled up. Just as I reached for the ignition key, I found myself staring at the garage door. Inside, Uncle Joe's beloved Silverado sat in its stall in the dark, where it would stay, possibly forever. The memories slammed through me again, and I lowered my head.

Fields touched my arm. "You okay?"

"I really don't want to leave the truck." My voice sounded like it belonged to a child.

"I know."

"I'd love to take it with us."

"We can't."

"I know. I still want to."

Fields squeezed my arm. "Just let it go, babe."

"This is ... really hard for me."

"I know. I liked it, too."

"That truck ..." A lump formed in my throat. "It ... saved our lives."

Fields was silent for several moments. Then she gently stroked my arm. "This van got us out of a few scrapes too, remember?"

Once again, she was right. The truck had served its purpose. Not only for Uncle Joe, but also for us. I turned to her and put my hand over hers. "Thanks, baby. I needed that."

She smiled, leaned over and kissed my cheek. "You're welcome. Now let's get out of here before we both change our minds. Harry Shaw's still waiting for us down near the main road."

I fired up the ignition, backed up and turned the van away from the garage. Then, as we crept down the gravel drive, I forced myself to ignore the tall square shape of the two-story house on our left and then the huge gray presence of the barn looming straight ahead.

An image shot past my vision. I saw myself as a child escaping the barn after Uncle Joe found me playing in the hayloft. I forced the humorous memory away and focused on taking the van down the drive, past the front of the barn. I didn't start breathing normally until I saw the truck sitting at the bottom of the hill, where Shaw waited for us.

"Where's Gresch?" I asked. "He didn't go on ahead, did he?"

"He might have. They didn't tell me what they were doing. It doesn't matter, does it?"

Once again, she was right. It didn't matter. The only thing that did matter was that our lives were being given a new beginning. I knew that something like that didn't happen very often. When it did, the only sensible thing to do was to look straight ahead.

"No. It doesn't matter at all."

Shaw pulled onto the deserted road and we followed him up the hill and away from my childhood home—the only place in the world that would continue to hold so many memories of my life.

***

It was a quiet, relaxing trip. Beside me, Fields sat staring at the road ahead. She didn't say much, but I could tell that, like me, she was excited and a little nervous about starting all over again. She began the trip with her trusty .45 in her lap, but once we got onto I-79 and went a few miles without encountering another soul on the road, she placed it on the floor between her feet.

A major step, of course, and one that made me wonder once again about our future. I was pleased there *was* a future, and this in itself told me we were doing the right thing by leaving. Shaw and Gresch had been right—how much longer could Fields and I go on living like two escaped prisoners? How long would it be before I went out to get the truck and one of Simon's thugs or someone else picked me off as soon as I left the house? Or when I opened the garage door? Or when I pulled out onto the road?

How long would it be before someone began shooting at the windows while we ate supper? Or while we slept?

Our only option was to find others just like us and begin living like normal human beings again.

So what if society was brought down again in the next few decades? So what if the new Powers That Be turned stupid again and let history repeat itself? That was what humans did, wasn't it? They worked hard to improve the situation and then sat back while someone else came along and destroyed it. Eventually someone else would come along and try to fix things again, but the process would repeat itself, and things would end up destroyed again. Man's legacy would never change. He would always destroy things when he tried fixing them.

And who was I to argue?

"Something funny?" Fields asked. "You're smiling."

"I was just wondering how long it'll take before the next big one comes along to end this one. If we'll be around to see it happen."

"Kind of cynical, but I see your point."

"I should say we've earned the right to be cynical, wouldn't you?"

"I just hope that if it happens again, we won't be around to see it. I can't possibly go through this again."

"If it takes another fifty years, we might see it, but I'll be ninety and you'll be in your eighties. We probably won't care about too much about anything by then."

Fields laughed. "We'll make a good team. You can ask me what's going on and if I'm still capable of understanding it, I'll tell you what I think."

"Sounds like a plan to me, but something tells me I won't even want to know at that point in my life."

She sat back. "Why worry about it? Whatever happens will happen—with or without our help."

I went silent and stayed that way for a few minutes. My thoughts began spinning again.

"What's on your mind now?" she asked.

"Just thinking."

"About what?"

"We didn't have a very easy time living on my grandparents' farm, did we?"

"No. We didn't. But it was home, and we made the best of it."

"And you were there."

"What are you getting at?"

"We were constantly looking over our shoulders, listening and expecting the worst, but for some reason, it just didn't seem that bad. I think it was because you were there with me."

She placed her hand on my thigh. She smiled at me, and I could see a glint of tears forming in her eyes.

I placed my hand over hers. "I just wish Reed could be here with us. I would've loved to see his reaction to all this."

"He'd be happy for us."

The image made me grin, and I felt tears of my own gathering in my eyes. "He really would."

"I'll never stop trying to guess who his friend was," she said.

Once again my vision of him came back, and I found myself wondering if it had actually been him, or if I'd just been dreaming. "He seemed very happy the last time I saw him."

"He probably was. From what you told me, he's been watching out for both of us all along. We were his friends. We shared his last days with him. It'll stay that way until we actually do see him again."

"I'm almost positive he was with me when I started looking for you."

"Since you survived, I'd say he probably helped more than both of us will ever know."

She was right. Whenever I thought of what happened that night, I knew I hadn't been alone. I realized now that I hadn't been alone from the time I left the house.

She patted my thigh and settled back in her seat. A few minutes later she said, "I've always hated moving, you know."

"So do I, but this different."

"It's like moving to another world."

"That's one way of looking at it."

"Aren't you intimidated?"

"I'm looking at it as a kind of second chance."

"I just hope we all take life a little more seriously this time around."

"We will or we won't. There isn't any other option."

At around four o'clock, we climbed a hill. When we reached the top and I saw the magnificent sight, my foot slammed down onto the brake pedal.

A cluster of giant wind turbines spun madly at the top of the hill just a few miles in the distance. There must have been thirty or forty of them in a long line. The sight took my breath away.

"I never expected to see anything like that again."

Fields turned to me. "Is your heart racing, too?"

"It's about to take off."

She took my hand. "I know this sounds stupid, but I'm ... well, I'm scared."

"Me, too, but even so, my foot wants to press down on the gas."

"Maybe it's your subconscious trying to take over, since you're obviously not capable of doing it right now."

I thought it could be Reed trying to help me make the decision again.

Reed? Is that you?

Do it, came the quick reply. *Do it for your mom and your uncle. Do it for Fields. Most of all, do it for yourself.*

Was it Reed's voice? Or was it just my gut telling me what I wanted to hear?

Did it matter?

Actually, only one thing mattered. I knew then that I had to stop questioning everything and just get moving again.

Just as I let my foot lower onto the gas pedal, I glanced in the rearview and saw a familiar truck pulling up behind our van. It was Gresch, but he wasn't alone. An old man with gray hair and a thick gray beard sat beside him, grinning and waving.

It was Walter.

"Who's that with Vaughn?" Fields asked, squinting at her side mirror.

"That's Walter." More tears filled my eyes.

"The old man you told us about? The one who helped you? Gave you his son's car?"

"That's him. I really glad Vaughn went back and picked him up. He deserves this, too. Besides, he wanted to meet you."

"Really?"

"Yes. He said you sound a lot like his wife."

"What did you tell him about me?"

"Just the truth."

"Think he'll forgive you for letting those kids destroy the car?"

The beaming grin on Walter's face told me the answer to her question.

"I think he already has." I wiped my eyes. A wave of warm relief shimmered through me, and all doubts and fears scurried away in an instant.

As we went down the next hill, I realized that even though death and destruction had once covered our world in heavy darkness, all that was about to change. As long as there were some of us still left with the desire to start living again, together we'd be strong enough to stand tall and lift the shroud.

Fields put her hand over mine and we both knew right then that the darkness had indeed lifted, and that daylight had finally returned.

ABOUT THE AUTHOR

David Berardelli was born in Pittsburgh, Pennsylvania, and grew up in Gibsonia, an agricultural and mining area north of the city. Formerly a jazz musician, he studied music at Duquesne University before being drafted into the U.S. Army. There, he served as a member of the 80th Army Band at Hunter Army Airfield in Savannah, Georgia, and performed in the Third Army Soldier Show at Fort McPherson in Atlanta. He also served as a bugler at nearly two hundred military funerals between 1970 and 1971. He has also been a caricaturist, a nightclub musician, and a data-processing associate.

He lives on a thirty-acre horse ranch in southern Mississippi with his wife Linda and their horses and dogs, along with a variety of birds, squirrels, raccoons, coyotes, foxes, and deer.

After Darkness Fell is the sequel to his apocalyptic novel *And Darkness Fell*. Berardelli's other published novels include *The Apprentice*, *Wagon Driver*, *Demon Chaser*, *Demon Chaser II*, *The Funny Detective*, *Just a Simple Errand*, *Stepping Out of My Grave*, *Escape Clause*, *Fatal Innocence*, *Colors*, *Working for a Mob Boss*, and *Demon Chaser III*.

ALSO BY DAVID BERARDELLI

THE APPRENTICE
THE WAGON DRIVER
DEMONCHASER I
"Death is Hell, but the shoes are great"
DEMONCHASER II
"One foot in Hell, but still with great shoes"
STEPPING OUT OF MY GRAVE
ESCAPE CLAUSE
FATAL INNOCENCE
THE FUNNY DETECTIVE
"Taking On the Orlando Mob"
JUST A SIMPLE ERRAND
A Funny Detective Novel
COLORS
WORKING FOR A MOB BOSS
A Funny Detective Novel
AND DARKNESS FELL
AFTER DARKNESS FELL
DEMONCHASER III
"It's Hell with the wrong shoes"
IN ANOTHER REALM
BEYOND RECOGNITION
LOOKING FOR A DEAD GUY
A Funny Detective Novel